"SHOOT OUT THE TIRES!"

Investigator Franklin leaned from the car window and fired three rounds at the left rear tire of the speeding DeLorean. The .45 penetrated, but it merely began to deflate slowly. At the wheel of the police car, Investigator Sands cut right and slammed into the guy's rear fender. He hit the brakes and countersteered to break contact. The white DeLorean fishtailed sideways and slid down the highway until its tires regained traction. The car continued in the direction it was pointing, crossing in front of the police cruiser and going off the road. It spun to a smoking stop, and the driver climbed out.

Franklin and Sands dove from the police car. The fleeing driver fired three shots. Sands fired eight. Franklin fired three.

The gunman was blown back to a sitting position, his back resting against the median divider.

"Who are you?" Investigator Sands shouted. "What's your name?"

The perp looked at the police officers for a long moment. "Santa Claus," he said. He bled from the mouth and died.

THE HARDER THEY FALL

TOM LOGAN

LYNX BOOKS
New York

DETROIT P.D.: THE HARDER THEY FALL

ISBN: 1-55802-053-5

First Printing/August 1988

This book is published by Lynx Books, a division of Lynx Communications, Inc., 41 Madison Avenue, New York, New York, 10010. The name "Lynx" together with the logotype consisting of a stylized head of a lynx is a trademark of Lynx Communications, Inc.

Printed in the United States of America

0 9 8 7 6 5 4 3 2 1

To Anthony G. Marshall, Esq.

The author wishes to acknowledge the invaluable assistance of Police Officer John Leavons, the Public Information Office of the Detroit Police Department, and Mike Martindale of the Detroit *News*.

THE HARDER THEY FALL

ON A FINE July morning in 1985, Tom Castleton drove to Handy Andy's Forest City to buy an eighteen-inch kettle grill. Strapped in the passenger seat, Kate Castleton, age three, looked at the passing houses and trees, chattering brightly and incessantly. When Kate wasn't talking she was singing, and when she wasn't singing she was whistling. Or asking questions.

"Daddy, why can't we see God?"

"Well, God is everywhere."

"That's what Momma said, but I want to *see* God," Kate insisted. She pointed. "Maybe God is up there in that cloud."

The sky did put Castleton in mind of the picture skies in the parochial schoolbooks of his youth, blue and gray patches in a firmament of bright clouds.

A friend had facetiously told Tom Castleton that people have children not to populate the earth, but to remind themselves of their childhoods. Kate's

1

question stirred dim recollections of his own childhood frustrations. He wondered what his father might have told him at Kate's age.

They arrived at Forest City and parked in front of the entrance. Walking across the lot they presented an attractive image, the bright butterfly of a daughter and a father who stood six feet two inches tall, with blue eyes and a square jaw, a cleft chin and a Roman nose. Castleton was forty, but his full mustache made him seem like a man hoping to look more mature than his years. Before going into the market, they stopped at the mechanized pony ride next to the exit doors. Castleton hoisted Kate onto a pinto that had lost its gloss and stood close by. She had her ride and asked for another.

He refused this indulgence, for he had to make other stops for ice and beer. A backyard barbeque had been planned for the afternoon.

As Castleton started to lift Kate from the pony, he felt a funny little shudder pass through his body, a queer, uneasy sensation that had become familiar to him in the course of his employment. He noticed two male individuals pushing an empty shopping cart toward him. Castleton kept walking. The men moved past him and entered the market. Castleton followed, his daughter holding his hand.

Castleton was a lieutenant in the Detroit Police Department. After years as a detective in the 14th Precinct, he was in the habit of being prepared. And so it was that he felt his instincts go to work. The two male individuals were dirty.

The skinny one, who walked like he was wired real tight, wore a black Borsolino and a Bill Blass jogging suit. The other wore black sweats, Bally gym shoes, and a black cap with a white stencil which read "Shoot Me, I'm Already Dead." He also seemed tense, concentrated. Psyched up to get paid.

There was going to be trouble.

Castleton was off duty but, as regulations required, he was armed. His nickel-plated .38 was stuck in the waistband of his slacks. He was expected to respond.

"We have to go back to the car, honey."

His voice was calm, but he felt his pulse quicken. He picked Kate up and turned back to his car.

"Daddy, I want to go in the store," Kate protested.

He had to wait for traffic to pass before he could cross the street to the parking lot. He looked for a patrol car but there was none in sight. If he was right, how long would it take them to hit the register and come out?

For a moment, he denied it to himself. Maybe his wife Mary was right, the job made him crazy. Maybe his instincts were lying to him. He hesitated, then glanced back to the store entrance.

They were coming out together. Except now they wore ski masks over their faces. The skinny one held a blue steel revolver. The other carried a sawed-off shotgun.

They were walking fast toward Castleton's position. He set Kate on the ground near the right wheel of the Chrysler, which he was using for cover. Then he stepped out in a crouch, squarely facing the male individual with the shotgun, his revolver held with both hands in the isosceles grip. Surprise gave him an edge. The man with the shotgun stared pop-eyed.

"Don't do it, don't do it!" he shouted. His pleading didn't jive with the stencil on his cap.

Castleton hesitated for a split second. The man pointed his shotgun and fired a round. Castleton fired two. Glass shattered. One was a hit. The man dropped the shotgun, but continued running east across the parking lot.

Later, Sergeant Raccaniello said, "It was that peashooter he was carrying. Somebody should'a talked him into buying a magnum and carrying some good, gut-ripping hollow points in it. That would have stopped the scumbag when he needed stopping."

Incredibly, cars passed between Castleton and his targets, the drivers oblivious to the drama. The wounded man rounded the corner of the building, ultimately arriving at a getaway car parked in an alley located north of the store.

Castleton spun about, looking for the other target. Out of the corner of his eye he saw him crouched low, running among the parked cars as swiftly as a deer in the forest. But he wasn't retreating. This new jack was actually coming after him, an unnerving realization. Still in a low crouch, Castleton fired two unaimed combatstance shots when the man flashed across his field of fire. One shot frosted the windshield of an Olds. When he saw the man again, he had moved to a position almost directly south of Castleton's position. Castleton and Kate were in a direct line of fire without cover. At this moment, Castleton became aware that Kate was standing up, to the left of his field of fire.

Traumatic reaction took charge of his perceptions. It was like time standing still. His emotions became detached from what was happening, as if events were observed by another person. He thought about his wife who was waiting at home for them. Seconds were hours.

"Kate, get down!" he yelled.

The explosive pop of a bullet shattered the air. Kate was on the ground, bleeding from the head. The blood rapidly pooled and a broad rivulet snaked relentlessly along the pavement.

Castleton stood up without regard for his own safety and looked for the male individual. He saw him trotting across the front of the store. Castleton fired his last two shots, both rounds hitting the front of the market. Pulverized concrete powdered his target, who escaped.

The first people on the scene found Castleton cradling his daughter's head in his lap. The back of her skull had given to his touch, a sensation that he would never be able to forget. It seemed to him that the crowd was just staring at him.

"Why aren't you doing anything?" he asked.

They only continued to stare at the man who sat with his little girl in an enormous pool of blood.

"I love you, Kate," he said. "We're going to make it. Just take it easy, honey, and lie and rest. We're going to make it."

Kate Castleton was taken to an emergency room at Detroit Receiving, where a medical team attempted unsuccessfully to save her life. Kate died at 7:53 P.M.

Mary Castleton said, "Why couldn't you have just taken Kate away from there? You chose to be a cop first. And you killed our daughter."

No arrests were ever made.

Tom Castleton moved into a motel on Eight Mile and stayed there through the divorce. When the department gave him some leave, he stayed in the motel. There he nearly ate his gun on several occasions, but he was a Catholic and believed in sin. Although he could no more go to confession or accept communion than he could stand before his wife, Castleton figured he was just enough of a Catholic not to shoot himself.

The psychiatrist from the Records Placement and Counseling Section wrote: "He has chronic difficulties sleeping, with nightmares consisting of the murder of his child, which he views as being caused by himself. He becomes shaky at unpre-

dictable times, though he denies experiencing
anxiety attacks. He is resistant to analysis. He appears somewhat irritable and distractible, requir-
ing a great deal of effort to avoid outbursts.
Subject should not be required to tolerate a great
deal of stress."

Returning from leave, Lieutenant Castleton
transferred from the 14th Precinct's Investigative
Operations Section to duty as administrative lieutenant, reporting directly to Commander Rivers.
He supervised the roll call officers, those who were
responsible for the assignment of officers to various duties as well as seeing that officers were informed of court appearances. He also oversaw the
time-records clerk, and the planning and statisti-
cal officer who kept the records for arrests and
summonses.

Sometimes Castleton forgot to wear his gun.
They didn't take it away from him, he just didn't
pack it. It was rumored that when he did, the
chambers were empty. It looked like Castleton
would always be a desk lieutenant, because after
two years he didn't recover. Nobody in the precinct felt he'd been at fault except Castleton himself, but his self-blame shook him up so much that
Commander Rivers agreed he'd be better off on
desk duty.

Chapter One

IT WAS DEVIL'S Night in Detroit.

It had become the custom among inner-city youth to observe the night before Halloween by burning down as much of the city as possible. Authorities knew they would be lucky if they had less than 200 fires to deal with. In 1983, when it all started, 553 fires had been set in a two-day period. Accordingly, the mayor canceled leave for 1,400 police and 1,280 fire fighters and put trash collectors, meter readers, and civilian volunteers on patrol with the police, who were expected to enforce a dusk-to-dawn curfew for anyone under eighteen.

The fires began before the moon rose, with the 14th Precinct getting the worst of it—seven fires in occupied buildings, fifty-three in trash, and one major warehouse blaze near the marine terminals along the Detroit River.

It was expected that the 14th Precinct would have the big numbers, because the precinct itself

was so big on the map. Lying beyond the sky-
scrapers of downtown Detroit, the 14th Precinct
was bounded to the east by the John C. Lodge
Freeway, to the north by West Grand Boulevard,
to the west by Dearborn, and to the southwest by
River Rouge. The 14th encompassed a great
sprawl of houses mixed helter-skelter with schools
and hospitals, the General Motors Cadillac plant,
a salt mine, warehouses, stores, and public buildings, all an unhomogenized amalgam of blacks,
Poles, and Greeks, railroad tracks and zoning
abominations. Other little ethnic communities—
Chaldeans, Croatians, Hungarians—struggled to
survive beneath the awesome glare of heavy industry. There were pockets of prosperity and
burned-out battle zones. One could find elm-lined
streets which had been elegantly paved with brick
in the old days, but now were potholed and
patched with asphalt, streets of once prosperous
wooden and brick houses with boastful porches
and backyard carriage houses that had declined
into crack houses and after-hours bars known as
blind pigs. Entire blocks had been abandoned by
families not because they were substandard, but
because it was safer to live in a shelter than in a
drug-infested neighborhood. In the 14th Precinct,
the war against poverty, drugs, and crime was not
being won.

For all that, it wasn't the worst part of town—
the 10th Precinct had the highest murder rate—
but overall the crime rate in the 14th was one and
a half times higher than the rest of the city. Pimps,
pushers, and small-time crooks peopled the
streets, along with the homeless and the jobless,
the factory workers and storekeepers. In the One-
Four, as in the city as a whole, there were more
guns than people, and the 14th Precinct made up
for a lack of downtown glamour with the ingenu-
ity of its criminals.

The streets surrounding the One-Four station house were an obstacle course of artillery potholes, loose manhole covers, discarded boxes, stray wooden pallets, and slabs of uplifted cement. The picturesque station house had been built in 1926, with two globe lights at the bottom of the broad exterior stairs. It was an architectural statement—that a police station should unmistakably look like nothing else. The ground-floor windows were grilled and had been since the day in 1971 when someone had placed a home-made antipersonnel bomb on a window ledge. A patrolman had been killed. The book was still open on that one.

A low retaining wall fronted the station house, topped by trimmed shrubbery. Desk Sergeant Charles Sudol was in the habit of running his hand along the space between the wall and shrubbery before he entered the building to begin his shift. He had discovered that certain individuals who had occasion to enter the station house often decided at the last moment to temporarily divest themselves of illegal items. It amused him to collect these.

In the lobby Sudol sat behind the long, dark wooden counter. It was four feet high with a gleaming brass rail running its length. The top of the counter was kept clear, except for a stuffed tiger which lived at the far end, wrapped in a banner that read "Bless You Boys." Though not clean, the lobby was painfully well-lighted by humming fluorescent lights that were fixed to the high ceiling and by fluorescent desk lamps on the booking and muster desks. High on one wall there was a large reproduction of the city's insignia, a cross-legged giant squatting with his arms raised, a blazing sun in the palm of his hand.

Settled upon his swivel chair, Sergeant Sudol examined his finds. Once before when he had been

doing this, a man leaving the station house had
had the nerve to ask for his partner's knife back.
This Devil's Night, Sudol laid out two switch-
blades—one spring, one gravity—a Baggie containing a dozen .22 cartridges that had been
crudely dum-dummed, and a half-dozen tiny zip-
locks, each with the brand name Rolls-Royce sten-
ciled on it. This was how heroin was commonly
packaged, but Sudol was quick to perceive that
the packs contained only talcum powder, the
property of a burn artist.

Sergeant Sudol was a heavyset man with dark
hair, a complete set of false teeth, and an interest
in the human comedy. He had grown up in River-
view, worked in the steel mill there and served in
the Sixth Fleet before becoming a police officer.
Today, Sudol had brought a copy of Schopen-
hauer's *The Basis of Morality* to work, and he
hoped later to discuss it with Lieutenant Castleton. Not that he had any time for reading on Devil's Night. Traffic was heavy, with juvenile
arsonists being brought in and responding officers
rushing out. There was constant movement. The
lobby seethed and shifted as groups formed, huddled, re-formed. Sometimes it was hard to tell who
was who in the confluence of lawyers, punks, and
establishment types. Cops hung out and gossiped
by the coffee machine. Behind the muster desk, a
patrolman on the phone was oblivious to all but
his conversation with his girlfriend.

To encourage and acknowledge outstanding
work by officers, Chief of Police Wilson Davies had
initiated a Police Officer of the Month award. The
selection was made monthly, and a board with the
officer's photo and a copy of the writeup was
prominently displayed in the station lobby.

*Inspector Campbell has displayed an inves-
tigative talent that only comes from years of*

experience and dedication. His other qualifications of judgment, dependability, and maturity qualify him as an expert investigator.

The writeup had been annotated. Between the words *Campbell* and *has*, an arrow underlined the phrase, written in longhand, "better known to us who love and serve him as 'Douche.'" Sudol had decided not to notice.

Twenty minutes into the shift, a cab driver staggered into the lobby bleeding from a wound below the neck. "This whore took me to a club on Rosa Parks. Said she'd give me a blow job free and then these guys came out from the bar and took my money and cut me."

"Would this be the United Civic Club for Community Action?" Sergeant Sudol asked.

"Yeah, something like that."

"Who do you drive for?"

"American."

"You oughta know better. That's one of the worst dives in the presink." Precinct was a word almost no one in the Detroit Police Department could pronounce. Other common variants were precin and precint.

"These are parlous times, my friend," Sergeant Sudol observed.

"Uh, yeah? Yeah, I guess so."

While the cab driver was making his statement, the dispatcher reported a ten eighteen—a fatality—at the scene of a fire on Livernois. Inspector Campbell charged down the stairs from the second-floor squad room, bound for the scene.

Several minutes later, a woman entered the station with a friend, complaining that a cab driver had stolen her house keys.

Sergeant Sudol pointed with his chin to a bench pushed against the far wall. The taxi driver sat waiting for transportation to the hospital.

"That cab driver?" Sudol asked, eager to please.

The woman was arrested. The cab driver was taken to Detroit Receiving.

After sixteen years as desk sergeant at the One-Four nothing surprised Sergeant Sudol, especially on Devil's Night, and he didn't so much as raise an eyebrow when the gorilla entered the lobby.

The gorilla suit was the whole schmear, glossy black fur from head to tuchus. Sergeant Sudol thought it needed a tag that read "Caution—Wearing a Gorilla Suit Can Cause You to Look Like a Jerk."

"May I help you?"

The gorilla cocked his head and looked at Sudol, but did not respond. Crouching and swinging his arms, the gorilla moved, crossing the length of the booking desk with surprising speed.

Gary Newman, the precinct clerk, looked up from the time-records log to peer over Sergeant Sudol's massive shoulder. "What is it?" he asked in his squeaky voice. "And what does it want?"

The gorilla stopped beneath the board with the photograph of Inspector Campbell and the encomiums. He took it from the wall and sniffed it. Then he humped the photograph, slowly at first but then in a mounting, savage lust. At last, looking about suspiciously, he tucked the board under his arm and departed, crouching and waddling through the heavy doors.

It was shortly after the departure of the gorilla that the dispatcher received a second ten-eighteen. The call came from Patrol Car 7, Officers O'Hallerin and Mallory. While giving chase to some kids who had set a trash fire in Riverside Field, they had found a corpse.

Riverside Field, courtesy of a bend in the Detroit River, presented Investigator Nick Sands with a stunning view of the Detroit skyline. The handsome twenty-nine-year-old policeman looked out upon the towers of the Ambassador Bridge and the giant illuminated Canadian Club sign on the Windsor side. His eyes followed the Detroit River past the bridge to the high-rise waterfront apartment towers, Cobo Hall and Hart Plaza, all clean lines and brightness, and beyond, the five futuristic tubes of the Renaissance Center. The cityscape was something from a dream, and overhead the three-quarter moon glowed with a reddish cast given from the flames of many fires. It seemed like the city consumed itself—no longer having enough industry to feed its fires, the fires fed upon the city.

Sands had just radioed Lieutenant Crear Starks of the Patrol Section to send enough officers to seal off the area, and the fire department to send lights. He and Investigator Dwight Franklin walked back to the corpse from their unmarked white Chrysler, crossing the ninth-hole green of the golf course.

"Something *would* happen to hold us up just before the gorilla went in," Investigator Dwight Franklin said peevishly.

"Perhaps it just wasn't meant to be," said Nick Sands.

"Bite ass, honkie," Franklin suggested.

"Hey, nothing personal, it was just a philosophical observation."

"Man, what a shallow remark. Shallow and obvious. Just what I'd expect from a cop."

"*You're* a cop."

"I got an excuse! Do you think I would have become a police officer if I were *white*? Absolutely not. I would only recommend a black to become a policeman if he had no other trade or schooling, like me. But you, Sands, I think you're afraid to face life. You're a cop because you're afraid to go out in the business world where you face real challenges."

"You sound just like Dad."

It was cold out and Sands wore a three-quarter length black leather jacket over a corduroy jacket, silk shirt, and bowtie; he also wore tan slacks and dark brown ankle boots with brass buckles. Sands was a stylish dresser. He also wore an upside-down shoulder holster, quick-draw model, on his left with a vertical refill row of seven cartridges, and a pair of handcuffs. The gun was a 9 mm Walther TPK, popular among plainclothed cops. He was good with it, and was known as the Ivy League Gunman in the squad room after he won the annual Chief's Trophy Match at the Rouge Park Pistol Range.

Sands was a tall man with dark eyes, a flamboyant mustache and cleft chin, all dominated by abundant curly blond hair. He had a focused intensity and concentration that could be unnerving. People liked him, but Franklin was his only real friend.

Sands and Franklin were steady partners. They did a good Mutt and Jeff during interrogations, Sands always the nice, pretty-boy Jeff and Franklin the mean, nasty Mutt. Franklin was high-spirited, the insult comedian of the 14th, but he had a look that earned him the sobriquet Terror on the street.

Franklin also wore three-quarter-length leather. Both men loved their black leather jackets. They did not show dirt and smelled nice. If they got knocked down, the jacket could be wiped off easily. They made excellent pillows for sleeping in a car, or in a broom closet or basement while on surveillance. And they were convinced that the jackets were very cool. Dwight Franklin also wore a black turtleneck sweater and a black leather pillbox cap, the kind Eddie Murphy sometimes wore. The turtleneck was pulled over a big black S&W .45.

Dwight Franklin was a black man with a mustache and goatee, and a medium-length ill-kept Afro. His girlfriend Chimene Green was always clucking her tongue and messing with his hair. She called him Cargo Cult, and laughed at her own wit.

Most of the excited onlookers at the scene of the crime were also black.

Franklin scowled at the crowd. He was in a bad mood because the two ten-eighteen's had spoiled his timing. The gorilla had arrived after Roger Campbell had left and before Dwight Franklin got to watch.

For his part, Nick Sands seemed cheerful, as did Officers Declan O'Hallerin and Sue Mallory, the patrol car team who had first found the body. Heading south on Twenty-fourth Street, they had spotted a gang of youths trying to build a fire on the N&W railroad tracks. O'Hallerin punched the pedal, Mallory hit the siren and the red-and-blue lights. The youths scattered, most heading for the protective flora offered by Riverside Field. The officers had entered the park in pursuit when, rounding a turn in the drive, they saw ahead of them the glow of a big fire. They forgot the youths. The fire was a car, completely enveloped in flames leaping fifteen feet high. The heat was intense.

Officer Mallory got on the radio. The Detroit Fire Department responded commendably. A pump truck that happened to be in the vicinity was diverted to the scene, and twelve minutes later the flames were out.

They had been horrified to see a blackened human shape lying across the front seat—which was why the responding officers, with the exception of the peevish Franklin, seemed cheerful. It was a law of cop nature. The worse a victim looked, the more cheerful cops were. Tonight they could barely keep from giggling as they stood at the edge

of the picnic area, careful of where they stepped,
touching nothing.

Sue Mallory was five feet five and quite the most
attractive female cop in the precinct—at least
among the uniformed cops. There was also the
matter of Investigator Claire Hopson, for those
who happened to admire more mature women.
Sue Mallory had developed a quick-witted repar-
tee after long hours of riding with O'Hallerin, the
precinct's playboy. O'Hallerin was likable, but he
was eager. Dwight Franklin hated eager. An over-
eager officer was a danger to everyone around
him. O'Hallerin was too anxious to move quickly
up the ranks. He got along okay with the guys, but
he was always heading in one direction—female
conquest. The other men felt slightly alienated
from him for this reason. They joked that O'Hallerin joined the force to fuck himself to death.

Dwight Franklin's comments on if, how, and
where Officers O'Hallerin and Mallory got it on
were frequent, loud, and lacking in subtlety. Nick
Sands thought that Franklin was slanderous. He
figured Officer Mallory knew how to put the freeze
on. She was too savvy to take O'Hallerin's macho
shit and love-'em-and-leave-'em philosophy.

Among the onlookers were the overcurious,
coming too close and threatening to sully the
crime scene. The trick was to isolate the area
without driving away important witnesses. Sands
and Franklin knew that their best chance in any
investigation was in the beginning, when recollections were fresh.

Even when the two inspectors were not together, they knew what the other was doing and
avoided overlapping. Usually one man would opt
to stay with the body, as Sands did this night.
Sands had a firm belief that it was the body that
would tell them almost all they needed to know to
solve a case.

Without discussion, Dwight Franklin walked off
to see if any of the crowd had seen or heard anything. Unfortunately, many of the potential witnesses were in violation of the mayor's No More
Devil's Night curfew, and their inclination was to
split.

Sensitive to leather jackets, Franklin saw a
youth wearing one try to edge backwards out of
the crowd.

"Come back here!" he demanded, not in his real
command voice but in a mock authoritarian tone.
Franklin was *on*, quick-moving and fast-talking.
He was, in fact, hopeless for undercover work. He
did not blend. On the contrary, people always
watched him. When he moved across a room, people found their eyes following. Franklin had presence.

The youth halted, and it seemed he and two others were together. They might have been the very
ones that O'Hallerin and Mallory had been chasing.

"Looky here," Franklin said, "I don't care *how*
young your ass is. By the power vested me by the
city of Detroit, I declare amnesty for any curfew
violators that I be looking at."

"We seen somebody awright," said a bony-faced
kid, underdressed in an Ollie North T-shirt. "He
run across the road in front of us. Then he seen
us and turned back. He ran along that field."

"Yeah," his friend said. "He ran to those bushes.
I bet he still there."

"What'd he have for threads?"

"Dark clothes, couldn't tell."

"Was he a brother?"

"I'm not sure. We weren't that close and it's
dark, baby."

Over the years Franklin had formed impres-
sions about the way people ran and the differ-

ences in their strides. Whites, blacks, and Chicanos all ran differently, he felt.

"Okay, watch me, watch me. Did he run like this?" Franklin ran bent forward at the waist, something in his motion suggesting that he was being jerked by strings. That was his rendering of a white man's run.

The yeahs and the naws sounded together, neither having it. Franklin was about to demonstrate his Chicano run when a girl interrupted him insistently.

"I saw two guys running through the park with guns. It was two black guys."

"Did you actually see them?"

"I sure enough did."

"Come over here with me." He led her toward his car and placed her in the back seat. He got out a pad and pencil and asked her to describe the persons she had seen. He quickly copied down the information and picked up his radio.

"Unit Twenty, set to copy suspects."

"Ten-four."

"Okay, first subject. . . . YBM, no age, about five seven, dark pants, a Levi jacket, and white tennis shoes. Break."

He turned to the girl. "You ever work with a police artist? No? You gonna love it, young lady." Back to the radio. "Unit Twenty, continuing. Second subject. . . . YBM, no age, about five ten, sweats, trenchcoat. Both armed."

A dozen units arrived at the scene, their pulsating bar lights adding to the excitement. Sergeant Kalina, the patrol sergeant, trotted from his unit, his pet stomach obscuring the spare cartridge case he wore in front of his holster. Sands heard him yell at O'Hallerin to put his hat on.

"Canvass the area," Sands ordered Kalina, "and look for anyone who matches the descriptions."

Soon a large number of patrolmen were searching tree by tree, shrub by shrub, flashlights slashing lines into the night. In the distance voices called to each other.

"I can't see nothing."

"Everybody get in a straight line and stay close. Don't anybody get ahead, 'cause we don't want to shoot you. Nobody get shot!"

"Okay, O'Hallerin, you're getting ahead of us. get back, get back. Everybody stay in a straight line. Popovich, you okay?"

"They could be in the bushes, they could be anyplace. We gotta go slow."

"Get that light off us! You're gonna get us killed."

Meanwhile, since it was Devil's Night, it had taken the intervention of the Deputy Chief, Western Operations Bureau, to obtain further cooperation from the harried fire department. Finally, they sent a truck mounted with high-powered floodlights. Sands directed them as the truck moved into place to illuminate the entire area.

The red lights, flashing blue lights, klieg lights, and blazing yellow lights added immeasurably to the theatricality of the scene, which now glowed like a stage. The spotlights fixed upon the burned Ford, near the picnic area, and they attracted yet more people. Someone said, "Hey, they're making a *movie.*"

Sands and Franklin waited for Homicide, who were required at the scene. They were late, but they were busy, the nation's busiest, dealing with a homicide rate triple that of New York's. Six hundred and forty-six people had been killed in Detroit in 1986, more than had been killed in all of Europe. A child had been shot for every day of the year. And this year the homicide rate was up twenty percent. It had gotten so bad that emergency room physicians couldn't take all the gunshot victims on the busiest nights.

They were also expecting Inspector Campbell, ruler of the Fourteenth Precinct Investigative Operations Section.

Sands dreaded the arrival of Roger Campbell. Campbell was always breathing down his neck, always looking to catch him up short, showing up at the scene and taking over for effect. Sands thought Campbell was an asshole.

Sands looked over the victim's Ford sedan. All the windows had exploded in the fire. The smell of blood and burned flesh clung and hid in every crevice and crack of the interior. The trunk was open, and in the blackened detritus he saw what seemed to be fragments of heavy rope. The glove compartment had also opened, showing nothing recognizable as a registration.

Sands listened to the deep-throated horns of seagoing vessels churning their way up the St. Lawrence Seaway. He thought about going overseas, taking a trip with a woman named Marlene Moro. At length he turned to scrutinize the body. If there had been a wallet, it had been destroyed. The face was no longer there. It looked weird. A partial disfigurement of the face was always hideous, but the change in this man was so total he appeared to have been transformed to another order of being. It looked as if he had thrown up his hands to protect himself, as if he had known what was happening to him.

Sands had already taken several shots of the whole crime scene from a distance. He took six more shots with his pocket Kodak, moving carefully toward the body. He took these for his personal record, always using a whole roll of film on each case and getting his shots in before the crime scene unit got there. Their photographer would take the official shots, under the direction of the Homicide officers.

Freehand, on a blank sheet of paper, Sands

made a sketch of the scene, noting the car, the tree, the green, and the relationship of the body to them. Even photographs taken from every conceivable angle give a distorted view of a body in respect to its surroundings, so he made exact measurements with his steel tape and added these to the sketch. While performing these tasks Sands bent forward intently. In the grass gleamed the copper color of a 9 mm casing.

It was in this position that Sands noticed that the rear license plate had not been destroyed. It was blackened and bent, but the numbers could be made out and the vehicle traced.

The crowd had grown dense enough to impede the parking maneuvers of the arriving Assistant Medical Examiner, Walter Van Loon.

The ME was in his fifties but he looked like a man who hadn't had a vacation for too long. He was clearly in need of sunshine, exercise, and a revised diet. He carried a small black bag.

"Where am I supposed to put the stethoscope?" the ME asked jocularly. He went through the motions.

"Tell us the truth, Doc," Franklin said. "Give it to us straight."

The ME listened intently and shook his head. "I don't think he's quite dead yet. We're going to have to give him another twenty thousand volts."

The ME was a riot. He was still laughing, then coughing, when Roger Campbell arrived on the scene. Campbell strode briskly toward them with his hands behind his back. He was a big man with broad shoulders and a thick neck. He had that I'm-Roger-Campbell-and-you're-not expression.

"What the hell are you doing, Sands?"

Sands, who had been squinting at the license plate, swiveled on his toes without rising. A large shape blocked out the klieg light by standing in the aura with hands on hips. A familiar Campbell pose.

It had taken Sands years to realize that underneath Roger Campbell's stony facade lay a heart of steel. He was pushing to become a star, headed for downtown headquarters or a precinct command.

"I see you're as professional looking as always, Franklin."

"I can't get over the way *you* look, Inspector."

Campbell stood arms akimbo and looked with disapproval at Franklin and Sands, the theatrical-looking lights, and the crowd.

"I wonder how many ways you and Franklin managed to fuck up in the time it took me to get here."

"We love you, too," Sands said.

Campbell was of the opinion that Sands and Franklin spent too much time together. They were both sharp-witted and just a little too smart-ass, and one of these days they were going to go too far with him and get their ears pinned back.

Campbell brushed by Sands and crouched down beside the body. Franklin watched Campbell's fat ass stretch the windowpane check of his slacks and murmured to his partner, "I suppose maybe Campbell wouldn't be so bad if he hadn't had that there operation."

"What operation?"

"You know," Franklin said, "the one where they cut them slits in his gut. So he could still see with his head up his ass."

Franklin had a direct personal beef with Campbell.

Some black cops and correction men gave a dance one night, and Franklin took Chimene Green. Franklin had to do an eight-to-four tour of duty. The dance was over at 3:00 A.M., and he was driving Chimene Green home when he stopped to

break up a fight between a man and a woman.
They were arguing over money, and the man had
taken the woman's purse by force. The man was
nasty so Franklin booked him into the station
house. While he was in the station house, Campbell was outside was propositioning Chimene. Two
days later she told him about it.

Campbell scowled at the body. "And who might
this be?"

"No ID yet," Sand said, "but that plate might
give us something. I don't think he drove the car
here himself, but he was still alive when he arrived."

"Hooray, the Homicide Section has sent us
Jackson and Johnson," Franklin said. Lieutenant
Jackson and Investigator Johnson were on one of
the Homicide Section's general assignment
squads, two black men in black raincoats, both
built like linebackers, who had worked together
so long that their personalities seemed to have
merged. On the street they were known as Heckel
and Jeckel. Sands and Franklin greeted them cordially. If their lieutenant had honored them with
his presence, Sands and Franklin would have been
less forthcoming. They had come to feel that it
was desirable to keep out of the way of any boss
from outside the precinct, because bosses from
outside the precinct were authority figures who
might report them to God knew what levels of
command at headquarters on 1300 Beaubien.

Johnson looked at the car and said, "How many
miles on it?"

Jackson said, "We'll give you two hundred, and
that's our final offer."

Campbell told them about the accomplishments
of his investigators—implying that it had been
done under his direction. They had witnesses, a
shell casing, and the license plate.

Jackson and Johnson made a painstaking search

for more shells and found none. The cartridge was labeled and identified with extreme care so that it would not be mutilated in any way. The crime lab would need the fatal bullet, fatal shell, and—they hoped, eventually—the lethal weapon itself. When two men from the crime lab arrived, they took the cartridge as evidence to be traced from the time of recovery so that a chain of legal evidence could be maintained. They carefully removed the license plate, wanting to check for latent prints before cleaning it.

A vehicle from the Tactical Services Section's K-9 unit arrived, carrying seven of the best patrol dogs in Wayne County. They were gathered at the front entrance to the park and were deployed one at a time in various directions: the golf course, swimming pools, jogging and bicycling trails. For more than an hour the dogs moved with swift determination, sniffing the thick undergrowth, searching the park for anyone hiding in the shadows or rocky ledges. As a final touch, a Bell 47G5 observation helicopter from the Aviation Operations Section flew over and begrn to play its searchlight frantically.

There was a lot of activity but nothing was happening.

Nick Sands found himself scanning the crowd.

Franklin was looking at him. "You thinking what I'm thinking?"

Sands put it to Jackson. "If they aren't anywhere out there, maybe it's because they're here." He said it softly, casually.

Jackson asked Johnson, "You figure the perps are in the crowd?"

"It occurred to me," Johnson said.

"Do you have any undercover guys in the crowd?"

"Yeah, we got one," Jackson said.

"Tell him to take shots of the crowd," Sands

suggested. "Don't make a production out of it. Get the guy to mingle."

At 9:12 P.M. the ME authorized removal of the victim to the morgue. Those who could see past the clutch of cops couldn't believe what they were seeing. When a person is killed by burning, a condition resembling rigor mortis immediately sets in and the body remains stiff until the onset of putrefaction. The paramedics engaged in a macabre struggle with the burned corpse, trying to bend arms and legs to get the body out of the car. The limbs kept snapping back to their original position, as if the corpse were offering spirited resistance. When at length the body was placed on a stretcher, it retained its death pose, lying on its side.

Things began to break up after that. Campbell went the way he had come—a man full of purpose. When he pulled out in his car he did it fast, and he used the siren. People got out of his way.

The crime lab radioed back to the homicide unit. When Jackson got out of the car it was obvious that his mood had changed from stolid to grim.

"You ain't gonna believe this. We got a make on the plate. The car is registered to Ed Tomack."

"Shit," Johnson said flatly.

"Who's Tomack?" Sands asked.

"A good cop. Our section. Felony Murder," Jackson said, stony-faced. "He used to be an investigator in your precinct."

"No shit," Dwight Franklin said.

"That was before your time, when men were men."

"I thought Tomack was on leave," Johnson said. "Maybe that wasn't him, just his car."

"You think so?"

"No."

"Gentlemen," Nick Sands said, "it looks like the shit has hit the fan."

At 1:30 A.M., the search was called off. At 1:45 A.M., Tomack's car was towed across town to the police garage on Jefferson.

Reginald Philpot went to meet Maurice Finnegan in Finnegan's room on the seventh floor of the Hotel Atlanta. Philpot was wearing a red maxi-coat, a white felt slouch hat with a wide black band, and Ellesse gym shoes. He hoped to make a good impression because he respected Finnegan for his accomplishments. In his career, Finnegan, with the assistance of various associates, had been involved in over two hundred robberies and six robbery homicides.

The dude was about six feet two, maybe two hundred ten pounds, with short hair and a stone face. His knit shirt showed undulant muscles in his arms and chest. Philpot couldn't help thinking Finnegan knew something he didn't. It was in the way he looked at him. Like he had some kind of animal understanding of what life was all about when it was stripped down to the raw.

In street lingo Finnegan was called a "new jack", which meant he was internally restrained by nothing. He had no religion, no concept of morality, no civic responsibility, and no fear. To survive, he was out there constantly preying upon others, probing for any human weakness, forever frustrated, restless, and anxious for some action.

Top Dog was there too, watching TV. It was he who had recommended Philpot. Philpot was all smiles, but now Top Dog regarded Philpot with disinterest and Finnegan snorted in disgust. "You look like a fucking pimp," he observed.

Philpot was proud of his getup and pimping had in fact been his career objective before Top Dog suggested he join Finnegan's crew. But Finnegan's remark, the way he said it, cut him to the quick.

"It's the latest thang . . ." His protest trailed off. It sounded lame, even to himself.

"It's the hat," Finnegan explained. "I hate your hat. If we're going to do business together in the future, you got to wear a business suit. You wear a medium-length raincoat, tan or black. You get your hair cut short. No flash, no cut, no glitz. You dress so that nobody can describe you, dig?"

"I hear you, man."

"Okay, let me see your piece."

Philpot drew his revolver from his shoulder holster and handed it to Finnegan.

"The fuck is that rig? Nobody wears shoulder holsters anymore, man, they're out. Even cops don't wear shoulder holsters anymore."

The first Finnegan did, just like a cop, was to flip open the cylinder and unload the revolver. In Finnegan's eyes the gun met with even less approval than Philpot's unprofessional attire. It was a silver-plated .32 with ersatz pearl grips.

"Man, this a lady's gun!"

Philpot had in fact borrowed the gun, after much cajoling, from Zahara Lane, the woman he considered the love of his life.

"This a fudgepacker's piece! Who you goan scare with this biddy thang, Reginald, your momma? The man got to be looking down a big black hole, something so big, so black, he got to urinate and defecate." Finnegan sighed. "I don't know, man, I try to help you, but you a fool, you know that, don't you? Like the chump you be over that skinny bitch, crying like a pussy."

Philpot realized that Top Dog had told Finnegan about Zahara. The trouble with his girlfriend started one evening when he pulled his used El Dorado into a gas station on West Vernor. A dude called Main Man was working there, and he insisted that Philpot pay for the gas before pumping. The two men used to hang out together but now Main Man was coming on like he owned the place, showing off for his friends. Philpot objected, and a loud discussion ensued. They started throwing punches and pretending they knew karate. Main Man's friends broke up the fight and jeered at Philpot when he drove away.

Twenty minutes later Philpot returned to the gas station, parking in the little lot. The crew was still there, and Philpot saw them take notice from the office. Philpot was cool, taking his time as he got out of the car and walked back to open the trunk. He removed a .44 caliber Strum Ruger carbine and methodically shot into the office until the magazine was empty, blowing the windows in, triggering the robbery alarm, and hitting Main Man in the shoulder.

Having made his point, Philpot turned and strolled back toward his car, super-cool. Until they started shooting back from the shattered office—pop-pop-pop, and then a shotgun blast. Realizing that he wasn't going to be able to reload or make it out in his car, Philpot ran across West Vernor and kept going, worrying about the visibility of his rifle and how he was going to retrieve his El Dorado.

He was able to stash the rifle and call Zahara from a phone booth, asking her to drive his car from the parking lot to where he was. He didn't have time to give her all the details.

Zahara made it there, got into the El Dorado and started driving. She was rather tall and wore a cap that concealed her hair. As Zahara drove away, Main Man ran after the car with a pistol in his hand. He thought she was Philpot.

At that moment a 14th Precinct patrol car arrived. Officers Popovich and Witoski stopped their car abruptly and, with guns drawn, went toward Zahara, who had also stopped in response to Main Man's shouting. As they approached the car, Main

Man was shouting, "That is the car. He got a rifle. Motherfucker *shot* me!" Officer Popovich approached from the rear on the driver's side, and Officer Witoski from the rear on the passenger side. They called out a warning, but Zahara was petrified and slumped down on the front seat, trying to conceal herself.

"Hey, that's just a girl in there!" someone shouted, but in all the excitement Popovich apparently did not hear. As the officers eased toward the car, a head with a hat suddenly popped up. Officer Popovich fired four times. He missed, but now Dim and Wit were in deep shit and Zahara was *really* pissed.

Meanwhile Philpot's Ruger was gone when he went back to get it, and worse yet, Zahara had been making him pay after that, just like a regular john. Philpot, his eyes filling up, had complained about the situation to Top Dog in a moment of weakness.

Philpot shrugged. "I'm in love, man, and I need her."

"You acting like a fool!" Finnegan said. "Ain't no man need a woman! Need a woman, shit! World's full a bitches. What you crying for, she won't give it up for free? Man, I pay for it!" Finnegan said proudly. "You got to be a man. Don't owe nothin' to a woman. Get serious about business and get you some respect. You can have a rep. You can be gone five, six years, come back and find your place again, *be* somebody."

"I can dig it."

"But you got to understand, you got to have commitment. When you do something, you do it absolutely." As someone who used violence successfully, he knew that the use of violence is not easy. It requires both physical and mental training. "If I tell you to cap somebody, you don't stop and think about it."

"That's right."

"If you're going to do it, be first and be fast. No warnings, no hints."

"Yes."

"Be final. You got to hurt somebody, you hurt him enough he can't hurt you."

"Yes."

"Be careful. We stay on our own turf and we don't relax too much. And we don't run our mouths."

"I hear you."

"You see, Reginald, when you do what we do, we show balls. We're not like burglars," Finnegan said, shooting a look at Top Dog, "sneaking around when nobody's home. We're honest. We don't play tricks on folks. We give people a chance. Every place we go people got guns, got security guards, got guards outside the dope houses, whatever. We play fair."

Philpot had never thought of it quite that way. He felt inspired. "Man, I am ready."

Finnegan stared at Philpot until he felt small.

"Maybe you be frontin'. I'm going to try you out. Tomorrow night, man, and dress like I told you."

The Tomacks lived in the precinct's Poletown, a neighborhood of workingmen's houses, proudly maintained bungalows nosed up to the sidewalk. Many of the frame bungalows had been home to the same family for generations. The white Chrysler was parked in front of a house with new aluminum siding and a tidy fringe of front lawn. The main warehouse for the Detroit Edison Company loomed large behind it. The first to emerge from the car was a big black man with sad eyes and hair that showed a lot of white. Cal Rivers was Commander of the 14th Precinct and an old friend of the family. Authoritative and dignified in his bearing, he moved slowly, looking at the house

with reluctance before opening the rear door for
his wife, Beryl, who regarded him with concern.
Lieutenant Castleton and Lieutenant Jacoby got
out from the other side. Jacoby, acting as the official department representative, had come to the
station house from headquarters.

The door was opened by a teenage boy, Martin
Tomack. His mother Cynthia had just received a
telephone call from the *Detroit Free Press* inquir-
ing about the shooting.

Cynthia turned. Already in shock, she evinced
no further surprise when she saw the group at the
door.

"Cynthia, who is it?"

"It's—it's someone named Ralph Thomas."

"Hang up the phone, Cynthia," Rivers said.

Quickly, she did so.

"Ed is hurt, isn't he?" she blurted, looking desperately at them.

"Well, yeah, Cynthia," Rivers replied softly, his
head lowered. "He's been killed."

He saw her face turn an ashen color. She
reached out to steady herself. "Oh, my God!"

Cynthia's younger son, John, had appeared in
the room, standing silently beside his brother. He
did not appear to understand what had happened.
But Martin reacted with denial and anger as Beryl
embraced his mother.

"I don't believe it," he said. Suddenly he drove
his fist into the wall, punching through the flow-
ered wallpaper. "Shit!" he cried.

Rivers lay a heavy hand on his shoulder. "Get a
hold of yourself, Martin," he said.

Again, the telephone rang. Rivers answered it.
It was Mike Tomack, Ed's brother, calling from
Lansing to say hello. "I guess you haven't heard,"
Rivers said after identifying himself. "Your
brother was murdered tonight."

He heard a gasp, silence, something said too far
from the receiver to make out."

"Mr. Tomack? I'm sorry."

"Excuse me. I just—just went out of it. What
happened?"

"We don't have details yet."

"Did he suffer?"

It was a question Rivers found hard to understand. Of course he had suffered; he had suffered
horribly.

"No," he said.

"Tell Cynthia I'll be right over."

Cynthia had begun to climb the stairs, slowly
and unsteadily, depending upon Beryl's firm grip,
while Tom Castleton was saying something to the
boys. Cynthia paused at the landing and stared
down at Rivers with a terrible bitterness.

"Cal?"

"Yes?"

"You and Ed are children," she said, "playing a
boy's game, dying for nothing worth having. For
what? A stupid, empty, silly death. You're fools
and asses to play such stupid games. Where was
the good of it? Did the drugs go away? Did the
streets get better? Did anybody care? Why die in
such a—humiliating way? Where's the honor in
it? Where's the glory now, Cal? You're not men.
You're nothing."

At the end of his shift, Nick Sands drove off in his
Morris Minor. It was past four in the morning and
eight-lane Jefferson was nearly empty. Sands
drove to a sandblasted apartment building in
Bricktown, a corner of downtown busily refur-
bishing itself in the hope of catching dollars spilling over from the Ren Cen. It wasn't working out.

His relationship with Marlene Moro wasn't
working out either.

Nick let himself in the front second-floor apartment with his key. He hadn't used the key since his last fight with her.

She was in the kitchenette, which smelled of very strong coffee, freshly brewed. Marlene drank coffee to relax. Not that it helped. She considered sleep optional. Tonight she looked tanned and rested. Nick surmised that she had just come in, probably having returned from a gallery opening, an event which he had known about but had not been able to attend.

Marlene was looking good. Tonight she was wearing a bold black-and-white smock, belted, over tights. For a second, Nick wondered if she'd taken off her skirt, but if Marlene wore it, it must be in style. Her straight, glossy black hair was unmussed, cut in severe bangs. She had a wonderful complexion, and extraordinarily clear eyes.

"Hello, stupid," Marlene Moro said. She was glad to see him. Her shoes were off and she stood on tiptoe to kiss him lightly.

She wasn't alone.

Felix Laurent sat at the kitchenette table drinking coffee. Felix was an interior decorator, and Marlene was his most valued employee. Sands had a horrible feeling that Felix was straight, even though he wore a long striped scarf, knotted artistically around his pale throat. He stood politely and offered his hand to Sands.

"I like your scarf. I'd like to wear one to work, but I don't think I could get away with it, you know what I mean?"

Without further ado, Nick passed on the coffee and left the kitchen. Trying to gauge the extent of his exhaustion, he entered Marlene's bedroom. He undressed, got into bed, and turned out the lights. Marlene and Felix spoke for another five minutes in low, indistinct tones. Then the door clicked shut.

He heard Marlene enter the bedroom and sigh

exaggeratedly before slipping out of her clothes. As was her habit, she put them away neatly and set the alarm. She opened the window three inches and checked the answering machine. Then she turned on the bedside lamp.

"How was the party?"

"Fine. We went to Clutch Cargo's after."

"Say, I wasn't being inconsiderate, was I—you know—getting in the way of anything between you and Felix?" Sands asked innocently.

"Oh, no, perish the thought. But I think it's time I made some trouble. I need a new conquest."

He didn't seem to be listening. He always did this. He didn't listen enough, didn't talk enough. But the thing about Nick Sands, apart from the obvious, was that he was absolutely genuine. When he was happy, in the right mood, he'd love her like no one else ever had, completely, all the way, nothing held back, until . . . Until he was all distance, intent upon something she knew nothing about, something he would not share. He acted as if he were complete in himself. In a way she admired his not needing her. It made him different from the other men she had known. It gave him the kind of authority women crave. It was the reason women went for cops, she supposed. She hated the whole situation. She was happy just to see him, be with him.

"Seriously now, folks, Felix is just a friend. I really don't want anything coming along and complicating my trip, which is constantly complicated and confusing to me anyhow, thanks in large part to *toi*."

Characteristically, he said something unexpected. "I've never been to France. I've never learned how to ski. Or whistle properly. Franklin can break windows across the street, and I can't whistle worth shit."

She held his face in her hands. "Tell me, did something big happen to you tonight, Nick?"

"What makes you ask that?"

"Something's sure different. You're acting like you need me."

Nick didn't want to talk about the burned man, he wanted to make love to Marlene Moro and forget all about it for a little while. He didn't want to put the image that was in his mind into hers as well. "You don't want to know about it."

"Right. Nick, are you aware that this is only half a relationship?

"Why, because I just can't give myself over the way you seem to want?"

"I want to be your friend but you don't make it easy. And most of all I don't want to play any games."

Chapter Two

DETROIT POLICE DEPARTMENT files characterized Dwayne Fernald as a good burglar; that is to say, the first order of burglars: a professional, a specialist who worked less often than other thieves, used extensive planning, selected targets of big value, and never carried a weapon. Fernald had spent several years in a penitentiary, and had only recently been released.

Dwayne was a jewelry and fur specialist who had taken a gemology course in order to evaluate and learn about the property he stole. He had jeweler's tools and removed stones from their settings to weigh and safely secure them.

His main targets were the homes of the wealthy in metropolitan Detroit. He visited the neighborhoods of the wealthy at different times to get a feel for their living patterns. He spent considerable time, before contemplating a theft, researching possible victims in order to build a profile of them. He searched the social register, the city directory, and the directories of corporate officials, as well as the financial and social sections of the newspapers.

Thus Dwayne read with interest about Thurston Clarke in the *Detroit News—Lifestyle Edition*: "Mr. Clarke, who divides his time between Detroit's posh Seminole Street and Willsboro, a lakeside Adirondack hamlet, inherited his taste for new cars and old paintings from his famed stepfather, the thirties raconteur and man-about-town. Clarke has tastes of his own and the cash to splash on them, if you know what I mean and even if you don't."

When satisfied that Thurston Clarke was not only likely to have property in which he might be interested, but also maintained a life-style which includes substantial periods away from home, Dwayne added him to a list of possible targets. The list included the name, address, and phone number of wealthy individuals as well as a nota-tion about any item that particularly interested him. Thurston Clarke went to the top of the list.

And then Dwayne began watching the house in Indian Village.

There were no Indians in Indian Village, an his-toric and exclusive neighborhood filled with enor-mous, well-kept three-story houses.

For this phase Dwayne liked to drive a decent, average car that started quietly. In it he cruised, observing everything in the neighborhood to see if anybody was watching him, and to pick up the pattern of when patrol cars came by. At night in quiet neighborhoods he would wait for another car to approach before hitting the gas, to mask his car's sound. Dwayne liked to park heading down-hill whenever possible, so he could just slide away.

He devoted several evenings parked in view of the Clarke residence, sitting over on the passenger side to make it look he was just waiting for the

driver. From his closest position he parked between houses, so the respective residents could
each assume he had something to do with his
neighbor. To vary things, he'd pull out of his spot
to slide by the house and park at the other end of
the street and watch through the rearview mirror.
Sometimes he'd check out another angle where he
could watch through the trees from a couple of
streets over.

Then one afternoon he went in.

The Clarkes had an unlisted phone number and
he needed it.

He parked on the street in front of the house,
threw his hood up and came right up to the carriage entrance wiping grease from his hands. He
explained to a divinely beautiful Somalian maid
that his car had broken down and asked to use
the phone. Thinking it would be the quickest way
to get rid of this odd, tense man, she led him to
the phone. The private number was printed right
on it.

The time for working alone was past.

Dwayne assembled his team. He called in Top
Dog, who was classified by the police as a known
burglar. The known burglar was less skilled than
a so-called good burglar but highly active, estab-
lishing himself with the police as a consistent
thief. He exhibited a less subtle style of entry,
went for volume rather than quality thefts, had a
substantial arrest record, a low to minimal planning capacity, and often brought weapons to the
job. The longevity in the trade of the known burglar was shorter than that of the good burglar. He
was either caught on a B and E or moved toward
robbery.

Dwayne had perceived that Top Dog's career as
a known burglar was in fact giving way to armed
robbery.

"I want something that takes real nerve. I ain't frontin' no more," Top Dog had told him.

"Shit, you have to be cool to do this, everybody knows you got heart," Dwayne had said. He hoped they would be more of one mind since they were both family men. Dwayne was an intermittently devoted father to little Tabby, and he was dead set against abortion. It was murder, in his opinion. Top Dog lived with three women, each giving him a cool place to lay, and with one of them he had a new baby girl.

Top Dog casually brought in JoJo and Skeets to complete the team. JoJo and Skeets were junkies, by far the most hapless, least respected, and least rewarded of thieves.

The junkie was generally the least skilled and most active of thieves. He had the longest arrest record. He stole the most available items, which were rarely of large unit value. While very systematic, a junkie exhibited almost no planning in his thefts.

Skeets was about five foot two and a hundred and twenty pounds, little more than lips and sneakers. He usually wore some kind of hat that was too small for him on the back of his head. Like most junkies, Skeets was always sniffling and shivering from the cold.

JoJo was lily-white, almost translucent, with thinning red hair. He was a good driver, but when he wasn't on the job he was on the nod, watching TV.

Since his wife Bernie had taken Tabby to visit her grandparents in Flint, Dwayne convened the team in the den he had set up in the basement. He had a stereo, and the walls were covered with colored drawings in the psychedelic mode, stuff he did on speed, black velvet paintings he'd picked up over the years, and various memorabilia. He had spent part of his high school years on an army

base in Germany, and had once won an art contest
in his school. He pointed out, his tone completely
innocent of irony, that the certificate was signed
by the base commander himself.

"Um huh, I see that," Top Dog said, winking at
Skeets.

Dwayne set the telephone down on the wire
drum table. "You dial the number," he told Top
Dog. Top Dog dialed Thurston Clarke's number
and held the receiver to his ear: "One ringy-dingy,
two ringy-dingy, three—" he counted. His broad
grin suddenly evaporated. "Who the fuck is this?"
Top Dog asked, and winced as the receiver on the
other end was slammed down. "Dude hung up on
me!"

"No shit. Well, boys, that's all she wrote."

"Wait a minute," Top Dog said. "Lemme see the
number again. I think I misdialed."

Dwayne grabbed the phone and punched the
numbers. There was no answer.

The four of them got in Dwayne's car, with JoJo
behind the wheel, and drove down Livernois,
passed under the Fisher Freeway, and turned onto
eight-lane Jefferson by the marine terminals. They
passed under the approach to the Ambassador
Bridge. The *Detroit Free Press* building and Joe
Louis Arena slid by. They stopped at a phone
booth to call the Clarkes again on the way. All systems A-OK. They swiftly passed under Cobo Hall
and passed Ford Auditorium and Hart Plaza. The
Ren Cen towers loomed large. The traffic was
light.

JoJo turned left on Iroquois and entered Indian
Village, pulling up to the curb a hundred yards
short of the circular drive of an enormous, three-
story French Gothic house. Dwayne checked their
two police radios and the walkie-talkie. JoJo let
them out.

It took Dwayne two minutes to circumvent the

laser alarm system in one of the basement windows. The crew slithered through, except Dwayne, who alone of the crew was overweight and had to struggle through.

JoJo meanwhile had proceeded to a phone booth and after ten minutes he called the Clarke home once more. If no one answered something was wrong, and he was to drive to their predetermined pick-up point. But Top Dog answered. JoJo gave him his number and began waiting at the booth, monitoring police calls and phoning his partners in crime intermittently to be advised of their progress.

In the Clarke residence Top Dog waited for the phone and manned the walkie-talkie. The first step for Skeets was to find the luggage to transport the property from the house.

Dwayne made a beeline for the master bedroom, where he set about dumping the contents of the drawers onto an enormous Tabriz carpet. Dwayne was into invasion of privacy. He was afflicted with the need to see everything the Clarkes had. It was the same when he was pals with a guy. He always wanted to look at all his stuff. It was an uncontrollable compulsion that had caused him serious trouble in the Louisiania and Texas prison systems, where he had spent many formative years.

Dwayne always wanted to take whatever things they would really feel they needed, stuff for which the insurance money would be of cold comfort. He made his selections among the furs and jewelry, and took some cologne he liked. So where was Skeets with the luggage?

Skeets was in Thurston Clarke's study, reclined on an ottoman. He liked to sit alone in a dark, still room that smelled of money, and pretend that it was his. He concentrated so fiercely for that intimate private moment between him and the envi-

ronment that nothing else existed. He was startled
when Dwayne Fernald hissed, "The fuck you doing, Skeets? You sleeping? Get your fingers out of
your ass."

They were nearly finished packing the Vuittons
when the phone rang. Top Dog picked it up. "Yo,
JoJo!" he said. And then: "Yes, this is the Clarke
residence. Who am I? I'm the fucking butler, what
else?" He put the receiver down and said,
"Dwayne? I think it's quittin' time."

They packed up hurriedly. Top Dog called JoJo
and they left as they came, walking casually with
their luggage to the pick-up point. In the car they
talked loudly, high-spiritedly, letting off steam. It
was a good score, a clean heist.

Of course, they didn't know about Skeets's double life as a stool pigeon for the Detroit P.D.

Taxi drivers were experiencing a rash of robberies. American, City, Radio, they were all getting
hit. Since the rash was citywide, it attracted the
attention of the Armed Robbery Unit of the Crimes
Against Persons section. The supervising lieutenant, Steven Passaro, noted that while the largest
number of holdups originated from the Greyhound station, they actually went down in the 14th
Precinct. Passaro's main headache was a string of
bank robberies, and he and Commander Rivers
decided that they had joint responsibility.

Thus it was that half a block from the Greyhound station on East Congress, Sergeant Joe
Raccaniello sat in an unmarked black Chrysler,
its color chosen because it was the least distin-
guishable car color at night. The car was free of
dents, decals, or bumper stickers, and had heavily
tinted windows and dark upholstery. He had
parked ahead of the taxi stand to watch through
the rearview mirror. Distance was always the answer.

The interior of the car reeked of the plastic-tipped cigar he smoked. He had switched from cigarettes to cigars when he realized they don't burn quite so brightly when inhaled.

The squat, balding, forty-five-year-old cop exhaled contentedly. He had a high tolerance for stakeout work. He felt like he was the sole observer of the night shift, the people who come out only after dark. He liked the city then, when there were no bright colors to distract him. He liked the way everything was black and white, like a forties movie. Night seemed more factual, more real. It was easier to identify people. Night gave him shape and movement. He liked to go by a set of shoulders, the way clothing was worn, gait, the things that never change.

He noted some gypsy cabs in the stand, not that he ever busted a hack for driving without a medallion. Gypsies were useful to him, they knew all the crooks, gamblers, and girls. They were in on all sorts of wrong business, from making a getaway for somebody to driving a dead body to the river. They were good transportation for burglars. If he suspected such had been the case and he wanted stuff back from a robbery, he'd tell them. They'd deliver the next day. If they didn't he gave them a hard time. They were usually willing to act as stool pigeons, and he didn't bother them if he could help it.

Raccaniello was watching the decoy cab, driven by Investigator Wally "Sinker" Barnes, who waited in the cab rank behind the wheel of a City cab. Raccaniello and Barnes were in radio communication with each other and with four of Passaro's men in another two unmarked cars out of sight on Cadillac Square.

They had used the borrowed old City cab before, taking turns playing passenger and driver. It was one way to cruise without being too obvious.

Tonight, though, Barnes was to ride alone while Raccaniello was to follow in coordination with the other unmarked cars.

The primary targets were two black males who had held up a Radio driver on Euclid and shot him after he had surrendered his money.

Raccaniello had shot seven people in his career. Five blacks and two Latins. Two of the blacks he had killed outright, and another was paralyzed below the waist. Raccaniello wished he'd fucking died. Internal Affairs had brought charges against him on that one. That was back when Raccaniello had participated in the controversial Operation STRESS (Stop The Robberies—Enjoy Safe Streets), in which fourteen blacks had been shot by undercover officers posing as marks. The first black he killed was the brother of the man he had crippled, who unwisely sought revenge.

The other black he had killed had been a woman named Vivian Miller.

It happened when he had been with Vice and License, working in the 10th Precinct. He picked up Vivian Miller for solicitation on 12th and Hazelwood, but she refused to go, pulled away, and hit at his stomach. He thought he had been punched, then realized he had been stabbed. Joe pulled his pistol, so mad, that he fired a shot into the ground, then hurled her into the entranceway of a building. Vivian Miller slammed against the door, fell through it, and it banged shut behind her. She had a chance to run for it, but Raccaniello didn't feel like chasing her.

He fired three shots. Vivian Miller didn't get away. She looked so bad that even he was affected. He couldn't eat chicken for a week.

Internal Affairs tried to fry his ass, but he wasn't about to express regrets. A few less miserable cocksuckers just saved the courts a little paper and time. His partner had gone along with an edited version of the shooting, and Raccaniello came out smelling like a rose. He always did.

No one in Vice and License would willingly partner with him after the incident, and, like other officers awaiting disciplinary hearings, he was dumped in the 14th Precinct.

He lit another cigar and kept his eye on the mirror as an American cab pulled out and Sinker Barnes pulled up to the head of the stand.

Barnes stirred uncomfortably behind the wheel of the City cab. The front seat had beat-up springs and Raccaniello had outfitted him with an unfamiliar left-handed holster, explaining to Barnes, "You wear this on your belt, on your right side, see? You got the guy, and you see he's gonna have to go, you take him out quick. You don't take it out of the holster, you just shoot through the seat. Then you can take the gun out and shoot over the seat and get the other one in the head. Rule number one, don't stop shooting until you're sure they're dead."

"That's not our policy," Barnes had protested.

"Hey, there's policy and there's reality. Stick with me, kid, and you'll be buried in a golden coffin."

Only a few people passed under the pink neon Greyhound Bus sign. A brace of pimps were followed by a madly grinning Indian, lurching on a stiff leg. In the decoy cab Barnes looked twice— the Indian was trailing an artificial foot which had come loose but was still attached to an unraveling rag. He took a place by the newspaper boxes.

Barnes wished he had taken another sip from the pint of Johnny Walker that was nestled in the inside pocket of his sportsjacket. He kept the radio on to a home game against the Indians.

Home runs were coming in droves for the Tigers. The previous inning, Lou Whitaker had connected for his second home run in the game. Willie

Hernandez was still on the disabled list. Spanky
Anderson was carrying ten pitchers.

Sinker had been a star relief pitcher his first
two years with the Tigers, until he caught a fourth-
inning line drive with his elbow locked and
jammed his left shoulder. He was a southpaw.
Sinker remembered how he watched the rest of
the game from the bench, unaware that his career
had just ended. He came off the disabled list the
next season but didn't make the kind of progress
he was expected to make and spent a year on the
Double-A level. His ERA level rose to 7.96. His ego
was bruised. He was mentally crushed. He had no
idea of what he wanted to do, and ended up join-
ing the police force because his father had been a
policeman.

Sinker Barnes was depressed. He was just another face going nowhere.

A young prostitute walked past. Barnes had noticed her on other nights, walking fast and wearing a fur-lined Pakistani jacket, her long blond
hair falling over the collar. Her round glasses and
leather bag were those of a student, but she looked
tough and self-sufficient.

A hustler named Cadillac had been standing by
the doors, wearing matching gray slouch hat, vest,
and creased trousers. He carried a light suitcase.
Busy hitting people for quarters "so I can put my
luggage in a box," he had no success until a priest
proved an easy mark. Cadillac saw Barnes looking
at him. He grinned and shrugged lightly, then
stepped up to the car.

"You got to have an angle," he told Barnes.

"You'll have to do better than that."

"It's just an experiment. Say, my man, have you
been contemplating the purchase of a diamond
ring?"

"No." Barnes tried to look around Cadillac, to
see if fares were coming out. Cadillac leaned

against the door, showing him the ring in his cupped hand. He looked away from the cab when he spoke.

"That's a real diamond, I don't lie, and all I'm asking is fifty-five. I'm not greedy."

"Why not?"

"The ones want it all for themselves don't get nothing."

A silver-haired wino, dressed in air force blues, made to join them, asking for spare change.

"You don't hit up the cabbies, man, don't you know that?"

"I'm a good guy," the wino airman said. "I know all the cabbies. I always put bottles up on the curb. I watch out for you guys tires."

"Beat it, willya?"

"I'm not like these other bums," the airman insisted. Then he said, "I'm sorry, I'm sorry," and leaning forward with outstretched arms, he put his hands on Barnes.

"Shove off!" Barnes pushed him away in repulsion, and the airman staggered back, recovering his balance with great effort.

Cadillac stepped over to the cab again. "It is lowly here, ain't it? Remember what Jesus said, look in low places and there you will find me, that's right. How about it? I'll give it to you for fifty."

"Give it a fucking rest, okay?"

Sinker sighed heavily. Another night in the zoo. He didn't know if he could take it anymore. The animals were making him crazy.

Someone rapped urgently on the back window. It was the blond hooker in the Pakistani jacket, and she couldn't get in fast enough.

"Take me to Brush, quick!" That was two blocks away. He'd barely have time to throw the meter. Raccaniello would have something choice to say.

He turned to protest, but she slapped the seat. "Let's go, please! Get me away from here!"

He shot ahead to Brush.

"Thanks," she said, sighing once, and she handed him two dollars. "That was a little too close," she giggled.

It was a giggle, all right.

"Bet that's the shortest ride you ever gave." She sounded like she had a cold.

"I suppose." He leaned his head around. She was really quite small.

"What's your name, foxy cab driver?"

"They call me Sinker."

"I'm Tish. You have a nice face, Sinker," the girl said, and she was gone.

On the return trip Sinker rolled down a window and smoked a cigarette that he had cocktailed with some sinsemilla. Once back in line, Barnes washed his hand over his face, trying not to grow inattentive. He turned the radio back on. Henneman was pitching an outstanding ninth inning. Henneman was twenty-five. It seemed to Barnes like yesterday that everyone wanted to slap his ass.

He was startled when someone came from behind, threw the door open, and hopped into the back seat with manic energy, sliding over for a second man. The first man wore a tan raincoat. The second man was younger and wore a beige raincoat and one of those big knitted caps. They were taking the cab at the end of the line, the one without a partition, after walking the length of the stand. They were definitely testing positive.

"Take us up Twelfth, baby," the older man said.

"Twelfth and what?"

"West Chicago. We got to pick up some luggage at my girlfren's and then we got to go to the airport. Can you wait for us a couple minutes?"

"Long as you give me some green to keep me cool."

"Thass cool."

Barnes threw the meter and pulled out. He drove past Kennedy Square, an all-concrete park popular with brown baggers in the afternoon, deserted as a lunar crater at night. The pool stood dry, having leaked on cars in the underground parking lot. In the rearview mirror he saw Raccaniello pull out after him.

Raccaniello worked his radio. "Nine two to three four. Barnes took off for Twelfth Street and West Chicago."

"Roger three four. We got that."

"Nine two. I'm staying behind him."

The passengers in the taxi were silent until they gone several blocks up Michigan.

"You wanna buy some hash?" the young one asked. "Good shit, Afghani."

"No thanks, man, I'm not in the market right now."

"You're not a cop, are you?"

Stopping for a light on Twelfth, Barnes turned for a good look at the pair. It was too dark, though for a moment light flashed across the younger one. His face was strangely immobile, like a mask but for his moist eyes. He seemed close to fright. His floppy cap was pulled down on one side of his head, nearly covering one eye. The other passenger remained in shadow, saying nothing.

"Do I look like a cop?" Barnes asked.

"Could be I'm paranoid."

The light changed and he drove up Twelfth, past an army of hookers. Three hundred yards behind the City cab, Raccaniello hung back and stayed in the right lane. Barnes was supposed to keep transmitting the conversation in the cab, but Raccaniello wasn't getting anything.

They were getting close to their destination

when Barnes realized that he had not left his radio on. An intense pounding started just under the center of his collarbone.

"Nine two to three four," the Armed Robbery unit radioed to Raccaniello. "Barnes is flying tonight. He just went through a red light. What's he trying to do, lose us?"

In the taxi, the older man spoke. "Turn there on Clairmont."

"I thought you wanted West Chicago."

"I know what I want awright! Turn on Clairmont!"

Barnes made the turn. His throat had grown tight and his heart felt on fire. These people were barely in control.

He didn't see any headlights behind him. He'd lost Raccaniello.

His left hand slid to the butt of his revolver, very slowly. He could take them alone if he acted now. It was time to do it, but he did nothing. He was mesmerized, and he knew then that he would be helpless until they made their move.

"Turn here!"

He had a strong grip now on the gun handle.

"Pull right in here, in front of the garage!"

His strongest sensation was an intolerable burning in his throat. He stopped the cab a yard from a white garage door that glowed harshly before the headlights.

"That my girlfren's place right there."

He barely felt the blow to the back of his head.

"Awright!" the young one screamed. "This is it! This is it!"

Barnes found himself upside down, the crown of his head resting against the brake pedal, and his feet poised rudely a short distance in front of the boy's face. Both of them were pointing guns at him, and he was pointing his gun at the older one.

No one fired.

"Get your feet away from my face, mutherfucker!" the younger one yelled indignantly, but Barnes did not obey.

"Drop that fucking piece!" the other yelled.

"Drop yours!"

"I'll blow you away, man. Don't make me do it."

"I'll blow *you* away."

"Maybe," the older one said. "The game ain't promised to nobody. Let's have the bread, man! I don' fuck aroun'!"

Barnes reached into the pocket of his jacket and offered him a folded wad of ones which he hoped would look satisfyingly thick.

"This all of it?" younger one asked uncertainly.

"Yeah."

They kept their guns trained on him as they let themselves out. "Now git!" the older one yelled, and they ran down the alley. Barnes got on the radio and gave his location. The cruiser and Raccaniello's car drew alongside, their red-and-blue lights swirling.

"What the fuck happened, Barnes?" Raccaniello asked.

Sinker had to tell him that he had been robbed, and it soon came out that he had not even identified himself as a police officer.

Raccaniello nodded skeptically. "Tell me something, Barnes, just between you and me. Are you behind this job or not?"

Chapter Three

THE BODY OF Ed Tomack was the first to be autopsied that morning at the Wayne County Morgue.

The underground facility on Monroe and Brush was filled to overflowing, and Tomack's body had first joined those in a refrigerated trailer that served as an annex. In the morning his body was brought to the autopsy room.

Commander Rivers walked down the hall to the autopsy room, his movements slow, almost cautious. A sturdy glasses case protruded from the breast pocket of his maroon sportsjacket. He looked more like the principal of a high school than the commander of a police precinct. But when he spoke, his deep, commanding voice was that of a man always in control of his needs and impulses.

Walter Van Loon asked, "Are you sure this is how you want to start the day, Cal?"

"Pretty sure, Walter."

Rivers seemed unresponsive, but the ME knew him well and could sense the depth of his anger and grief.

In the autopsy room bleak fluorescent lighting burned out every shadow. The pathologists wore green surgical gowns and heavy rubber gloves, the cuffs turned up. The ME performed the autopsy himself, dictating as he examined.

Before the grime and remnants of clothing were removed, closeup photos were made of the body. The police had not asked Cynthia Tomack to identify the body, which was quite unrecognizable. It had been hideously damaged.

Cal Rivers watched, and remembered.

Ed Tomack had come from Hamtramck, where his father and uncle ran a pharmacy. They wanted something better for Ed who, like Rivers, was the first member of his family to attend college. He was going to law school nights while working in the Records Department when he decided to enter the Police Academy the same year as Cal Rivers. By the time he passed the bar, he told Cal that he couldn't change gears. The job had gotten into his blood.

The clothing fragments were removed and an identification tag was put on each piece before it was placed under a drying lamp. When they had dried completely, they were laid flat, with butcher paper between each article to avoid the possibility of any transfer. All articles in the pockets were catalogued.

The body was placed on the autopsy table. The upper half of the sloped metal table had a grated surface, at the foot a shallow tub ran beneath the grating. Through the tub flowed a continuous flow of water. A wooden block under the shoulder blades thrust the chest upward and caused the head to fall back.

Ed used to throw his head back to laugh. Rivers remembered how Ed had once lured him to the Polish Century Club with praises of pierogis and kielbasa, and made him dance a polka. The whole clubhouse exploded into applause. Ed threw his head back as he danced, radiating pure joy.

Suspended from the ceiling, a microphone recorded every step as dictated by the ME, who fell into the formal jargon of the forensic pathologist: "Ha-hmm ... this is Walter Van Loon, Assistant Medical Examiner, office of the Wayne County Medical Examiner. We will conduct a post-mortem examination on the body of Edward Tomack." He gave the time and the date. "The body is that of a well-developed, well-nourished white male fifty-three years of age. ..."

Ed used to make his own kielbasa and pickled herring and *sznycelki cielece*. On summer evenings the Tomacks transported feasts to Riverside Park and joined the families gathered on the piers to catch the river breeze. So close to where he was to die.

"The arms and legs are almost burned away, as is the chest wall, and the skull vault appears fractured. Probably the skull damage has been caused by the heat, bursting it outwards ... we'll see ..."

The ME made a coronal mastoid incision, cutting a track from a point just above the left ear all the way around to the right ear. He then peeled the anterior portion of the scalp forward over the brow, exposing the skull.

"There is a large, ragged, irregular-shaped apparent gunshot entry wound over the left side of the head. The wound extends to the anterior attachment of each ear. The vertical dimensions measure twelve centimeters and transverse dimension measure six centimeters. The massive loss of tissue had removed the facial features. There is a blackening of the skin over the ventral aspect of this wound, extending for a distance of six centimeters. When probed this wound penetrates left laterally toward the midportion of the left zygomatic arch."

"At least a thirty-eight?" Rivers asked.

"At least."

The ME went on to find gunpowder residue in the pocket that the heat had created between the skin and the skull, which had been blackened by the tremendous heat. Charring converged from the outside of the wound toward its center. The muzzle of the gun had been held in close contact.

The wound was examined microscopically to scrutinize the powder residue.

A Y-shaped incision was made in the chest and abdomen. A triangular portion of the rib cage was removed. When the throat and neck had been examined, the ME removed the heart and lungs.

"The lungs show carbon traces," the ME noted.

"Does that mean what I think it means?" Rivers asked.

"Yeah, it means that the head shot didn't kill him outright. You know what they say about Polacks. He was alive for at least a few seconds after the fire started."

The kidneys, pancreas, liver, spleen, and intestinal tract were taken from the abdominal cavity after the heart had been examined, and dissected on a black dissection board. A sample of blood was taken and blood type established. Finally, the pelvic contents and genitalia were reviewed.

Ed had saved Rivers's life during the Livernois sniper incident, after the sniper had nailed him. Rivers had been negotiating for hostages who, it turned out, were already dead. Ignoring Rivers's protests, Ed had carried him out of the line of fire, calmly giving the sniper a clear target for four shots.

The cerebellum was fixed by an injection of

formaldehyde. The ME used a scalpel to slice away the connections and arteries that held the brain in the cavity. He held the brain in his hands, a mottled, purplish sponge. "Lots of trauma. Bullet track. You can see it clearly, Cal, look at this."

"Any fragments? Any sign of a slug?"

"If there are we'll find them."

Enough. Good-bye, Ed. Cal Rivers left the autopsy room. His friend's brain was weighed on a white metal scale and segmented.

The press conference was held in a conference room in the City County building on Woodward and Jefferson. A long, gleaming wooden table dominated the huge room. Only an event on the level of a presidential visit, a riot, or a cop killing could convene this gathering of police brass. The room was packed solid—reporters from every television station, newspaper, and magazine in Detroit were present. Chief Wilson Davies stood behind a flock of microphones on a wooden lectern. On either side he was flanked by deputy chiefs, who were seated along the table.

Chief Davies was in full uniform, with a four-starred epaulette on each shoulder. He stood six foot two and he had a thrusting, heavy jaw and a small, tight mouth. His eyes were entirely without warmth, lacking even a trace of compassion. He looked like a politician, despite the uniform.

He made the usual brief statement to the effect that he wanted to assure the public that the investigation into the death of detective Tomack was being vigorously pursued, with all leads being followed. His death was mourned by the entire department and the community, and had brought them all closer together. The public would be provided information as the case developed.

Then he took questions. When he was asked,

"Why does the homicide rate continue to climb?" he was off.

"Detroit is infested with the most dangerous predators on eath—the two-legged ones. These predators range freely. They have choked out the life of the city. People live in fear. They don't go out, and they buy guns. Predators strike even within the boasted enclaves. We mollycoddle young criminals and release unreformed hoodlums to prey anew on society. The bleeding hearts, particularly among the judiciary, are so concerned for young criminals that they become indifferent to the rights of law-abiding citizens. The only course left is to restore order. And that requires a strong police department, not a department affected by layoffs and a long-term hiring freeze, not a department with a force that has declined to just under four thousand. When it's safe again, the city's many advantages will draw wealth back."

Among the reporters was Ralph Thomas, a small, wiry man with a blond beard, shoulder-length hair, and wire-rimmed glasses—a sixties holdout who had been a reporter for the *Detroit Free Press* since its counterculture days. Davies had put off taking a question from Thomas until it threatened to become too obvious that he wished Ralph Thomas did not exist.

Thomas was a pain in the ass, but he had an enthusiastic readership. People loved his exposés, which had all the inside details of corruption among the rich, the powerful, and the talented.

Years before, Thomas had arrived at the perception that civilized middle-class types nearly always shrink from head-on rudeness. As a rule they back down, back off, look away, stammer hastily. He made himself a master of confrontation. He lived by a fierce, stripped-down honesty, and he projected that quality obnoxiously.

"Chief Davies, if we understand you correctly, Lieutenant Tomack was on leave at the time of his death. What hypothetical motives might the police be contemplating? I mean, he must have been into something to get himself killed."

There was a moment of stunned silence.

"I know," Commissioner Davies said, "that the *Free Press* is a fair paper, it will be just and true to the facts. Right. I know that. None better. You will seek the truth, and the truth you will report, as you find it. Right? But you cannot get the truth from smutmongers who are the enemies of the police. You will listen to us, too, to me. You will want the news. Well, I control the news from the police department, and I can give and I can withhold the news."

Though the threat was delivered cordially, an eddy of tension swept the room.

A last few questions were asked, more because questions must be asked at a press conference than because anyone wanted to ask them. As the news reporters filed out, Thomas was overheard saying, "What was I supposed to ask him? What's the capital of North Dakota?"

To assure that there were officers on the streets of the 14th Precinct twenty-four hours a day, three eight-hour shifts of officers patrolled daily. Each patrol officer was assigned to a squad of five or eight, commanded by a sergeant.

The men and women taking the four-to-twelve filed into the rows of folding metal chairs. Most of them were wearing Eisenhower jackets, many carried night sticks. Some adjusted the knots of their black neckties before Kalina, the supervising sergeant, came into the room. An overbearing son of a bitch and an irritating bastard, Kalina went out of his way to make things aggravating for the troops. Kalina had never gotten over 1975, when a Federal court ordered preferential treatment in hiring for minorities and women. Roughly eighty percent of every rookie class had to be black and fifty percent female. Only twenty percent could be white males. That practice was later declared unconstitutional by the Supreme Court in a suit supported by the Reagan Administration, but as far as Kalina was concerned the damage had been done.

A few moments later the room came to attention. Inspector Mike Mouzakion walked in, followed by Lieutenant Crear Starks.

Starks, a tall, utterly self-possessed black man, began calling the role in his slightly mournful singsong. "Ott."

"Here."

"You'll be riding sixty-one—also covering sixty-four. We're short again this shift."

Ott groaned a protest as the lieutenant went on. "O'Hallerin."

"Here."

"Riding seventy-four with Mallory. Popovich."

A husky man responded.

"Popovich, you've got Witosky."

After Lieutenant Starks finished the roll call, he read a letter from a female citizen who complained about police service, and then invited officers to drop by any time after 6 P.M. He added, "I won't make any further comments since there are ladies present." Then he said, "Fellas, the inspector has a few words to say to you before we get into the daily bulletin."

The room became extremely quiet as Mike Mouzakion came forward and spoke. At forty-nine, Mike maintained a powerful physique, a bold black mustache, and black hair, though he was almost entirely bald on top. He had the complete attention of his officers.

"We've got a partial description on those two

individuals who had a Mexican standoff with Investigator Barnes last night," the lieutenant said.

The men began clicking ballpoint pens and adjusting clipboards in their laps.

"Both suspects are black males . . ."

"Hey, can you imagine that, Frank?" an officer whispered to the man next to him.

"Must be a mistake."

"Suspect Number One," Mouzakion went on, "around six two. Two hundred pounds. Thirty-four to thirty-six. Plaited hair and a short beard. Last seen wearing a tan raincoat. Suspect Number Two. About five eleven. Hundred seventy pounds. Twenty-two to twenty-four. Last seen wearing a light-colored raincoat and a knitted cap."

"Probably no more than a few thousand like that in the city," Declan O'Hallerin said.

"Consider these two clowns extremely dangerous, and have a nice evening."

"Okay, men, listen up," the lieutenant said as Sergeant Kalina began handing out the daily bulletin. It contained a lengthy list of reported crimes in the precinct for the preceding twenty-four-hour period, as well as descriptions of suspects and vehicles to be on the lookout for.

Starks finished the reading file, and the men and women began collecting flashlights and other pieces of equipment from beneath their seats.

"Oh, one other thing. I hate like hell to keep bringing this up, but we're still getting complaints from your sergeant about officers being out of their cars with no hats on. Let's not disappoint Sergeant Kalina. Dismissed. Nail 'em and jail 'em."

The men and women began filing out, laughing and talking with one another.

When signing out, Popovich looked at Sue Mallory's chest and remarked, "How long do you think she can float?"

Sue Mallory marched over and pressed her nightstick against his sternum. "When you see me coming, turkey," Sue said, "just act like you don't see anything."

"Sue, he didn't mean any harm," Witosky said, "but I just want you to know that you have the biggest breasts I've ever seen on a policewoman."

Let them talk gross, Sue thought. It showed their immaturity but she stopped it before it got to the point of upsetting her. They were like schoolboys who tried to dip girls' braids in the inkwell to get a reaction.

"Here, you drive tonight, Sue," Deck said as he tossed her the keys to the patrol car. "I'm getting tired of doing all the work."

"Then you keep the book," Sue said. At the start of every tour each officer began a new activity log for the day in a memo book, a leather-bound book that had to be carried at all times. In this was recorded the complete activity of that tour, including assignments received, activities performed, absences from post, and the time of completion of the tour. This record was critical in recalling occurrences at a later date for court appearances and departmental complaints.

They had pulled the four-to-midnight shift on a rainy day that saw the temperature drop. Sue almost welcomed the cold. Sometimes it was slow when it was like this, even bad guys didn't want to come out in the cold. Sometimes it seemed the police department simply hadn't the bodies to do the job. Ten was the standard number of runs a patrol car could responsibly handle in a eight-hour shift, but they had been averaging twenty-two. Officers were overworked, and morale was falling. Every patrol officer passed on stories about backup that never arrived, refusals to handle dangerous situations alone, and willful disregard of calls for service because of exhaustion.

But they had to come out and cruise the streets alertly, watching for anything that seemed out of the norm. During the early hours there was little action. They stopped two cars for flagrant traffic violations, cautiously checking drivers' licenses and writing tickets, standing in the cold rain.

They saw flagrant street drug-dealing, but it was so pervasive, open, and well organized that they could rarely make busts. Often kids nine and ten years old, who couldn't be prosecuted as adults, had been organized as runners, peddling brand names like Murder One and Rolls-Royce.

"Off the hook, off the hook!" they shouted up the street to the dealer as the patrol car slowly cruised past the king of the corner. A flashy youth no more than nineteen, hung with gold chains like Mr. T, was sitting in a black Mercedes sedan.

They couldn't ask him to open his trunk—it would be illegal. They couldn't frisk him without having reason to believe he was a felon.

And then, as happened every once in a while, they found a situation. They stopped a car that weaved as it exited off the Edsel Ford Freeway. The driver had been having a few beers after his shift at the Cadillac plant. When Sue asked for his license and registration, he threw it down on the ground for her to pick up. "No broad can lock me up. Why don't you arrest some niggers? I want to be arrested by a white man."

O'Hallerin came around, fast, from the passenger side. "Hey, no problem."

"Back off, Deck. I'll make the collar."

"I doubt it," the drunk said.

"Don't, because if you give me any trouble you're going to get shot." In fact, her revolver was drawn, though she was just holding it against her side. "If a man was locking you up and you gave him trouble, he'd beat you up. I'm so confident that I couldn't beat you up that if you hit me I'd probably get hysterical and shoot you."

"I see what you mean," the drunk conceded, new respect in his tone. He kept his own counsel all the way to the station house.

Deck and Sue were back on the beat, still laughing about it in intermittent gasps and guffaws when Kalina's unit drew abreast of them on Livernois. After being turned out at the start of a shift, it was customary for officers on patrol to be checked by the supervising sergeant twice—usually two hours after the tour had begun and two hours before it ended. This was called giving a see. But Kalina checked on O'Hallerin and Mallory incessantly, sometimes doubling back after only ten minutes in hopes of catching them drinking coffee or fucking in the backseat cage. He might give them a see half a dozen times on a tour when the moon was full.

They pulled over behind the sergeant and got out of the car as he strutted over, a thickset man with a thin, acidulous mouth, his eyes murky and vague. He looked like a hood, actually, but then so did one of the precinct commanders and an executive deputy chief. Kalina was maybe two inches taller than Sue Mallory, and it was widely believed in the station house that he had a Napoleonic complex from being a little guy.

"Tell me the truth, Sue," Kalina asked. "You really don't like this job, do you?"

"I love this job," Sue replied. "I never had a shift where I couldn't wait to get to work."

"Even on a night like this? You can level with me, Sue. Even I don't like coming to work on a night like this, and you're a girl."

"I'm a woman, dammit, Sergeant."

Kalina ignored Sue and addressed O'Hallerin. "I don't envy you. Me, I just don't like being around bitchy broads. You know, there's nothing worse than working with a woman." Kalina had a way of talking about Sue as if she weren't there and creating the feeling that O'Hallerin agreed with him. "If you happen to be the only guy there and they had a fight with their husband, you know, they'll walk over and put the screws to you."

"Aw, Sue's not like that."

"Let's be real. Who would want a hundred-and-twenty-six-pound girl as a partner? I certainly wouldn't."

It was a rule among patrolmen that you don't take on the patrol sergeant by yourself, but O'Hallerin said, "Sue is a dynamite officer. I'd rather have her than most guys as a partner. She might not be as strong, but I know she'll be right there with me."

It was a fact that together they had earned two citations, the first after they revived a twenty-month-old baby suffering from an electrical shock whose heart stopped en route to the hospital, and the second after they were first on the scene at a house fire at Twenty-third and West Vernor. They woke up the occupants and led several confused and frightened elderly residents out, and O'Hallerin scaled the side of the burning house to rescue a woman trapped inside a second-story room.

"Don't let me see you get out of your unit without your hats," Kalina said in parting.

They had proceeded down the commercial strip, checking out the small shops, black and Arab, when the radio crackled with a call about a domestic dispute on Euclid. The complainant had called the station to say that a man was threatening to kill his wife.

O'Hallerin sighed heavily. He had joined the department believing that police work primarily involved the officer in crime fighting; all the cop shows had convinced him that he would spend the working day apprehending criminals. He had learned that the police could not eradicate crime even if it were their only responsibility, and that most of the patrol officers' time is not devoted to law enforcement. Most citizens' requests are for service, or involve situations in which the officer is pressured to act as a controller or social mediator.

With some difficulty they found the building, between two burned-out neighbors on a block where the houses were jammed together like cartons. The screaming was coming from *under* the first-floor stairwell. Sure enough, there was a door, splintered and looking as if it had been recently kicked open.

The woman who opened the door had small, reddened eyes in a face white as library paste and a fresh contusion over one eye. The space under the stairwell had been made into the smallest apartment O'Hallerin had ever seen, but it had a little window and a sink. "Get fucked, pigs," she said, and shut the door. O'Hallerin took an instant dislike to her.

As O'Hallerin knocked on the door again, he heard the woman say, "You so scared of the pigs, you open the door."

This time the door was opened by an Indian, tall and light-skinned, with high cheekbones. He looked like he had been crying.

He told them he was separated from his wife and was to take his daughter out for the afternoon. The girl was living with the mother, and he arrived late to pick her up. The mother had by that time locked the apartment and left, leaving the two-year-old inside.

"And he showed up drunk!" she protested. "You can tell he's been drinking. Look what he did to the door."

"How long was my daughter locked up in there?"

"I had to go out. José said Delphina would take care of her. She was supposed to pick her up this afternoon."

"That's where you were, weren't you? Fucking José?"

"No."

"Then where, tell me that!"

The woman stared steadily at her hands and said nothing, childishly clinging to silence.

"Ha? Who is your husband, ha?"

"You."

"José's lost a friend, I can tell you that," the Indian said, beginning to choke up. "He better not come near me again!"

He lunged at his wife. O'Hallerin restrained him, wrestling him into the hall and out to the cruiser. He made the Indian sit in back. Now that he was in the cop car the Indian calmed down.

"You okay now?" O'Hallerin asked.

"Yeah. I'm just upset."

"How long you been together?"

"Six years. What happens now? Am I busted?"

"That depends whether or not she makes a complaint."

"*I* got the complaint. She's on crack. I quit, I'm clean, but she won't quit. I found out she's been seeing her dealer on the sly."

"You know the guy?"

"I know he'll kill me if I talk to you."

Sue returned to the cruiser. No complaint.

"Well, I'm not going to do anything to you," O'Hallerin said.

"Can I take my kid now?"

"No, but you can talk with her."

"I want my kid."

"I understand how you want to see your daughter," O'Hallerin said patiently, "but you'll have to come back sober tomorrow."

They left the scene feeling depressed.

"I felt sorry for the guy," O'Hallerin said.

"I'm thinking about the baby under the stairwell," Sue said.

The rest of the tour was uneventful. They answered calls to assist other officers but found nothing serious. A call to a department store netted them a shoplifter whom they arrested and took to the station house to be booked. They filled out the necessary papers and turned the shoplifter over to detectives.

Before they left the station house, on an impulse, Sue Mallory ran the man's name, Merle Clemets, through the computer.

"Deck? Merle Clemets is wanted on a bench warrant for petty larceny. We should have arrested him."

"The hell you say."

Sergeant Kalina caught them in the hall. "Someone just called to complain about brutal behavior toward him on your part."

"Let me guess," Sue said. "Was his name Merle Clemets?"

Then it was back to the cold streets, O'Hallerin brooding until they stopped to eat at a diner.

At the table opposite him sat a husband and wife and child. The husband and child had their backs to him. The wife was facing him and she was really cute.

He looked at her and she was smiling at him whenever he was looking away. One time he looked, and she ran her tongue across her upper lip.

"I think I've got something going here," he told Sue.

"Tasteless," Sue said.

"I bet I can get a date with her."

"Deck, you are sick. Anyway, the woman is with her family."

"No problem, the guy's going to the restroom." He made a hand gesture. She wrote something on a piece of paper and gave it to the kid who ran over. It was her address.

Chapter Four

COMMANDER RIVERS GLANCED at his watch. "All right, let's get over there. We don't want to be late."

Rivers thrust his heavy hands into the pockets of his trench coat and walked slowly down the station-house steps, toward the waiting squad cars. It was a cold Sunday morning but the commander was bareheaded—he had a thing about hats. He instinctively rejected them, even in the winter. His gold shield was pinned to the outside of his coat, a black band stretched across the face of the badge. Inspector Campbell and a half dozen other detectives followed closely behind.

They made their way through morning traffic, the engine of the squad car spewing clouds of white vapor. Inside their squad car, Inspector Campbell and one of the senior detectives, Vern Szabo, reminisced about the years when Ed Tomack had been with the 14th.

"When he was Inspector, that was when we had

the mother who was tired of her baby shitting his diapers, so she sewed his asshole shut," Campbell recalled.

"There was a guy in the squad shot his own car to make it look like he'd been in a shootout," Szabo said. A barrel-chested detective in his late forties with a lived-in face and a pair of powerful, ham-sized hands, Szabo struggled against claustrophobia in the overcrowded car. "Tomack put the car in for the Memorial Medal."

They laughed, and recalled other stories. Reminiscence helped them to mask their real feelings, for under all the rough talk the detectives felt angry, sad, and bitter.

When the car pulled up to the church, they got out and joined a sea of blue: row upon row of police officers standing in ranks; young patrolmen in pressed navy blue uniforms and dress white gloves; detectives and older commanding officers in trench coats; state troopers and sheriff's deputies in dress uniform; and some FBI agents, all standing silently outside the church.

The muffled thumping of a dozen drums began to echo through the street. The thumping grew louder, then closer, moving slowly and inexorably toward the church.

A uniformed sergeant raised a megaphone to his lips. "Ten-*shun!*" he barked, and the army of uniformed cops went rigid.

Down the street, step by deliberate step, the honor guard marched.

A hearse glided up from behind, followed by three dark, sleek limousines.

The casket was covered with an enormous American flag. The police pallbearers carried it on their shoulders up the church steps.

"*Pree*-sennnnt *arms!*" the uniformed sergeant barked again.

Thousands of white-gloved hands snapped to salute.

Cynthia Tomack and the children followed the coffin. Mike Tomack, the victim's brother, embraced her supportively as they mounted the steps.

Seated inside the church, near the family, were the mayor, the police commissioner and other city officials, Chief of Police Wilson Davies and other high-ranking officers.

The eulogy was simple yet eloquent.

"I am the resurrection, and the life: he that believeth in me, though he were dead, yet shall he live."

Cynthia Tomack crumpled forward in her seat. Mike Tomack's shoulders began to quiver. He dropped his face into his hands and unabashedly wept.

Sinker Barnes stared at the big casket. It was absurd, monstrous to think that he also might die out there. The realization that it could happen, did happen, was numbing. He didn't want to die out there. Not like Tomack. Not in the prime of life.

He could feel the sensation coming over him again, just as it had before. Fear. It had become an intensely personal thing. Fear had a face. At odd times he felt the symptoms—a tight ball in the pit of his stomach, an indescribable and recurrent dryness in his throat. Cold, moist palms. A rush of adrenaline. Standing in the packed cathedral, it began as a vague uneasiness that unexpectedly drifted across him like a fog. It seemed that fear was always hovering close by, mocking him, stalking him.

"And whosoever liveth and believeth in me shall never die," the priest continued.

Tom Castleton stared at the casket, thinking that such a funeral should have been his own. If

only *he* had been killed in the parking lot of Handy
Andy's Forest City.

The priest folded the book in his hands and
stepped back.

As the casket was borne back down the church
steps, three helicopters from the Aviation Section
swooped low in formation, passing directly over
the church.

"Present arms!" the sergeant's voice commanded. There was silence for a moment, then
from somewhere unseen a lone bugler began to
play taps.

Cal Rivers's stone gaze followed the casket as
the final notes of taps sounded and the blue rows
held their salute. Sergeant Kalina noted that Officer O'Hallerin, handsome and young, showed off
very well at the end of his rank.

Sue Mallory felt a thickness in her throat as the
tears began welling involuntarily in her eyes. It
was strange to be crying for someone she had
never met. Perhaps she cried for herself, because
she realized that every policeman there must be
thinking the same thing.

Maben drove out of the Detroit-Windsor Tunnel—
back in the good 'ole U.S.A.—emerging between
Hart Plaza and the Ren Cen. The afternoon traffic
wasn't too bad and his car, a gleaming stainless
steel DeLorean with Ontario plate, made good
time on Jefferson Avenue.

A diminutive man, Maben wore designer dark
glasses and a conservative suit. His hair, neatly
trimmed but longish, was entirely white. People
who stared admiringly after the DeLorean assumed Maben to be an elderly, top-level executive
in the automotive industry.

In fact Maben was forty-two and not really the
executive type.

However, he was making a business trip, and

knowing his requirements at such times he slapped Schubert's "Trout" piano quintet into his tape deck. The classical rhythms insured calm thought patterns.

Maben headed west along the riverfront and then onto the John C. Lodge Freeway. He took the exit past the giant red Stroh's Beer billboard and followed West Grand River past Henry Ford Hospital, eventually turning onto Woodrow Wilson. He found the address across from a stripped Chrysler, all four tires gone and KILL spray-painted across the body. Maben parked in front of a house with a sagging porch and several broken windowpanes, wedging the handlebar of an over-turned plastic tricycle under his right front tire. When Maben got out of his car, Dwayne Fernald's voice issued from the house.

"Far out!" Dwayne opened the door for Maben and gave him a hearty handshake. "How you doing, man?"

"I'm doing it, honey."

Dwayne looked at the DeLorean. "Jesus. Is this vehicle registered to you?"

"That's my short. Check it out."

"Come in first, man. I wasn't expecting you so early and I haven't got my shit together."

The door opened directly into Dwayne's chilly and mildewed living room. The blinds were closed and seemed as if they always had been. A television and an aquarium gave the room what light it had. A *Road Runner* cartoon was on the television. A brand-new, matching living-room set that smelled of plastic and a cherrywood secretary laden with porcelein Scotties and frauleins bespoke prosperity. The room was also filled with debris—soda cans, milk cartons, pizza napkins, candy wrappers and back issues of *The Watchtower*.

"You should see my basement," Dwayne said.

He was drinking a glass of milk. His pink eyes looked small and far apart in his acned, hillbilly-type face. Coming down off some speed, Maben supposed.

"What'd you do, join the boys in blue?" Maben asked, smiling at Dwayne's uniform trousers, black with wide blue strips running down the sides, and a blue shirt with a badge pinned to it.

"Shit, I'm a rent-a-cop, working the graveyard shift."

"With your record?"

"My brother-in-law's the boss. It's all right."

"You always were a police buff, weren't you, Dwayne?"

Dwayne shrugged. "I coulda been a good cop if they gave me a chance. Anyway, this is an easy gig. And it leaves me plenty of time for my night work."

"That oughta put you in solid with your parole officer, I tell him you said that."

"I can always snow him, no sweat."

Maben laughed. "Dwayne, I do believe you're the luckiest dude I've ever known. I mean, you were doing life at Milan, right? I never expected to see my sweetie on the outside."

"First thing, my sentence was reduced to twenty years. Then I got released on parole."

"How the fuck did you swing that?" Maben asked in an admiring tone.

Dwayne grinned. "I'm still good with locks, and I work for the best, the best. I can't get hurt, believe me."

"Yeah, I heard something about that. I heard all good things about you, Dwayne. You're connected, right?"

"Yeah, I'm with Jason Lemons," Dwayne said. "Lemons knows the right people. He's the one fixed up my parole. Got me out and working again. Only problem these days is getting good help. The guys on my last score, JoJo and Skeets? They're not the kind of people you'd want to associate with, believe me. Make yourself comfortable, man. I'll just get out of these things."

"You do that."

Dwayne was in the bathroom a long time. He had a bath, combed his hair carefully, and put on cologne before pulling on jeans, a cowboy shirt studded with mother-of-pearl, and a pair of green cowboy boots. When he emerged from the steamy bathroom, he found Maben sitting in front of the TV, cracking a can of Stroh's. He had changed the channel. A laxative commercial was succeeded by a news update, a talking head, and then five seconds of a big cop funeral flashed on the screen before the head came back.

"Hey, how about that detective getting hit?"

Dwayne stared for a second, his mouth actually open. "I don't know nothing about it."

"You oughta read the papers, or at least watch the news sometimes, 'steada that *Road Runner* crap."

"*Road Runner* ain't crap. In my opinion," Dwayne said with dignity.

Maben had been about to say the name, Tomack, just to see the look in Dwayne's stupid face, but he decided to let it go. No point.

"So where's the wife and kid?"

"Bernie and Tabby went to visit her parents. Her folks won't even talk to me, so fuck it, I don't go."

"What's the problem? They prejudiced against ex-cons? You paid your debt to society."

"Yeah, but they excommunicated me."

"The fuck? I thought only the Pope could do that."

"Man, we're Witnesses. Bernie got converted while I was in Milan, and I went along with it.

Jehovah's New System, the whole nine yards. I mean, what the hell, I believe in God."

"So how come you're out?"

"Bernie complained to some of her fucking Sisters that I tried to have oral sex with her."

"Oh." If Bernie was still as fat as Maben remembered her, Dwayne deserved a medal for even trying to *find* it.

"Dwayne, how would you like to get laid?"

Dwayne hesitated. He couldn't look at Maben. "Things are different now," he said at length. "We're not in the joint anymore."

"What a guy! I love this guy!" Maben laughed. "You dumb fuck, I'm talking about chicks. I'm talking pussy, Dwayne. I'm talking slit."

"Oh."

"You got big plans of your own for the afternoon, I won't press it."

"Nah."

"Great. We'll go for a ride in my fancy car and I'll introduce you to a couple of chicks who work a topless place in East Detroit. Suki and Marilee. They owe me, you can get it for nothing, man. And I mean get it."

Dwayne looked torn, like he was fighting himself over it. "Thing is, I'm not supposed to leave Wayne County. And Bernie might call. She just would."

Maben sighed. Spending too much time with stupid people put him in a foul mood.

"Come on, man, you owe it to yourself, the treatment you've been getting. We're gonna get *laid*, honey."

"Okay, let's do it."

Outside, Maben lifted the gull-winged driver's door for Dwayne. "You drive, baby. This is going to be a real experience for you."

They took East Jefferson, the heady Detroit skyline as their background, both men grinning. They drove east along Windmill Pointe past the expansive lakefront homes of Grosse Pointe Park and took East Jefferson all the way to Lake Shore Drive and kept on, the greens of the Country Club of Detroit to the left, Lake St. Claire to the right.

"How far now?"

"We're not far, honey."

"You don't think we shoulda turned left at Nine Mile?"

"Onward, onward."

The scene was changing into a landscape of the rural rich, houses hidden in pines and surrounded by desolate fields. Dwayne shifted in his seat, sneaking a glance at Maben.

"What's with this?" Dwayne asked. "Why are we going so far?"

"Turn right up there. I want to show you something."

Dwayne hesitated and Maben decided it was time to show his gun, a .22 hammerless High Standard, his weapon of choice. It was too bad the manufacturer went under.

Maben said, "Somebody wants to talk to you and it don't make no difference to me either way. I don't want to hurt you, man, just drive on and I'll show you where to go."

Dwayne said, "Who, man?" He'd gone all pasty-faced.

"You'll see when you get there. Just drive on, man."

Maben tried to maintain a conciliatory tone. He wanted to manage things properly. Dwayne had to be sufficiently aware of potential danger to co-operate, but he should not believe that death was a foregone conclusion.

"Jesus, what do they want with me, man?"

"Hey, be cool, baby. As far as I know they just want to talk to you. Don't cause me any trouble, Dwayne, because I don't want to do anything to you. Just go where I tell you."

Maben knew better than to listen to his victims.
If he did, they would try to change his mind.
Dwayne had already started crying, with sweat
popping out on his forehead.

"Stick that tape in. That one there." It was
Schubert's "Symphonic Fragments in D Major."
Good.

Tears kept coursing silently down Dwayne's
cheeks. "What is this? Is there a paper out on
me?"

"Dwayne, would I shoot you while you're driving my DeLorean? Really, Dwayne."

Dwayne looked at Maben and then looked
straight ahead. At that moment, Maben saw, he
knew. Then he was supposed to deny it to himself,
like all the others. But Maben had the sense that
he had failed to reassure Dwayne. "Turn there."
A dirt road wound through thick woods and
stopped dead at a scenic overlook; there were
guardrails where the stratified rock fell steeply to
the water.

When he turned the first corner, Dwayne
slammed on the brakes and lunged at Maben hys-
terically, trying to claw at him like a woman. Maben struck Dwayne just under the nose with the
heel of his hand and Dwayne's head snapped back.
It took him some moments to recover from the
pain and disorientation.

"Dwayne, Dwayne, Dwayne," Maben intoned
gently. "Poor honey."

"What *is* this? What'd I do?"

"You know what you did, what the fuck you
did."

"Watcha mean?"

"I mean you were seen, in Riverside Park."

"What are you talking about? You're crazy! I
don't even know what you're talking about."

"Who the fuck are you? Ya fuck, you come from

nowhere anyway, ya hillbilly. Who you been talking to?"

"I don't know what you're talking about. What can I tell ya?"

"You gotta go, honey."

"I'm innocent! You wanna kill me, what the fuck, what can I do? What can I say?"

"You can say hello to the Big Dark."

Maben shot Dwayne in the gut. "Oh!" Dwayne exclaimed at the impact.

"Get out of the car, man, or I'll shoot you again."

"All right," Dwayne said weakly.

Dwayne got out of the car and staggered away, trying to run. Maben backed the DeLorean out of the ditch and lit a Parliament with the dashboard light before he started walking after him.

Dwayne stumbled and began to crawl desperately toward the low shrubbery ahead, as if it offered sanctuary. Maben followed unhurriedly, holding the High Standard loosely at his side. He stopped at the edge of the shrubbery and leaned forward just a bit to look down at Dwayne. As Maben casually extended his arm, Dwayne continued to scratch at the ground and shift his legs. He stared with utter concentration not at Maben but straight ahead, as if at a goal he must reach.

The evenly spaced reports of the .22 were mere pops in the underbrush.

On the return drive Maben played Schubert's "Auf Dem Strom," for soprano, horn, and piano.

Rosa Parks Boulevard, still known as Twelfth Street to many, had once been a mecca. It was a major business center of the black community. At Twelfth and Hazelwood, there was Bosky's Restaurant. Drugstores, appliance and furniture store, clothes stores, and pawnshops lined the street. Along with its bustling stores, hot nightlife, and periphery of black middle-class homes, the

neighborhood had in its midst an undeniable
ghetto. From West Grand Boulevard to Clairmont,
the neighborhood suffered from an enormous
number of substandard dwellings, the largest
number of unemployed, and the highest crime rate
in the city. In 1967, the ghetto had exploded, and
Twelfth Street never recovered from its devasta-
tion.

The ladies of the evening were out in force. Sa-
shaying up and down the street, their hips sway-
ing seductively, they scanned the street for
prospective customers.

"Want a date, baby?" asked a bosomy black
woman in her sultriest voice. She was wearing
spiked high heels and an outrageous blond wig,
and she fluttered a pair of eyelashes that looked
as if like they must have been made of plywood.

A middle-aged man carrying a briefcase stepped
up to negotiate the price. A moment later she was
clutching him demurely by the elbow, and they
strolled around the corner to the ten-dollar-a-night
hotel.

A few doors down, another woman was standing in a darkened doorway studying the passersby with cool detachment. She was black and
petite, clad in a tight, form-fitting blouse, miniskirt, and white leather boots. Despite a thick
frosting of rouge and lipstick, her face was quite
attractive.

A car cruised by, the driver slowing for a long,
lingering look. Then he accelerated and turned the
corner. A few miles later, the same car returned
for a second pass. Again the driver eyed the little
fox with keen interest. Again he drove around the
corner.

A moment later, having parked his car, the man
came sauntering around the corner on foot and
headed straight for her, finally ready to make an
overture.

"Hi, baby," he said.

The woman was wary. She looked first to the left and then to the right before giving a tentative "Hello."

The man grew bolder. "Whatcha doing here?"

She could not lie. "Working."

The man smiled slyly. "How much?"

She played coy. "For what?"

The man stepped closer and lowered his voice to a murmur.

"That's a lot, baby. How much can you spend?"

"Twenty-five dollars."

For an instant, she glanced just past his shoulder, to a spot a few doors up the street. Then she gave a telltale nod.

The man smiled again, his anticipation building. "Can we go now?" He was unaware of the two burly vice detectives who stepped from a doorway and quietly moved up behind him.

"Mister," she said, with a new and surprising tone of authority to her voice, "I'm sorry to tell you that the only place you're going tonight is the stationhouse. You're under arrest." From her shoulderbag she whipped out a policewoman's badge.

"Say it isn't so." He realized he had just propositioned a cop. He staggered backward, into the arms of the plainclothesmen.

"Tough luck, pal," said Sue Mallory, the decoy prostitute who had just collared her first unsuspecting john of the evening.

She hated it.

Working the "pross detail" was one of those assignments that policewomen loathed. The city was in the midst of a campaign to crack down on vice and clean up Rosa Parks Boulevard, a never-ending crusade.

In addition to rounding up the streetwalkers, the police department had decided to sabotage their trade by busting their patrons. So, on a rotating basis, policewomen were ordered to disguise themselves as prostitutes and arrest at least two johns a night. The female officers felt demeaned and degraded by these assignments, especially on the occasions when they were borrowed from the 14th Precinct to do decoy work in the 10th. Sue was so resentful that she once showed up for duty in her regulation uniform, and Sergeant Kalina had promptly lodged an official complaint against her and ordered her home. She was threatened with suspension of pay for dereliction of duty. Commander Rivers brought her up to his office to talk it over. He explained that in the old days the precinct dealt with the local people; they were left pretty much to themselves as long as no major disturbances attracted unwelcome attention to the precinct. But times had changed and a precinct no longer owned its turf. The management cops centralized much of the decision-making power of the department and took away much of the discretionary decision-making power at the precinct level. Also, they increased the number of activities for which both the individual officer and the precinct were responsible, to include the farcical "pross detail." He didn't like putting her on the assignment but there was no way to refuse it.

It was just the kind of talk that convinced Inspector Campbell that Cal Rivers was a poor supervisor.

Still, Sue felt better afterwards. Some of her tension had been discharged in his office, and she knew Commander Rivers was a street cop at heart, on her side. She decided to make her arrests as quickly as possible on each tour, then come back to the station house and busy herself with paperwork for the rest of the evening.

While deceiving the passersby was easy, deceiving the real prostitutes was not. They always made her the second she hit the street. When Sue returned to her corner to bust her second john, she had the sense that she was straining the tolerance of the hookers. Some tried to stare her to death, and one began to berate her. She was familiar to Sue, a too-thin woman named Zahara whose protuberant buttocks were barely covered by a vinyl miniskirt. "What you comin' back here for, woman?" Zahara asked "You done made your collar already. Now you interferin' with our business!"

"Zahara, how can you do this? How can you sell your body?"

"Shit, woman! What else I got to sell? I sell it, I still got it, dig? At least I gets money for it. But you just give it away for nothing. You the dummy."

Julie Mills was an emergency room nurse at Southwest General Hospital. When she got home from her shift, she was looking forward to lingering under the shower, then turning in early.

Her apartment was a spacious one-bedroom. The building was only three blocks from the 14th Precinct station house, and for the tenants the proximity seemed to guarantee an extra measure of security.

After flipping on the lights, she locked the front door and walked into her bedroom. She had started to unbutton her blouse when she heard her cat meowing from the kitchen.

"Yanni! Come here, Yanni!"

The cat ignored her calls.

Walking to the far end of the hall, she found that her cat planted itself near a closet and was hunched on all fours, sniffing purposefully at the base of the door. The door appeared to be firmly shut.

"Silly cat," she scolded, running her hand along his orange back. "Didn't you like your chicken livers?" Yanni was half Siamese, seventeen years old, demanding, and hard to please.

Once she had opened a fresh can of 9 Lives Super Supper, she finished undressing and headed for the bathroom.

She turned on the shower and stepped inside. The mirror over the sink fogged. She drew the plastic curtain shut and hummed a tune as the jets of hot water luxuriously splashed down her back. "Ah," she murmured to herself, "hydrotherapy!"

Suddenly an unseen hand ripped the shower curtain open. Julie whirled. She screamed.

A man stood there. He just stood there watching her. A nylon stocking was pulled over his head, grotesquely obscuring and flattening his features. In his hand he held a long, gleaming bayonet.

A part of Julie thought: "This can't be real."

But it was. He was there, holding the bayonet at his side, staring at her. He seemed very calm. Paralyzed with fear, Julie looked through the taut nylon into his eyes. They seemed huge and protuberant. Julie had to look away.

"Don't scream," hissed the voice. "If you make another sound, I'll kill you." Covering her naked body with her arms, she cowered in a corner and, despite the hot water that descended just as before, she shivered.

"Please. I have money and jewelry. Take them, but don't hurt me," she whispered.

"Wash the soap out of your hair," he ordered "Then dry yourself." The funny thing was he had a nice voice, a voice she would envision with a handsome face.

His eyes were riveted to her body. "I'm going to have you three ways," he said, no more passion in his nice voice than if he had told her how he liked his eggs. With a sweep of the bayonet, he motioned her out of the bathroom, down the hall toward the bedroom.

"Lie down on the bed," he commanded. "Turn your face toward the wall. Don't you look at me!"

The man removed his clothes. Then he peeled off his mask and crawled onto the bed with Julie. Like a mating tiger, he bit her on the neck and held fast with his teeth.

"No, don't," she sobbed.

He started babbling, whispering that he had seen her before. Coming out of church. On the People Mover. Jogging in Palmer Park. Coming back from dinner with her boyfriend.

He turned her over—"Don't you look at me!"—and teasingly drew his bayonet down the side of Julie's cheek, across her breasts and belly, cutting off bits of her pubic hair, threatening to slash her pudenda.

"How does this feel?" he asked. "Sharp, isn't it?"

And then he raped her.

Between grunts of passion, he asked her questions.

"You have a nice body. How do you keep in shape?"

"Exercise," she managed to say. "I—I bicycle a lot."

"Nice tan."

She almost said thank you, but was silent. He went on in his nice voice, asking her what her sign was. She told him.

"We're very compatible. Don't be afraid. Think of me as your boyfriend. Try to enjoy it. You do like it, don't you?"

"It's great."

"Tell me you love me," he moaned.

Even after everything he had already done to her, she felt resistance to giving herself over to

him with words. She felt him waiting. Yanni had
begun to yowl, and it got to him.

"I'm going to get rid of this fucking cat!" he
hissed.

Julie's eyes widened in horror. "No!" she
pleaded. "Please don't kill my cat! Oh, please!"

Abruptly, he jumped off the bed and put his
clothes back on. He pulled his mask back over his
face and reached for his bayonet.

"Walk back to the bathroom."

He followed her through the bathroom door. He
seemed in a hurry now.

"Wash off," he told her. "Wash thoroughly, very
thoroughly, and nothing will have happened."

Julie stepped back into the shower and did as
she was told.

But the man was not satisfied. "More!" he
shouted at her. "Again! Scrub!"

Finally he relented. "That's enough. Stop. Now
stay here for twenty minutes." Drawing his bayonet close to her throat, he said: "If you move before that, I'll have to come back and kill you. Don't
think I won't know. Don't you look at me!"

He pulled his mask up, leaned forward, and
kissed her shyly on the cheek.

Her eyes closed, she gave him a sisterly peck on
his cheek. Strange, she knew, but it seemed the
thing to do at the time.

And then he was gone.

She heard her door slam.

She waited twenty minutes.

When Julie ventured out of the bathroom with
a towel wrapped around her, the apartment was
empty. As soon as she had locked the front door,
she was stricken with an anxiety attack. For a few
minutes she could hardly breathe, and it seemed
as if steel bands were wrapped tight around her.
When the attack passed she had a good cry. Still

trembling, fighting back the tears, she reached for the phone.

Behind her his voice was flat. "You bitch." His voice wasn't nice anymore. "You lied to me. You're just like all the others."

Ten minutes later Julie's rapist was in his car, heading home. The eastern horizon had turned blue. Soon night would be driven away. Waiting for a traffic light at Buchanan, he noticed a man asleep in his idling car. Indiana plates. He pulled over to the curb and walked back to the car. He rapped on the hood and motioned for the startled man to roll down his window.

"Listen, mister," he said, "don't sleep with the engine running. Carbon monoxide. Two friends of mine died that way in California. Got stuck in a storm in the mountains and fell asleep with the engine idling. Or the wrong sort of person might come along, know what I mean? There's a lot of creeps and kooks in this town. Think about it."

The man rubbed his eyes. The guy talking to him seemed trustworthy, almost professional in his concern.

"Hey, I guess you're right," the man said. "I just meant to rest my eyes. Appreciate it, pal."

He watched the man walk back to his car, thinking, there *are* nice people in Detroit.

"What the hell is gbahzajamah?" Dwight Franklin asked.

"Try it, you'll like it," Chimene Green said. "And order some fufu on the side."

"Fufu. Right."

Franklin's squad worked according to a duty schedule that put them on a day tour for four or five consecutive days, gave them two days off, and when they came back it was to a night tour. Dwight had just come off nights and hadn't got

adjusted yet, but his stress symptoms were too
faint to obscure the object of his desire. Chimene
Green had a beautiful, broad, serene visage. Her
smile was like a promise of peace. Her black hair
was heavy and glossy. Her body was every boy's
dream, and she was statuesque, fractionally taller
than Franklin, so there was a lot of her.

They hadn't been out to dinner together in
weeks. Chimene knew the place, Chez Lila. Tie-
dyed tablecloths, waiters in African garb, reggae
music pulsed throughout the place. Chez Lila was
in. Franklin recognized a city council member sitting with some dudes who looked like visiting African dignitaries, wearing the colorful flowing
robes of their native land.

Dwight Franklin met Chimene when he walked
past a ground-floor elementary school classroom.
He looked into a window and saw that the teacher
was kind of attractive. Pretty as could be. He
looked back as he passed the last window and saw
her, smiling, in the act of bending down to have a
last look at *him*. He turned on his heel and entered the school, found the classroom, and demanded a date.

On their first date they walked for four hours,
ate Cuban-Chinese food, ran into a mutual friend
they had shared for years, shot a few baskets in a
corner-lot game, and visited Chimene's grand-
mother in a city nursing home. He hadn't had
enough imagination to dream up a woman like
Chimene.

Chimene at first thought she would feel safer,
going steady with a cop. But it wasn't like that.
Instead, she became more aware of how dangerous the city had become. And there was another
problem. Dwight was subject to all the tensions
and conflicts that arose from police work, but the
conflict was compounded for him. He was a
guardian of a white society, viewed by many as a

traitor to his race because blacks were not bene-
fiting from the protection he offered.

They had driven to Chez Lila in Chimene's car,
because someone had taken the whole ignition out
of Franklin's Buick, smashed it, and left it out on
the street. Purely malicious. And it was because
he was a cop.

"The white guys carry guns off duty mostly because the department says they're supposed to. I
carry one because I've got to. I don't so much as
dare take a leak in a gas station or run down to
the store for a quart of milk without a piece stuck
under my shirt."

"You bastard, half the time you enjoy it!" Chimene said.

"Okay, it's true. Part of the reward of the job is
knowing you've survived another day, knowing
you're still alive. The fact that you're smart
enough to get through an eight-hour shift with the
conglomerate of bastards that are running around
this city today . . . it's kind of exciting."

"You're you, but . . ." When Chimene started a
sentence, she would look down, taking in a breath
before raising her eyes. Franklin couldn't get
enough of it.

"At the same time you're a symbol of accom-
plishment to others. Like me," Chimene said.

Dwight couldn't help it, he felt good. It was like
having the cute fourth-grade teacher say you had
the best book report in the whole class. Sincere
and innocent. He twisted his glass of Chinese beer.
Chinese beer didn't seem very African, but as Chimene had said, whatever the Chinese people put
their minds to they did well. The beer was full-
bodied and tasty. Cold, too.

The gbahzajamah turned out to be a stew of
greens, goat meat, chicken, and bony fish, which
added a sardine taste. The fufu was a doughy

paste made of pulverized cassava root. It was good.

And so was being with Chimene. Gold rings gleamed on eight of her slender fingers. Dwight spaced out a little, watching them. "Now That We've Found Love, What Are We Gonna Do With It?" filled his ears. Third World. He'd been to a concert once. Great group.

Nick Sands came up in the conversation.

"Is the Ivy League Gunman really rich?"

"His daddy rich."

"Is that story true, about his family?"

"Yeah. Nick says, 'Dad, I've got a new career plan. I'm going to become a police officer.' Dad goes, 'If you do that, leave here and never darken my doorstep.' So Nick leaves the room and he hasn't seen his old man since."

Chimene thought that Nick Sands brought out the worst in Franklin. Actually, they brought out the worst in each other. Too much irony and gallows humor. She had the sense that together they tended to function in other than the procedural mode. Someday, if they stayed partners, they were going to get into trouble.

Chimene glanced over Dwight's shoulder as a happy entourage of young, attractive people made their way from the back room, on their way out. They were led by a man who seemed about thirty. He had a trim mustache and an Afro. When he moved he looked very together physically. Chimene was surprised when he called to them from the group. "How are you, Dwight? What's happening?"

Franklin turned and saw the man who had spoken. He faced a handsome, blue-eyed black man who wore a conservative suit and heavy horn-rim eyeglasses. One arm was draped around an attactive black girl. It was Jason Lemons.

"How you doin', Dwight?" Lemons remembered

Franklin's name, even though he had not seen him since Franklin had brought the notorious drug dealer in for questioning about a double homicide, the year before. "Still partners with the yuppie?"

"We're in love. How's business? Still getting folks high?"

At first the talk had appeared to be casual, but a cool intensity emerged from their stares. Lemons's entourage seemed unaware of the eddy around them.

"I get folks high on money."

"You get rich on the blood of our people."

"Hey, listen! You talk about getting rich on black men's blood. What's the average income of a black man in Detroit? What's a fryer cost him in his own neighborhood? Go over to the suburbs and you get a better fryer for less. Everything is cheaper in the richer neighborhoods. That's exploitation, not me. Say, aren't you going to introduce me to your lovely friend?"

For a moment, when Lemons looked at Chimene, his gaze conveyed a certainty that she could as easily be with him. It was subtle, insulting, scary—and against her will she liked it a little.

"I don't think so," Franklin said.

"The man sure is exploiting the shit of you, Dwight," Lemons continued. "This is what they think. You are a good nigger. You are different. The man says, 'You are one of us.' But that is a lot of bullshit. We are not like them and they sure as hell are not like us." He beamed at Chimene and took his leave.

Through the plate-glass front doors, Dwight Franklin and Chimene watched him enter a custom-silver Eldorado with all-white tires. The driver who opened the door for him wore a suit that clung and shimmered with colors and a broad-brimmed hat.

"Get fucked, scumbag," Franklin muttered to himself, but Chimene heard.

"Who was that?"

"That was Jason Lemons, Detroit's number one heroin dealer."

Lemons was the chief executive officer of a major-league heroin- and crack-selling ring, one with a sophisticated system for laundering profits, using paper corporations to shift them out of state and shelter them under different names. Chimene knew him by name because he didn't hide his existence in the shadows but boldly made himself a public figure in the precinct, a provider of parties, a dispenser of largesse, something like a Tammany ward boss or an old-fashioned mafia don.

"He wasn't at all what I expected," Chimene said.

"Everyone gets taken in. He's like a hero to school kids."

"Local boy makes good?"

Franklin shook his head. "He grew up in Russell Woods, a nice middle-class boy. Top of his class at school. Then something happened. His father, stepmother, her mother, and her nurse were murdered. Traces of semen were found on the bodies. Guess whose?"

"Lordy."

"Jason was tried, but after a mistrial all the charges were dropped. Lemons is as lucky as Ronald Reagan. He collected his father's insurance and went into the drug trade. If he'd gone into a legitimate business he could have had it both ways, the fast life and a longer one. Like in records maybe, 'cept Motown is gone. Lemons is smart enough and tough enough to run any kind of business. But he'd break a head open on a whim.

"Now he's the biggest in Detroit. We know he has at least three hundred people working for him, mostly gang kids who don't risk heavy sentences. And those are just the couriers. He runs his people like a military outfit, with street dealers called soldiers and lieutenants. And an 'A-Team' for the enforcement. I think he's into more than pushing dope, though. I think he's into regulation and control of practically everything that goes down."

"But he seemed so young, so poised, so soft-spoken. . . ."

"So fucking charismatic? Every cop and prosecutor that's ever gone after him finds him so fucking likable, despite how they feel about his business. Anyway," Dwight said bitterly, "let me tell you something. The white cops downtown don't give a fuck about drugs. They don't give a fuck about nothing. They think maintaining order here is a losing proposition. They think black people will inevitably kill or maim people or tear up each other's property. But I take it personal. Particularly when people try to make Jason Lemons a goddamn folk hero when he tells you how dope provides jobs for the downtrodden! The man needs to be taken out. If I had a chance, I'd take Jason Lemons somewhere when nobody be looking and put two in his head. Quick."

"Dwight!"

"The man has got to go. He's a symbol for kids. They see him with his diamond pinkie ring, throwing money around on the softball teams and dances. They start as couriers and he buys them gold jewelry. Those who do well get flashy cars. And an attitude. Because they not only sell dope, they don't give a fuck about anybody else. Kids beat up on people after they've already given up their wallet, or they set somebody on fire. Lemons is out to prove to the world how cold-blooded he is, and now you got kids who want to prove the same thing, just because they're mad at the world. They don't care, and they'll do anything."

Dwight Franklin's point was graphically illus-
trated at Chez Lila's twenty-five minutes after he
and Chimene Green departed.

Finnegan, Philpot, and Top Dog entered the restaurant, identically garbed in raincoats, ski masks,
and surgical gloves. The cashier had a clear view
of them a full fifty feet away. The big man in the
lead, walking fast, aimed an oversize handgun at
his face. Top Dog remained at the front while Finnegan and Philpot started toward the back. They
opened their raincoats and swung out identical
short-barreled twelve-gauge shotguns. Made in
Brazil, they had quaint exterior hammers, like the
Sicilian *lupara*. They waved their shotguns and
screamed obscenities at the startled patrons, some
of whom were dropping to the floor. A table fell
over with sounds of breaking glasses. The reggae
played on. Finnegan vaulted the bar. Philpot had
the whole dining room covered.

"Every motherfucker on the floor and start
throwing out your wallets!" Finnegan roared.

Philpot stepped among the prone bodies and
collected valuables efficiently until he came to the
city councillor. Philpot nudged him with his shoe.
"Where the money at?"

"I'm not giving you any money."

"We're not fooling, we're for real!" Philpot insisted.

"Waste him," Finnegan said. Philpot obediently
stepped back and cocked both hammers.

"Okay, okay, take it," the city councillor said.

Philpot stepped over him to another, younger
man who hadn't given over. "Don't you have any
money?" Philpot asked.

"No. I just found out they don't take credit
cards. I was wondering how I could skip the
check."

"Then don't worry, we're not going to hurt you."

Finnegan overheard the exchange, and though

he was disgusted with Philpot, he kept his peace. He understood the necessity of maintaining the appearance of cohesiveness in front of the victims. It was a serious mistake to criticize the behavior of someone on the crew when things were going down. It looked real bad.

Finnegan took the manager to the back and cleaned out the safe. They were getting ready to go when one of the African dudes with the councillor got up from his table to hassle Philpot.

"What's your problem, jack? You some kind of mental?"

The African shouted angrily in his strange tongue, and tried to pull Philpot's ski mask off. Outraged, Philpot jabbed the stock of his shotgun into the man's stomach. He keeled over and tried to rise. Finnegan blew him down with OO buckshot.

When the shooting started, Top Dog yelled to the other African dude, "Run, motherfucker, run!" When he started to run, Top Dog laughed and shot him in the leg. The second African writhed on the floor."

"Now what you do that for, Top Dog?" Philpot asked.

"Shit, Finnegan shot somebody. I figured it was time I did, too."

Chapter Five

THE 14TH PRECINCT'S central squad room was a cavernous, high-ceilinged office adorned with metal chandeliers that, like the toilet facilities and the large, old-fashioned windows dated from the 1920s. It was a warren of drab, beat-up metal desks and wooden tables butted together, file cabinets, telephones, a Mr. Coffee, a GE battery charge box for radios, a detention cage, two banks of flickering fluorescent lights, a wall display of mug shots, a black-and-white TV, and a poster of Porky Pig in police uniform saying, "Up ag-ag-against the wall, m-mother f-f-fu-fu . . ."

This was the room that never slept. The color scheme was an institutional light blue—that included walls, typewriters, desk tops, and most of the telephones. Here detectives reported for duty, got assignments, and received special instructions.

The central room was surrounded by Commander Rivers's cluttered office, Inspector

Campbell's tidy office, and an office with a type-writer and phones to the outside world. Adjoining the squad room was the windowless interrogation room, about seven by eleven, which held three folding chairs, an old office table, a wall of built-in shelves where closed case records were stored, and a window with a reflective surface. A short corridor led to the cells for female prisoners.

When the detectives came into the room at the beginning of the four-to-twelve shift, few sat behind the desks. Typically, Joe Raccaniello sat down on a desk, picked up the chair, slammed it down in front of him, and put his feet up on the seat. Sinker Barnes had to handle some paperwork. He went directly to a typewriter with a harassed, don't-talk-to-me look and started typing.

Dwight Franklin and Nick Sands, the only man in the room wearing a shoulder holster, were reading the *Detroit Free Press* account of the Wild West robbery at Chez Lila. "Gbahzajamah," Dwight Franklin said. Sands laughed. It was an inside joke.

Munching on sunflower seeds, Vern Szabo roamed the room gregariously. His pockets bulged with slips of paper containing names of informants, phone numbers, and addresses. Two ball-point pens protruded form his trouser pocket below the holster on his belt. He got a handshake from everyone. He liked to be liked.

Claire Hopson was the last of the detectives to enter the room. Her red-gold hair had a severe, short cut; men were always telling her she looked like Shirley MacLaine.

When first promoted to investigator, she had to do a great deal to prove herself but now nobody doubted her competence and nobody bothered her. At thirty-eight, she was a jaded cop with no illusions about criminals or the administration.

Her colleagues had long learned that there was no use picking on her. They couldn't get to her. The only one who still tried was Inspector Roger Campbell.

Campbell came out of Commander Rivers's office. He filled the doorway, his black shoes glittering, tie in regimental stripes knotted hard up against his thick, muscular neck.

"Ten-hut, you faggots!" He walked straight into the central room without further acknowledgment. He did not need to be liked. He liked himself.

The killing of Ed Tomack and the rape/murder of Julie Mills had affected the mood of the squad room. There wasn't a hell of a lot of small talk.

"What about the Tomack case?"

"Homicide hasn't given us any chores."

"He used to be one of us," Nick Sands protested. "Somebody killed him on our turf. Why are we out?"

"Leave the case to the powers that be."

"What's going on? Do they have something?"

"How should I know? Do I look like I've been sleeping with Jackson and Johnson?"

"Our plate is full anyway. We have to work the double shooting that occurred last night at that restaurant. We need action on this one, it's an international-type incident. The two victims are both critical. They were the Liberian consul and his brother."

"No shit," Dwight Franklin said.

"Could it be the fellas the Armed Robbery Unit wants?"

"Let us get them, Inspector. Barnes is in love with them."

"Armed Robbery's not operating under that assumption. The last tour brought in witness descriptions, for which we have squat. Two of the perps were of the same general physical type as those Barnes encountered. All we have is a nickname overheard by two of the victims: Top Dog. Do we know him?"

"Where's the File?"

The Nickname File was an essential index, because half the perps in the city knew the other half only by a nickname. And the file had to be constantly updated as Mange, for instance, became Heavy Lester. Nicknames could be a problem for the perps as well as the cops. Once Sands and Franklin had busted Slick, a salesman for Jason Lemons. Nobody bailed him out of the joint right away because Lemons's lieutenant didn't know the name he was booked under. Slick couldn't understand the neglect and started jiving that he was going to bring the whole thing down. Sands and Franklin got excited for a while, but the lieutenant did finally find him and bail him out. Word of his bad attitude in the station house got out. A few days later Slick fell from a rooftop.

The Nickname File did exist as a document, but the File the detectives referred to was human— the precinct clerk, Gary Newman. Newman had a photographic memory for sports statistics and case histories. The detectives often used him as a shortcut to their files. He'd have been an attorney years ago, but he was psychologically unable to pass the bar exam.

They found Newman chatting with Sergeant Sudol and gave him the name and the physical description.

"Top Dog? We have six on file, but only one is pudgy, five seven, a hundred and eighty pounds. He's Eugene Yarrington III, and he has a string of arrests for robbery and assault."

"Okay," Inspector Campbell said. "Raccaniello and Barnes. Get Top Dog and we'll see what we have. Next, the rape and murder of Julie Mills.

Homicide wants us to assist their investigation. I have the autopsy report." Campbell paused for a moment and looked at the document in his hand. "Which I shall now share with you. Bruises and welts on her face indicate that Miss Mills was severely beaten, possibly with clenched fists. A ligature around her neck suggests she was strangled, not with the Venetian blind cord that was used to bind her wrists and ankles in a spread-eagled position to the four bedposts, but with a length of string that laboratory technicians determined had been broken off from the ceiling light fixture in the bedroom closet. The wounds in her chest indicate repeated stabbing, undoubtedly done with a 1898 U.S. Army bayonet that Jackson and Johnson found bloody on the bedroom dresser. They also found her missing left breast atop the dresser."

Claire Hopson gave a small start of repulsion, banged her knee on the edge of the desk, and exclaimed "Ouch."

"What did you do, dear," Campbell asked, "break a fingernail?" Campbell was always making mock attempts at flirtation. This included exaggerated door ceremonies, remarks about her appearance, and questions such as "Are you *sure* you're getting any action?" She was expected to appreciate him as a virile male.

"No, Inspector," Hopson replied coldly. "What was the method of entry?"

"There was no sign of forced entry, but it was a ground-floor apartment and the jalousied kitchen door at the rear was discovered to be unlocked. Maybe it was unlocked when the killer entered the apartment. He might have come in with her, someone she knew."

"Wasn't there a bayonet involved in an attack last month in the Second Precinct?" Claire asked.

"Go to the head of the class," Campbell said. "Yeah, some kind of long blade."

"So we're looking for someone who's making a habit of this? Like someone with a collection of war surplus bayonets?"

"Maybe," Campbell allowed. "Only thing that's for sure, whoever did this is a sickie of some magnitude."

"He's a fuckin' beast," Vern said. Szabo was one of those people who could casually coin a nickname and make it stick. Without even intending it, he had done it again. From that point on the precinct detectives referred to the perp as the Beast.

"All right," Campbell said. "You're going to canvass the neighborhood until we find everyone who saw anything. Sands and Franklin, you're on it, too, along with some of the Patrol Section. Get to it."

He turned, walking away heavily on his heels.

"What about the pizza connection?" Franklin asked. He referred to the fact that there had been fifty-four robberies of pizza deliverymen, eight involving injuries, in the precinct since September.

Campbell put a large hand around the molding and leaned back into the room. "Franklin, we have priorities. Let me think about it over the next few days, and I'll get back to you."

"Roger, chief."

As the detectives filed out of the squad room, they saw Lieutenant Castleton. They didn't know how long he had been standing there. They all felt a little embarrassed to see him upstairs, they about to hit the street, he the burnout.

Castleton knocked on the door to Commander Rivers's office.

"Can you give me a minute, Cal?"

"Sure, Tom." Rivers looked up from the desk in

his tiny office, with its synthetic curtains, an un-
happy avocado plant, three telephones, in and out
trays, and reproductions of Haitian art tacked to
the cheap paneling.

"You know I used to work with Ed Tomack."

"Of course. So did I, before you. He was a good
man."

"I hear that Homicide is putting together a task
force to investigate the murder. I keep thinking I
wish I was part of it."

"So does every officer in this precinct, Tom."

"Ah, who am I kidding? Everyone in the department knows I'm a burnout. I suppose I should put
in for early retirement."

"Tom," Rivers said evenly, "you can't leave now.
You've been around too long. It's in your blood.
Take it from me, you'll be miserable as hell if you
quit. There's nothing sorrier in the world than an
ex-cop."

"I'm an ex-cop now."

"You're a street cop, always were."

"I can think of some people here who would re-
spectfully disagree."

Rivers knew he was thinking of Campbell.
"Since when did you care what certain people
think of you?" He leaned across the desk and
looked Castleton straight in the eye. "Tom, I need
you."

The attack on Julie Mills had taken place on the
ground floor of a nine-story building. Vern Szabo
and Claire Hopson parked their cruiser in front.

"Onward, Fosdick," Hopson muttered with
mock enthusiasm. The two officers went through
the glass doors into the building.

One thing that had made Claire uncomfortable
in police work was that the average policeman
didn't have very many categories to put women
into. They were either having an affair with some-

one or they had no relationship whatsoever. She found it difficult just to develop friendships with the men she worked with. Most policemen didn't have friends who were women.

Vern Szabo was an exception. He had never been partnered with a woman before, and in the beginning of their working relationship he refused to even speak to her. Eventually a warm, mutually respectful, and efficient relationship had developed between them.

One thing about Szabo was that he was hopelessly profane, and he was beyond making any attempt to curb his salty language in her presence. Claire had become utterly accustomed to it.

Witosky and Popovich were standing outside the apartment door. "You're gonna love it," Witosky told them.

In the hall a sickeningly sweet smell lingered. The smell of death.

"What a fucking scene," Sazbo said when they entered the bedroom.

The walls were a mess, so much blood had been thrown against them. Then there was the mattress. And the dresser. A drag mark on the mirror indicated that the breast had been placed or hurled against the glass, stuck there momentarily, then slithered down to the top of the dresser. At the same time, Claire took note of her reflection.

She turned away. "Okay, Vern, we've seen it."

They stepped back into the hall and Szabo, nosy, opened the closet door with his toe.

"Look over here!" Vern shouted. "I found a cat. A dead cat. The fuck is this? You'd think Homicide would either take the cat to the crime lab for some fucking reason or dispose of the fucking thing."

"We can pick the cat up later and give it a decent burial, okay? Let's get out of here."

* * *

One of the strangest aspects of police work was
how horror was succeeded by boredom.

In the many hours of work that followed, the
14th Precinct Investigative Operations Section
conducted a major canvass of the apartment block
and the streets and alleys surrounding it. Patrol
officers made the initial interviews, merely asking
whether or not anyone in the area had seen or
heard anything during the hours surrounding the
attack. If they got a positive response, which was
rare, then they gave it to the detectives. Out of 143
canvass contacts, they found only seven people
who might have relevant information. It was bor-
ing work.

From all the evidence, it appeared that Miss
Mills' murder did not occur until approximately
3 A.M. One basis for that assumption was a statement by Alonzo Smith, a neighbor who got up at
that hour to go on his milkman's route. He recalled hearing a muffled female voice, like a moaning, and also a low, angry male voice but without
distinguishing any words. Thinking that neighbors were quarreling, he didn't think about it
again until he came back from work in the afternoon and heard that Julie Mills had been killed.

Hopson and Szabo paid special attention to the
apartments across the back alley from Julie
Mills's apartment, where people had a clear line
of sight into her bedroom. That's how they found
that a retired electrician, Richard Petunato, and
his wife Rita, had been spying on Julie Mills for
months. They had seen someone draw the bedroom curtains, something Julie Mills had not been
in the habit of doing.

Mr. Petunato thought it had been a light-skinned
black man or possibly a swarthy white man. His
wife thought it might even have been a woman.

The canvassing team searched gutters, bushes,

sewers, and trash cans for anything that might look like evidence, such as discarded bloody clothing. They found nothing.

The detectives always wanted to know whom the victim had been sleeping with—"who was fucking who in general," as Vern Szabo put it. A sensitive fact about Julie Mills emerged as soon as the investigation turned to the people in her own life. She was bisexual.

"There you have it," Szabo said. "A woman did it. Women can be more fucking possessive toward their lovers than men."

"Get serious," Claire Hopson said. "One of the interns did it."

There were two prime suspects, each of whom considered himself engaged to Miss Mills. Both men were interns at the hospital where she worked. One saw her weeknights, the other saw her on weekends. As it turned out, neither man knew about the other. Each was shocked to learn of the other's role in her life.

Szabo discovered that Julie Mills had also been seeing a policeman for three years. "I guess she was a love junkie," Claire said.

On Sunday, the IOS squad had the day off.

Once a year every officer in the department went to one of the ranges to qualify. Sinker Barnes had been a very good marksman—on the range—and he thought he was doing well that morning on the Rouge Park pistol range.

"Pull those shots down," Raccaniello said, his voice rising above the sound of simultaneous gunfire.

"Come on! Let's go! You're running out of time," he exclaimed from behind Sinker.

He fumbled with the gun's cylinder and the empty shells spilled onto the ground. He began reloading with uncooperative fingers.

"Move, dammit!"

Only a few seconds left. Sinker dropped into a crouch position and thrust the weapon forward at waist level. The paper man was an amorphous blur somewhere in front. One. Two. Three. He counted the explosions and kept on pulling the trigger.

The range whistle sounded. The staccato noise of gunfire was replaced by a numbing silence. Raccaniello stepped forward and tore the human silhouette target from its backing. "N.F.G.! Start grouping your shots," he said, handing it to Barnes. "You should be trying for gut shots! Like this," he said. He clenched a fist and held it in front of his stomach.

"But look," Sinker protested. "I have one here in the head and two more in the chest."

"That's just fine. This kind of shooting is okay as long as we're talking about a piece of paper. I've never known one of these things to kill a cop."

"But any one of those three shots would have been fatal to a real person."

"What do you think would have happened if this sonofabitch had been real? Maybe coming at you with a gun or a knife?"

"Why, he'd be dead, of course."

Raccaniello poked two fingers through the holes in the paper man's chest. "Yeah, he would probably croak from either one of these, all right," he said.

"Then what's the problem?"

"The problem," he began in an irritated voice, "is that he just might not have died until after he'd first killed you or somebody else. That's why you shoot for the gut. You hit somebody in the chest and he might not stop. But a gut shot's different—it'll double him up, stop him cold right where he stands."

"What about my head shot? It would have killed him instantly."

"It would have if you'd gotten lucky enough to hit him in the head. And that's just what it would have been—pure luck. In a situation like that you've got to allow for the effect of fear—panic. Like what happened in the cab."

"Where was my backup? They had the drop on me."

"Just as well you didn't start shooting. You were so scared you were lucky you didn't shoot yourself."

The Rivers family had a secret—a nice secret. Not that they went around cross-stitching it on samplers or even said so out loud, but they were a happy family. Cal and Beryl had married late and bought their house, an unexceptionable nine-room ranch, in the mid-sixties when real estate was reasonable. They raised their kids there, in a good neighborhood with nice neighbors who had the habit of dropping by when they smelled a cookout and expected you to do the same. The kids walked to school, and both of them, Randy and Anne, were kids whose teachers loved them.

"Randy is the nicest boy I've ever taught," his first-grade teacher had written on his first report card; Anne's teachers had similar things to say. The Rivers kids weren't the smartest in their classes, but they were so normal, so unaffected, and so good-natured that they got moved into special academic programs with the brainy kids just to balance things out.

Beryl loved to garden, and she had planted the front and back yards with forsythia, dogwoods, lilacs, and a lawn. Of course, there was a basketball hoop on the garage. In April people came from blocks away to walk by the daffodils in bloom. She

also raised Pixie tomatoes in wooden pots by the
back door; they filled the refrigerator in August.

Cal Rivers had worked through the night and
the following morning, and in the afternoon, when
the smell of burning leaves had taken him back to
his own childhood, he came home to a tense scene.
As soon as he entered the kitchen, his daughter
Anne gave him a "you're in trouble look" and left
the room. Randy, who never even slowed down,
was planted at the kitchen table, looking like he'd
lost his poster collection.

"Hey! Whaaa . . ." Rivers said, his spirits falling
fast.

Beryl stood at the sink, her back to him. She
didn't turn around and her body language was all
wrong. He knew he'd forgotten something. Christ,
it wasn't her birthday, was it? No, he knew her
birthday was in May.

"We had a nice time at the concert," Beryl said
in a small voice.

"Oh, shoot," Cal Rivers said. "I'm sorry."

"You missed the whole thing," Anne said.

Rivers remembered with a rush that they had
all planned to go to the concert at Randy's school.
Randy had played the alto sax for two years and
was almost worth listening to.

"That's all right, Dad," Randy said.

"Well, I am sorry! Hey, team! These things happen in the big world. What else is wrong?"

"I read an article," Anne blurted out.

Cal pulled out his chair, the one nearest the Mr.
Coffee and the telephone, and sat down heavily.
He brushed past Beryl and saw to his horror that
she had been crying.

"Sit down. Family powwow. What article?
Where? About what?"

Beryl hesitated, then dried her hands and joined
the family at the kitchen table.

"I read an article by Ralph Thomas, honey, and

I just freaked out. I mean, we all know you have a dangerous job, and that you love it, and we are all proud of you. Anne is so proud of you that she's doing a report on the importance of police in our society. But, honey, it said right in the *Free Press* that the average police officer lives to be fifty-nine; only one in ten lives past sixty."

Cal reached out and the four of them joined hands, just like they did on special occasions like Thanksgiving. "Hey! Team!"

"Yes, Dad?"

"Nobody knows the future but the Man Upstairs, but He sometimes gives me a tip. And what I see is all of us sitting here when Anne dresses for her weddin' and when Randy comes home with a college degree!"

"Dad!" Anne protested. "I'm not ever gonna get married. I'm gonna be a doctor!"

"Okay, okay, whatever you want, honey. Hey, Beryl, you ain't studying to be a gay widow, are you? Isn't this old daddy enough?" Under the table he gave her knee a special squeeze, warm and strong.

"More than enough. I know I was just being silly," she said.

"You sure were," he said standing to kiss her gently on the cheek. "You sure were."

Claire Hopson's small apartment was cheerful and inviting, brightened by a colorful collection of small abstract paintings done in delicate pastels. Vern Szabo had done them. Of the squad, only Claire knew that Vern was a secret painter. She liked his work and she was right to do so. Szabo had a lot of spirit and it showed in his paintings, which made the whole apartment sing.

Without really trying, Claire was a homemaker with a strong sense of individual design. She had picked up most of the furniture at Goodwill and

Murphy's Second Chance, but it was all solid, well-polished, and neat. She had made the curtains, which were tied back neatly with black grosgrain ribbons. She had found the antique Shiraz carpet for fifty bucks—it was worth a couple of grand. Plants sprouted from pots on the carpeted floor and crept from copper bowls on the window sills. Claire had a policy of keeping the living room free of kids' paraphernalia, and it was not easy to uphold.

In fact, there wasn't anything she wouldn't do for her kids. The oldest was almost grown and in a rebellious stage, but they were still solid. They liked each other. Sometimes Claire worried that her daughter was too adult, too self-reliant. At twelve, she had won the citywide competition for selling Girl Scout cookies. For Claire's birthday she had baked not a mere cake, but a Gateau St. Honoré that had been described in the *Free Press*. The kid had gone to the public library and looked up the recipe in a French cookbook. It was a masterpiece of cream puffs and whipped cream. Claire had nearly cried when she saw it. Now Wendy had a job at a D'Angelo sub shop and paid for all her own clothes. The kid was all right.

Claire had always felt an extra measure of motherly concern for her son Timmy ever since his near-fatal illness in infancy. It was hard not to overprotect a kid who had been through something like that. It was true that he was not very strong, but he was charming, a trait that would see him through. He had personality. He loved old people. He loved children. He could talk to anyone. He had everything going for him. He was a character.

She knew she was neglecting him with her job but it had to be done. On four-to-twelve she didn't see him at all, but she made a point to call him once a night. She felt guilty about it. On the street people could call her names and that didn't bother her but if some man said, "Why aren't you home taking care of your kids?," that upset her.

Her daughter walked into the den. A full inch taller than her mother, Wendy was a striking blond-haired girl, dressed in designer jeans and high heels.

"How was your date last night? Plenty of action with Philip?"

"Wendy!"

"Well?"

"I'm afraid the relationship may have self-destructed," Claire said.

Philip Linton edited GM in-house publications and wrote official biographies of the top execs. It was a job that paid well, very well, so well that Philip had to hire a shrink to keep him from feeling guilty. He was tall, dark, handsome, divorced, and urbane. Claire had been dating him for several weeks, but she had realized the night before that they had nothing going.

They had gone to the London Chop House, but Philip was sulky, brooding over his Scotch. "You look like you've had a rough day in the executive jungle. Care to talk about it?"

"Forget it."

To Claire this was a hateful phrase, but she persisted, "It can't be that bad."

"The hell it can't."

Claire was beginning to run out of patience. For once she decided to lay some of her work problems on Philip. She told him about Julie Mills. She described the mirror against which a severed breast had been hurled.

"My God, that's terrible," Philip allowed. "I guess you're running into tragedies like that all the time. That's a rough job you do." He took a sip and brooded some more. "The thing with me is, that damn project I've been working on—I've misplaced a memo and I can't find it. It's driving me up the wall. It was the best memo of my life."

Memo? Claire thought. Memo? He's upset about a memo. She had the clear feeling that she was in the wrong place at the wrong time, certainly with the wrong man. Memo? Inappropriately, she had laughed, and Philip frowned at her, crumpling his napkin angrily.

Vern Szabo's wife began each morning by asking when he was going to make a change. He had refused a transfer to a much easier job with the Residency Unit. All he would have to do with his days would be to investigate complaints that employees of the department were not residents of the City of Detroit. Instead of chasing criminals, he could chase police officers and their families back into the city from the suburbs.

The main change that Vern Szabo wanted was a divorce. He wanted to move to a quiet, clean room without a screaming TV and a fat woman padding about on large swollen feet. If in his youth he had been afforded a glimpse into the future and seen the enormous bulk that would be his wife, he would have run screaming into the night. He wanted to get away from the everlasting fight with his son. Ben was just fourteen and he was into drugs, truancy, and petty thievery. Vern was pretty sure that Ben and his punk friends occasionally rolled queers in Palmer Park. Szabo often lay awake in the night thinking, Where did it all start? He wished he had a magic wand. But he didn't.

His wife wanted another TV set. She didn't like to sit by the television in the living room when he was out prowling the precinct because the old wood-frame house was drafty and cold at the temperature she had to maintain on their budget. She wanted a set in the basement recreation room, where the oil burner gave a cheery glow within a radius of four inches. She was a stubborn woman. It wouldn't do to move the television they had.

At least it gave him reason to get out of the house.

While Vern Szabo was shopping for a secondhand television, Nick Sands and Dwight Franklin were doing lunch with Skeets.

The oozing, festering sores on Skeets's arms made an unappetizing spectacle, but that didn't deter them from taking him to a Syrian delicatessen between Eight and Nine Mile in St. Claire Shores. The place had home-cooked baba ghanough and great meat and spinach pies. It also had the advantage of being far from the boundries of the 14th Precinct.

Skeets sighed. "I'm starving."

"No wonder," Franklin said. "You never buy any decent food."

"This my big chance, huh?"

"On one condition," Sands reminded him. "Please control that mouth of yours. Everybody here knows me, and I don't want you embarrassing me. So no swearing."

"Right, Nick."

Skeets was their personal snitch, their ally against Jason Lemons. Skeets had come into the picture after he and JoJo had ripped off some furs in cold storage, a lot of them. Skeets was unused to handling property in such volume and sought to make a quick deal. He approached a fence with whom he had had satisfactory dealings, only to find that he, appreciating his predicament, was bent on taking some advantage of it. Unwilling to let his efforts go so cheaply, Skeets began to survey other fences to see if he couldn't negotiate a more equitable bargain. It was then he discovered that the word had gone out. Other fences had been alerted to the prior claim placed upon the merchandise by the original fence. Knowing the exigencies of Skeets's situation, they had agreed to uphold their colleague's territorial rights. Knowing he could not expect a fair price or even the original offer, he took the furs to Chicago and sold them. On his return, the local industry's displeasure came at him in the form of two of Jason Lemons's enforcers. He was beaten and his money taken.

To get Skeets to squeal on Lemons also required a cash incentive. Sands and Franklin didn't like to think that police department money was going to feed a junkie's habit, but it was better in the long run to pay Skeets. That way they'd have a shot at keeping him around for years.

One of the funniest facts about Skeets was his vehement denial that he was a stool pigeon. Whenever he left the station after trying to peddle some information, he would complain on the street, "The cops pinched me again, but they don't have nothing on me. I didn't tell the pigs a fucking thing."

In fact he sold information to Sands and Franklin on a regular basis. They had established a routine. Skeets called Franklin at an unlisted number and arranged to meet him, usually in the lot of a gas station on Oakwood, just across the River Rouge bridge. Half an hour later, while Franklin and Sands waited in the car, Skeets would slip into the back seat and sell absolutely reliable information about whomever or whatever he happened to have picked up on the street. And once a week Sands and Franklin took Skeets out to lunch.

Skeets had become an unofficial but crucial member of the team. The basic rule with informants was to pay them only if the leads they provided panned out, but Skeets was so consistently accurate that they sometimes paid him upfront.

They knew that the twenty or thirty dollars they paid him for the tips would be spent on drugs, but they never offered him narcotics in exchange for information.

The more he became part of the family, the more concerned everyone became for his health, especially Franklin. That Sunday Franklin had brought Skeets a waterproofed poncho with a hood, figuring Skeets needed it more than he did.

His eyes half-closed to Skeets's uncouth table manners, Nick Sands asked, "What's on the grapevine? I'm busting with anticipation."

"Dwayne Fernald knocked over a house in Indian Village last week," Skeets told them.

"Dwayne who?" Sands asked.

"Shit, man, he only one of the best thieves in Detroit."

"Oh, that Dwayne," Franklin said. "I thought he was in prison. He got life. Dwayne wasn't supposed to see daylight for a *long* time."

"He out now. He says the fix was in, you know, acting all puffed up about it. Someone got paid off to get him out early."

"You don't say. Sounds like something's rotten in Denmark," Franklin observed.

"Rotten is right," Skeets said. "It bother me to hear a judge say, 'A year,' and the dude is out again in six months. If he stip'late a year, it oughta be a year. If he stip'late life, it oughta be life. If he stip'late one hundred years, it should be one hundred years. None of this frontin' and confusin' bullshit."

Sands and Franklin looked at one another. Part of what drove them crazy about their life was the number of times they had to drag a violent criminal back in front of a judge before the son of a bitch finally got a sentence that would slow him down a while. Then they had the parole system throwing them back.

"Who was on Fernald's crew?" Sands asked.

"A few guys."

"How did you learn about it?"

"Little birdie." They let Skeets slide. They had an understanding. Sands was relieved that Skeets hadn't said anything vulgar so far. In fact, their snitch was just getting around to it.

"Hey waitress, what you got for fucking dessert?"

The waitress turned red and hastily handed him a menu. After glancing at the choices, he said, "Gimme the lemon meringue. Got a sweet tooth, babe."

"Well, I'm sure you could get something for that information in the Fifth Precinct," Franklin said. "But we need to know about Ed Tomack, the Chez Lila robbery, and the rape/murder of that nurse, shit like that."

"Man, I don't associate with perverts. What would I know about that? You talking about the restaurant, I'll keep my ear to the ground. Now about that D. T. in the park, I don't know, but people say the cop knew too much about something. Things were getting too hot for some guy. So he offed him."

"Who is he? What was this guy into?" Sands asked.

"Hey, I don't put my name on that, this is just the rhythm of what people saying. I'll work on it. But what about Dwayne? Man's a master criminal."

"What'd he do, Skeets, stiff you on the job?" Franklin asked.

"Dude gave me chump change," Skeets admitted. He turned to the waitress and shouted, "Where the fuck is my pie?"

As the mortified Sands looked apologetically at the offended waitress, Skeets grinned.

* * *

Even Maben was required to remove his shoes before walking on the new, thick pile carpet.

The living room was in immaculate order, in pastels of brown and red, subdued in hue and without a hint of sleazy opulence. The carpet was deep red. Curtains were drawn behind a long brown sofa that faced a large color television. Along one wall was an assemblage of high-quality electronic gear, with Lear Jet amplifiers. In one corner was a broad velvet lounge chair shaped in an undulant continuum like a gentle wave. Bookshelves along one wall held hardcover editions of encyclopedias, black philosophy, biographies, and the complete works of Ayn Rand. Two full-length mirrors mounted on closet doors on opposite sides of the room provided a double reflection.

Jason Lemons pulled the curtains and pointed down toward the streets. It was a cold afternoon, and the air over the city was unusually clear. From the balcony high up in the high-rise waterfront apartment tower he could look northwest to Woodward, the spine of the city, dividing east from west, north to the Wayne County Jail, and beyond to the rise of the Frank Murphy Hall of Justice.

Just to the east lay Greektown and the restaurants on Monroe Street, and to the south rose the five tubes of the Renaissance Center, its spires and glass glinting silver and green-gold in the afternoon light.

He turned to the white-haired hit man. "Look out there," Lemons said. "Look at those marks and hustlers and cops. This city is a fast place, Maben. Fast and tough. And they got the best police force in the world. So here I am. The way I look at it, I must be one of the fastest hustlers in the world, right? I gotta figure I'm one of the fastest because here I am." He let the curtains fall back and turned to face Maben, raising his eyebrows. "Right?"

Tom Castleton was spending the afternoon sitting alone at a table in Maxie's Mainstreet, listening to a blues jam session and ordering one glass of water after another.

He used to drink. He felt the killing of his daughter had destroyed him mentally, and he got to the point where he couldn't sleep. When he did sleep he had nightmares.

Castleton nodded appreciatively at the riffs of the bearded alto-sax player, a barrel-chested man whose eyes bulged as his sax wailed. He felt he owed his life to him. The Reverend Leo Harris was a Baptist minister who used his pulpit to advocate for the poor in the 14th Precinct. He coordinated a shelter for the homeless and was part of a community task force working to respond to an unparalleled rise in juvenile homicides.

The blues quartet wrapped up "Born in Chicago," the sax down and dirty, and went straight into "Livin' in the U.S.A." When Reverend Harris stepped up to the mike to shout the lyrics, the effect was so rousing that people stood and crowded the little stage.

Harris acknowledged the applause and announced a break. He joined Castleton at his table. He had come to Maxie's directly from his storefront church, and, since he had another gig with the Lord in a few hours, hadn't bothered to remove his clerical collar.

"You look like a refugee from a seminary," Castleton said.

"Why aren't you in church?" Harris asked. "You take communion today?"

Castleton didn't answer, but asked, "Why aren't you trying to convert me to your denomination, Leo? Is it because of prejudice?"

"The problem ain't that you're white, but that you can't sing."

Castleton laughed, and Harris got serious. "You won't go to confession for the same reason you won't go to your wife. But you know that."

"I do? Go on, you're telling the story."

"You'll know you'll be forgiven, 'cause there's nothing *to* forgive. But then you'll have to forgive yourself, and you can't handle that."

Castleton couldn't respond, couldn't meet Leo Harris's clear gaze, and didn't see the embrace coming until Harris had enwrapped him in a bear hug. He sensed Castleton's embarrassment and, releasing him, said, "I like to lay my hands on my people, it's the way I am. The Lord made me black, funky, and demonstrative. Thank God!"

It was time for another set. Castleton decided to pass the comforting on to someone else. He left Maxie's and drove to the Tomack house. Cynthia Tomack took a long time coming to the front door. She was alone, the kids spending the day with their grandparents. He declined her offer of a drink and they sat on the living-room sofa.

"Maybe it's not a good idea for you to be alone," Castleton said.

"I thought I needed a good, uninterrupted cry," Cynthia said. "But I can't cry. I keep trying to think, to understand what happened, but nothing comes together. I feel they're lying to me about what's really been going on."

"Who's been lying, Cynthia?"

"Ed's . . . colleagues. I feel so mixed up. They act like they don't know anything, but they must. I certainly don't know what was bothering Ed."

"Something *was* wrong?"

"I can tell you, Ed was drinking too much. I'd never seen that before. We started arguing. He was out at night a lot, even though he was on leave. I thought he was seeing another woman. He

wouldn't talk about it. We'd scream at each other
and he'd get in his car and drive away. He was
obviously fighting himself about something."

"But it wasn't another woman, was it?"

"I don't know. Tom, I feel like I'm trying to
climb out of a hole, but the rungs are missing from
the ladder."

Castleton took Cynthia's hand and gave her an
understanding smile. He could assure her of nothing, but he knew then that it was his job to put
the rungs back.

And to do that, he'd have to climb down into the
pit.

The Michigan Opera Theatre was presenting *Fal-
staff* at the Fisher Theatre on West Grand Boulevard. The voice of Luciano Pavarotti soared and
swirled, filling the auditorium with a spine-tingling
aria. Maben leaned back in his chair and hummed
along softly, totally and blissfully entranced.

Dwayne Fernald was submerged among reeds
about eight feet off St. Claire Shores. His torso
and limbs had swollen into grotesque, balloonlike
shapes by the body gases released during decom-
position. His belly exploded, spilling rotting in-
nards that fish nibbled.

For Sue Mallory, Sunday was a working day. In
addition to the dreaded pross detail, she sometimes pulled matron duty, searching and guarding
the female prisoners who were lodged overnight
at the precinct until they could be arraigned in
criminal court the following morning. Most of the
prisoners were streetwalkers, often rounded up
en masse by Vice undercover men.

It was the pits, worse than pross detail. The girls
were a bawdy and boisterous lot—"Hogarthian,"
Sergeant Sudol had said—strutting, jabbering,

and cursing, clamoring for coffee or candy or cigarettes the moment Sue locked them in their cells.

The most difficult part was doing the search. The women often concealed joints, penknives, or razor blades in their purses, clothing, or sometimes in various orifices. As soon as Sue ventured near, they began to squawk like chickens.

"Oh, don't be doin' that," Zahara protested as Sue reached for her purse. "The policewoman the other night didn't go looking in there. Nobody else makes me do that. Now you ain't got no cause to be looking in my purse, officer. Don't you be touching that . . ."

Patiently, Sue would persist. "Now, c'mon, honey, you know I have to look in there. You're no stranger around here. You've been locked up plenty of times before. You know the rules."

"I sure do. Do you think I could do . . . what you do?"

"Do what, honey?"

"Be a police lady."

"You kick that stuff and get back for a little schooling, and you could do it better than me."

Prisoners who were not regulars like Zahara got a good looking-over before the body search. Sue had learned that appearances could be deceiving. It was not uncommon to suddenly discover that the female she was searching was not really a female after all.

About 2 A.M., Popovich and Witosky brought in a scruffy-looking hooker. As they hustled her up to the front desk, she began to scream and curse and kick out at them, indignant over their rudeness.

"Got one for you, Sue," Popovich said.

An hour later, Sergeant Sudol called her. "Sue, Witosky and Popovich are on their way back to the precinct to pick you up. Lieutenant Starks wants all of you to take a run over to Detroit Receiving and get shots for infectious hepatitis. That doll you searched? They think she's a carrier."

Riding to the hospital with Witosky and Popovich, Sue remembered how she had joined the department to help people. If only she could get a chance to do something that mattered.

Chapter Six

DOWNTOWN AT 1300 Beaubien, the Crimes Against Persons Section had noted similarities between rapes in the l4th Precinct and others in the city. The Section sifted daily reports and made connections, and came to the conclusion that a homicidal rapist was walking around. The Deputy Chief of the Criminal Investigation Bureau directed the Sex Crimes Unit and the D.A.'s office to form a joint task force, to be overseen by Assistant D.A. Caroline Bodner, to pursue the investigation.

According to scuttlebutt, Bodner was part of a clique of tough D.A.'s. She kept to herself. She was committed to her work and the public good. She didn't cut corners, and she had a fierce integrity. And she lorded it over cops. If she told you to shit, as Vern Szabo put it, you had to squat. She had a reputation for being stuck-up, snotty, even a lesbian. Once she compared the thrill of hearing a jury return a guilty verdict to the ultimate sexual experience.

What the precinct detectives saw at their first meeting conformed to their expectations. The D.A. was beautiful, in her late thirties, with blond hair, delicately sculptured facial bones, and grace of movement. She was a zealot in a city of sin.

The beautiful ones were always bitches, sticklers for detail and proper procedure. Sure enough, she entered the precinct squad room harried and tart of tongue. Bodner was accompanied by Lieutenant John Wartiainen of the Sex Crimes Unit. He had a good reputation but the precinct detectives had always found him mysterious. A Finn from the Upper Peninsula, Wartiainen was a dedicated, obstinate man with a broad, impassive face and a controlled voice. He was so uncommunicative that some thought he must be shellshocked, while others thought he was brilliant. Tibbets, a porcine detective who had come with Wartiainen, called out to Claire, "Hey, baby, how'ya doing?"

"You don't know me that well," Claire responded. "When I tell you my name is baby and ask you to address me that way, okay. Until then my name is Investigator Hopson."

"All right, people," the D.A. said. "We're going to catch and convict this person. I have a reputation for getting a damn lot of convictions, and I do it by making certain that when I go into court, the odds are in my favor. Judges shy away from hard sentences, and they don't like seeing their calendars cluttered with cases that could have been plea-bargained away. That's not going to happen to us."

Nick Sands brushed his lower lip with his thumb and looked at District Attorney Bodner speculatively. He didn't seem to notice when she stared back, hard. Her ears were tinged with color as she continued.

"If we develop a case, ladies and gentlemen, I'm going to want extra depth in the evidentiary material and three or four paths leading to conviction. I see nothing to be gained in proceeding without evidence in depth. I want this understood right now. A reasonable chance of success will not be good enough."

Lieutenant Wartiainen reviewed the information at hand. A forensic odontologist had gotten photographs of the bite marks on Julie Mills's shoulders, taken with a centimeter rule in the shot. There were so many variables in bite size, in wear patterns, in fillings and occlusions, in the pattern and distribution of teeth, that bite marks were as good as a clear latent print in a court of law.

The degree of bruising and tissue destruction proved that it had been done while the victim was still living.

An attempt had been made to lift latent prints off the victim's body. A technician who had been trained in the Kromekote film technique had performed the operation at the scene. But latent prints were useless unless a specific suspect was under investigation. The FBI Latent Print Section in Washington could only search for similarities in a few areas. There was no computerized filing system that could be tapped into for some magical whole-system check. The search had to be directed by name and FBI print number. Still, a latent print would nail a suspect once the man had been taken into custody. It was something that Caroline Bodner could use to convince a jury.

"What kind of person is the Beast? Do we have a profile?" Claire Hopson asked.

"One is being developed. Probably someone whom no one would ever suspect," Lieutenant Wartiainen said. "People have the idea these guys have to look like creeps, they have to look dangerous and act weird. Actually, they don't. They look like the guy next door. Their particular problem is usually a very separate thing from their normal everyday life."

The Sex Crimes people set up shop in the squad room. They began the tasks of creating a voluminous card file on the cases, cross-indexing names found common to previously separate precinct-level investigations, and tracing the movement of suspects. They began a map of the killing zone showing the locations of the attacks.

And precinct detectives hit the streets to track down reluctant witnesses and interview past offenders.

Barnes and Raccaniello were still trying to locate Top Dog. While searching for the suspect who might assist them in their investigation, Raccaniello carried no fewer than three "second" guns with him. A snub-nosed .38 was strapped to one leg, a .45 Derringer was kept in his coat pocket, and another was in his belt. In addition, he carried his cowboy gun, a .45 revolver with a six-inch barrel.

They went to a place where they thought they might get a lead on Top Dog, an abandoned house on Pingree that was used as a shooting gallery from time to time. The proprietor was a cousin of Top Dog's named Elroy.

They stood to either side of the door, guns at the ready, and Raccaniello knocked. "Elroy! Police! Open up!"

"You got a warrant?"

"Nope. Open up anyway."

"Not by the hairs on my chinny-chin-chin."

"Elroy, this is not a bust. We can get a warrant and there are five Narcotics detectives sitting in the station house right now who will gladly come over for a visit. Is that the way you want it, or are you going to talk to us?"

The door was opened. Elroy was a wily, wiry man wearing wire-rim spectacles. "What you want?"

"Top Dog," Barnes said.

"What's he gone and done now?"

"I thought you'd know," Raccaniello said.

"Shit, no. I ain't seen the sucker in a year. We don't keep tabs."

"Nice place you got here. Mind if we look around?"

Elroy shrugged. "Nobody here, as you can see."

Raccaniello pointed with his chin toward the back room. "Check it out, Barnes," he said, "while I keep Elroy here company."

The room was grimy and dark, illuminated only by the flickering light of a one-inch candle stub. It took him a moment to make out a huddled form lying on a dirty, bare mattress, a young woman who watched glassy-eyed as he looked around.

"I thought you said nobody was here," Barnes called back.

"She ain't nobody," Elroy insisted.

As Sinker turned to go, she suddenly spoke.

"I know why you're here," she said.

"Tell me and I'll tell you if you're right," Sinker said.

"Because of what happened last night, at that restaurant?"

"You know something about it?"

"You gonna help me out?"

Barnes and Raccaniello looked at one another.

"Sure, honey," Barnes said. "What's your name?"

"Zahara."

For the price of a fix, she told them she had been watching television with her boyfriend in her apartment when Top Dog hurried in, bragging about a big score.

"Who's your boyfriend?" Raccaniello wanted to know.

"Never you mind about him."

"Where's Top Dog laying now?" Sinker asked.

"I don't know. He lives with a lot of girls."

"Where's he hang out?"

"Sometimes he be at the Sportsman's Palace."

They knew the place, a social club and blind pig, as a spot with a rugged clientele. A guy had to puke twice and flash a straight razor before they'd let him in.

They drove to Sycamore, just off Twelfth Street, and stopped in front of the social club. Sinker asked, "We gonna go there without backup?"

"In this neighborhood mommas make their loud kids quiet by telling them that 'Rakinello will come and ketch you.' I am feared here. In fact, you better go in alone. I'd just spoil it."

"You're kidding me, right?"

Raccaniello grinned. Sinker shrugged. He walked to the door without looking back and plunged into the Sportsman's Palace. The place was crowded and loud, voices obscured by Aretha Franklin on the jukebox. There was a fluid movement of people in and around the bar where contacts were made, deals consummated, debtors and enemies sought. Sinker shouldered his way between a massive black man wearing a sleeveless, wide-mesh pullover and a floppy red cap, and an old man wearing a calfskin highboy, whose wizened eyes gleamed with street wisdom. Red lights fixed to the ceiling were reflected luridly in the mirrors behind the bar. The bartender's hair was processed and his head was shaped like a pear. The only white face Sinker saw was his own.

When the patrons saw him everything stopped. They regarded the cop with cool intensity.

"Hi, there, everybody," Sinker said. "Top Dog
been around lately?"

In the quietude that followed, Sinker felt that
he had failed to break the ice. The only voice was
Aretha's, and that suddenly stopped dead. The
hush became a quiet rush as men made for the
doors, the stairs, and the fire escape. Raccaniello
had come into the room quietly to stand behind
Barnes after pulling the plug on the jukebox.

"You see, Barnes," he said in a low, amused
tone, "every one who has been doing anything
wrong has beat feet. They think I know everything."

The remaining crowd was small and joyless.
Raccaniello leaned back against the bar and casually surveyed the men who were trying to stare
him to death. He was beaming, like Pavarotti leaning against a piano, thriving on antipathy. He
pointed to one man.

"I know you! You did five years at Milan for
B and E. Don't you know Top Dog?"

"I don't know nothing. You want to take me in
for questioning? Am I under arrest, man?"

"Why should I arrest you? I'm just gonna take
off all your drugs and flush them down the toilet.
My partner and me, we haven't ruined anybody's
day yet."

"Shit!"

Raccaniello shoved the man up against a wall,
and quickly frisked him, removing an ample sup-
ply of marijuana and several small envelopes of
cocaine. He tore open the joints and dumped out
the coke, smearing it on the concrete floor with
his foot. Repeating the process with two other
men, Raccaniello left a green and pink trail of
crushed pills on the floor. He hummed contentedly all the while.

He turned to the bartender. "Tell Top Dog to
drop Raccaniello a line when you see him."

As they drove away, they watched men sneaking back into the Sportsman's Palace.

"I don't think I've ever been hated by so many people at one time," Barnes said.

"Don't worry about it. They'll soon be happy again," Raccaniello observed.

Sergeant Sudol was staring at a suspicious package. Over the years he had received a lot of bombs with timing devices. They had to be disarmed by the Tactical Services Section, of course, except for the ones that went off. He received scores of suspicious packages every year. He never knew what he was going to get. Once it was thirteen sticks of dynamite in a lunch box. This package was addressed, in block letters, to Inspector Campbell.

Gary Newman approached diffidently. "Are you gonna inform Inspector Campbell? Are you gonna call Tactical Services?"

Sergeant Sudol, intent in his concentration, sniffed at the package. "Human offal," he pronounced. "This is a shit bomb."

At 3:15 P.M., John Hendrick, an employee of the gas company, arrived at the home of Mrs. Darling on McGraw, where the noise from the Edsel Ford Freeway was constant. Mrs. Darling, a mother of four, was told that she owed eighty dollars to the gas company. Mr. Hendrick approached the residence and went to shut off the gas meter at the side of the house. Mrs. Darling angrily approached Mr. Hendrick, screaming that she would not allow him to disconnect her gas service. She then struck him with a shovel, bruising him on the arm. Mr. Hendrick retreated from the Darling house. He returned to his office and filed a report. The gas company reported the incident to the Detroit Police Department, which notified the 14th Precinct.

Mr. Hendrick called the police dispatcher and requested a patrol car to join him at the residence. Mrs. Darling emerged with her shovel. The police dispatcher placed the call and Officers O'Hallerin and Sue Mallory acknowledged it.

As they approached the house, Mrs. Darling yelled at them, "You're not coming up on my lawn, motherfuckers, you're not going to turn off my gas!"

O'Hallerin rested one hand on the butt of his revolver and pointed at Mrs. Darling with the other. "Drop that shovel, lady!"

Mrs. Darling called O'Hallerin a cocksucker and told Mallory that she could lick her ass. "Use your gun, if you're going to use it!"

Mr. Hendrick and various neighbors were waiting to see what would happen.

"Deck," Sue said, "I think we're in danger of losing control of the situation."

"Officers," Mr. Hendrick shouted, "make your arrest! This woman assaulted me!"

They looked at Mrs. Darling, who was weeping now, having dropped her domestic weapon.

"Are we in this together?" Sue asked.

"I will if you will," O'Hallerin replied.

They backed away from Mrs. Darling and approached Hendrick. "Drop your complaint, Mr. Hendrick, and we'll take care of the bill," Sue said. "Give us Mrs. Darling's account number and I'll write you a check."

They left the scene and were coming down Livernois when they saw a white guy and a woman in a fancy Cadillac. He was double-parked, blocking traffic in both directions. He didn't care. They pulled alongside the Cadillac and O'Hallerin said, "Can you do me a favor, please? Move the car. You got the whole lane blocked."

The man said, "Haven't you got anything better

to do? Is this all you got to do to keep yourselves busy?"

"You better move this car right now or you're going to be the sorriest cocksucker around, I'll tell you that right now."

"Why don't you go arrest those black people? Why don't you go to the ghetto? You're scared of them so you're here bothering white people. You're scared of those people, so you just bother us!"

The excitement began when a Civilian Radio Patrol volunteer radioed from a bombed-out stretch of Twelfth Street. He had seen two men stalking up the steps of the United Civic Club for Community Action from a car idling out front. He did not need to slow down to see that they were carrying shotguns. Two minutes later, the volunteer also flagged a patrol car—Officers Mallory and O'Hallerin.

"I just saw two guys going into the Civic Club. They looked like they were gonna stock up a gun store—wholesale." He sped on.

O'Hallerin cut a squealing U-turn while Sue Mallory radioed Sergeant Kalina.

"Jesus," Kalina said, "anyone planning to induce those customers to submit to a holdup had better carry an arsenal."

He ordered all available units to the scene. "Ten twenty-two. Cars sixteen and eleven proceed to Livernois and Otis. CRP has reported a tavern robbery. Use extreme caution. Suspects are believed to be armed with shotguns. Robbery in progress. Car is a two-tone Plymouth Fury, about nineteen seventy-eight, red and white, license nine four three Fox Easy Boy."

Inside the social club, Finnegan and Philpot had lined up the fourteen male and twelve female pa-

trons against the wall opposite the bar while Top
Dog kept the car ready outside.

"Everybody strip off your duds!" hollered Finnegan. Even though shotguns were being leveled
at them, several of the women giggled as they
wriggled out of tight-fitting slacks.

"I'm gonna blow some ass away unless you
hurry up," Finnegan said. "Everybody toss the
stuff right here in the middle of the floor."

As the clothes piled up, Philpot rifled through
them, throwing valuables into a plastic shopping
bag from Fretter's. Top Dog appeared at the entrance. "How long you going to be with these
folks? I feel ex*posed* out there."

Finnegan handed the bag to Top Dog. "Take this
and stay in the fucking car like I told you."

"Awright, awright."

Only two blocks away, Barnes and Raccaniello
caught the ten twenty-two on their radio. Barnes
drove, without using the lights.

"It's probably a big fucking nothing, but . . ."
Raccaniello reached under the seat for the short
twelve-gauge double-barrelled shotgun he kept
there. Unless specifically assigned, it was strictly
against departmental regulations for a detective
even to have one inside an unmarked unit, let
alone carry it. A man could get a two-week suspension without pay. But he knew that. Humming, Raccaniello opened the cylinder of his big
.45, dumped the cartridges into a handkerchief,
and reloaded with hollow points—dumdums—another violation.

They were first on the scene, which looked desolate and abandoned. Nothing suggested life behind the doors of the social club, or a felony
robbery. One car, a wide Plymouth Fury, was double-parked and idling.

"Let's swing up so we can come up behind him,"
Raccaniello said. "Hold on now."

The Plymouth suddenly started driving down the street. The car moved too slowly to be an unconcerned motorist. The young black man who was driving nervously looked back at the unmarked police car in disbelief.

"Do you see who I see?" Sinker said.

"Top Dog!"

Raccaniello jumped out with a shotgun aimed right at the car. Barnes held out a searchlight, illuminating the suspect's car but also blinding Raccaniello, who trained his shotgun on the windshield of the Plymouth.

"Freeze, police! Put your hands on the wheel! Put your hands on the wheel! Put your hands on the wheel where we can see them! Slow!"

Top Dog placed his hands on the wheel slowly, with a deliberate, unnerving sullenness.

"Now keep your hands on the wheel or I'll break your fucking thumbs!"

Top Dog slowly complied. With speed that impressed Barnes, Raccaniello reached into the driver's side of the car to grab Top Dog by his forearms.

Inside the club, a blast of buckshot tore into the ceiling. The room filled with plaster dust and cordite. A woman shrieked and Philpot whipped around quick, ready to fire.

"Cool it," said Finnegan. "I was only telling them to speed it up. These cats just don't want to strip fast enough."

The detectives heard the report. Raccaniello momentarily relaxed his grip of Top Dog's forearms. Top Dog punched the pedal and the Plymouth shot ahead.

"Shit!" Barnes crouched with his Walther held in both hands, wondering if he could hit a tire.

"Let him go!" Raccaniello shouted. They raced to take position behind their car. No one came out. Three patrol cars converged almost simultaneously, the officers spilling out of their units. Barnes shouted the license of the Plymouth to Sue Mallory, who radioed the description in.

Inside, Finnegan and Philpot were ready to take their leave. Philpot paused for a moment on his way back out, noticing the backsides of some of the women. They were stripped to panties—except for those who had not worn any.

"Lotta slit," he murmured.

"Quit staring at ass and get the fuck out where you supposed to be," Finnegan said.

Philpot took three steps when he saw patrol cars at each end of the block with cops behind the cars, their guns trained on him. Frozen, he saw more patrol cars pull up in silence, followed by another unmarked car carrying Sands and Franklin. Philpot scampered back inside.

"The pigs have got us surrounded!"

Finnegan hardly seemed flustered.

"Everyone get their clothes back on, quick!" Finnegan ordered. The patrons knelt to pick out their things from the pile on the floor. As they dressed, Finnegan and Philpot tore off their ski masks and unbuttoned their own shirts so they would also look hastily dressed. They hid their weapons under the tables and behind the jukebox.

The last thing Finnegan did, before stashing his shotgun, was to club himself once, hard and without hesitation, with the barrels. His scalp split, and rivulets of blood ran down to his brow. Philpot watched wide-eyed. The man just wasn't afraid of pain.

"Okay, we're gonna march out with hands up, together," said Finnegan. "Anyone points a finger at us, we'll see to it you get capped." He looked around the room. He had that ability of crazy people to make each person feel that he was focused upon him or her alone.

Outside, the officers waited with weapons and

lights trained on the door. "Don't nobody shoot!"
a woman's voice cried out. "We coming out!"

Officers watched the column of half-dressed
blacks march slowly down the stairs to the sidewalk, their hands up. "What were they doing in
there?" O'Hallerin asked Sue Mallory.

"Parlor games?"

Sands and Franklin were the first to storm past
them up the stairs and into the club. Except for a
mess of leftover clothing, a card table piled with
valuables, and the guns and surgical gloves, the
room was empty.

"Okay, where are the holdup guys?" shouted
Franklin.

Everyone shrugged.

"Come on, who is it?"

"Maybe they got away out back," a girl volunteered.

"We had the back covered," Raccaniello said.
Now, if nobody is going to help us out with this
goddamn problem, then we'll just lock everyone
up."

"It was him," said Finnegan, pointing to a half-
dressed man beside him.

Raccaniello walked up to him. "I believe it was
you."

"Fuck off, man, you think I hit my own face?"

Sands took Raccaniello aside. "I can see this
isn't a crowd of police buffs. All these people
might be stoned, but they're scared, too."

They ordered the patrolmen to take them aside
one by one and ask confidentially who the robbers
were. No one was talking.

"Call in some wagons," Raccaniello said. "We'll
have to take them all to the station house."

This was done amid loud protests that began on
the street and continued amidst the congestion
and confusion at the booking desk. The computer
system had a printout for virtually all of the pa-

trons of the Civic Club. None were without criminal records. One attorney arrived at the station house within minutes and buttonholed Commander Rivers.

"I understand that you have been bothering Mr. Perry, claiming he is involved in armed robbery or some such thing."

"Oh, you mean Diamond Duke?"

"I don't know anyone of that name. I'm talking about Mr. Virgil Perry. I happen to know that he is a very honest and respectable citizen, and if you don't want to get the black community on your back, you'll stop harassing this poor man."

"This isn't harassment, counselor. If Mr. Perry is respectable as you say, he's one of the victims, and we're protecting his rights. Excuse me."

Rivers stepped into the interrogation room. Each of the arrestees in turn stood behind the mirror window for the lineup as all the other males were led through. Still, no one was willing to make an identification until one woman drew in her breath sharply at the sight of Finnegan.

"That's a make," Inspector Campbell said.

"There's no way I'll testify in court, no way."

Campbell slowly turned to face the woman. "Lady, you're talking obstruction of justice. Do you know what that means?"

"Baby, I know what I mean, and I mean what I say."

Campbell gave the woman an intimidating look, but Rivers touched his shoulder and dismissed the woman courteously.

Finnegan was kept in the interrogation room. Sands and Franklin and Barnes and Raccaniello took turns yelling at him.

"We have your guns."

"Ain't mine. You got prints to prove it?"

"We can get latent prints off anything."

"Bullshit."

"We can do ballistics and connect you to the Chez Lila robbery."

Finnegan crossed his muscular arms across his chest and rested his head against the wall. Hundreds of suspects had done the same over the years, making a distinct impression in the plaster. "More bullshit." He seemed totally at ease, even to enjoy all the attention. He stared insouciantly at the window with the reflective surface, behind which Commander Rivers and Campbell watched.

"He looks a little old to be carrying on like a new jack," Campbell said.

Rivers felt he knew the man. "Finnegan is the kind of psycho who always survives. The only thing that kills him is getting bored and taking too many chances. And that's what makes him so dangerous."

They left the room and stood in the crowded hallway as Finnegan was led up to the detention cage. He passed Philpot, and assuming that he also would be made, he murmured, "Be cool."

"I know that," Philpot said. Sands and Franklin brought him into the interrogation room.

Caroline Bodner was ending a long day, but she had sufficient energy to observe the proceedings and give an opinion in Cal Rivers's office.

"You don't have sufficient evidence to press charges against Finnegan."

"I know."

He saw Philpot being led to detention, and asked Nick Sands into the office.

"How'd it go with Philpot?"

"He's cool, Commander. He's not talking."

"If you can't produce a witness willing to testify, they'll have to walk," Bodner said.

"We'll hold them the full forty-eight hours and hope for a break," Rivers said.

* * *

While the interrogations were in progress, Sergeant Sudol received a call from a woman asking for Officer Mallory. The call was transferred to Sergeant Kalina, who acted as a funnel for cases that had to go to the second-floor detective squad room. Ultimately, Inspector Campbell took the call.

She coolly informed him that she had one of the robbers in her apartment.

"I'm calling from a pay phone. He sent me out to get some HoJo's and some wine."

"What's your name?"

"Zahara."

"Where are you?"

"Erskine and Wood'ard."

"Lady, don't move a goddamn inch." Campbell slammed down the phone. "Sands, Franklin. Check it out!"

They were there in fifteen minutes. Zahara stepped out of the shadows of a doorway.

"Top Dog come to my place all excited, said he had to ditch a car he stole. He nervous, watching the door with a gun, but I can fuck him to sleep. I let you know when you can take him easy."

She asked only that the detectives pay for Top Dog's Roma Tokay and HoJo's. Zahara hurried off to the corner package store and returned to her building. Franklin and Sands moved their car so they could watch the stairs leading down to the basement apartment. About an hour later she was back at the window of the unmarked car.

"He's asleep on my bed."

"Good, we'll go and get him," Sands said.

"Wait a minute, just let me run back to make sure that everything's all right."

"Let's go," Sands said a few minutes later.

They descended to the hall and quietly moved past the super's apartment, which emitted heavy bass vibrations from a rap record. Gripping their guns, they stood on either side of the door, and Franklin slowly turned the doorknob. It had been left unlocked. Sands made the rush while Franklin stood behind and at an angle, ready to provide cover fire.

Sure enough, Top Dog was asleep there, sprawled on the bed. His naked torso revealed a muscular physique. Zahara got up and moved away. She did a good job of being surprised.

"Put your shirt on, buddy," Sands said as they roused him out of his stupor. "You're coming with us."

"Whuffo?" Top Dog started to rise.

"Questioning, baby," Franklin said. "About the robbery you were in on tonight. Stay down. Hook your right foot over your left calf." Franklin grabbed Top Dog's left toe and kneeled on his right leg. A little twisting pressure persuaded Top Dog not to struggle. "Now put your hands behind your back." He slapped handcuffs on Top Dog and Sands stood him up for a proper frisk.

"What you talking about? I didn't do no robbery."

"Yes, you have," Sands said with mock patience. "You've been holding up people at the Civic Club."

"Why, looky here," Franklin said. He pulled a shotgun from underneath the bed. Sands dug roughly into his pants. "And look what you have in your pockets, Top Dog. Shotgun shells. Nice guy we got here."

They searched the apartment for the money, but found nothing.

Sands read Top Dog his rights and they hustled him out to the car. Top Dog had been docile up to that point, but once he was in the cage his mood suddenly changed. He began to shout obscenities and throw himself around the back seat.

The detectives stood outside the apartment with

Zahara, Franklin asking, "What was he doing at your place?"

"I know him. Sometimes he come around, that's all."

"Where's the money, babe?"

"I don't have it," she said emphatically.

"You know, I'm beginning to suspect you had something to do with the robbery," Franklin said.

Zahara insisted she didn't know where the money was.

"Aw, come on," Sands said, "can't you see the lady wants to help? Let's not spoil things by talking about money. Zahara, I bet you could help us make the leader of the crew, the man who led Top Dog astray. There could be a small fee involved."

"Don't be asking me that," Zahara declined firmly. "He's dangerous."

Chapter Seven

"**I** WANT THE names of the people you were with tonight," Dwight Franklin said.

"I don't know what people you talking about," Top Dog whined. Franklin stabbed at his chest with a finger. Top Dog tried to climb the wall behind him.

"Tell me, babe."

"I got nothing to say to you."

"Talk to me, fuckface. This is survival time. You're gonna tell me what you did with the money."

"I'm not gonna tell you shit."

"We're gonna get an indictment. We got enough to put you into the robbery and nail you for it. That's not guesswork, that's hard evidence. A jury's gonna look at and convict you in about fifteen minutes, and the judge is gonna send you away for something like ten or twenty years."

"Maybe longer," Sands said. "They figure because you won't talk, you'll have to hang for the others. The judge won't care that we'll get them eventually. All they know is that we've got you. And we've got you, Eugene."

"Were you involved in the Chez Lila robbery?"

"I don't know anything about that," Top Dog said.

"Let's book the sonofabitch," Franklin shouted. "Throw his ass in a cell." He focused his gaze on Top Dog's eyebrows. It was his theory that it was more intimidating than eye contact. "You're going away for a long time and I hope you rot."

Sands raised a hand to interrupt. "Take it easy, Dwight," he said. "Maybe Eugene wants to help us. Maybe he wants to cooperate and see if the court will give him a break because of his attitude."

Franklin smashed a hand down on the desk. "Book him. Lock him up and throw the fucking key away. Flush him down the toilet."

"Dwight, cool it. Give it a rest, okay? Go get a drink of water."

Franklin glared at Top Dog, turned his shoulders from side to side, and left the interrogation room.

"Whew!" Sands exclaimed. "Franklin gets pretty hot sometimes. I think he got frustrated talking to your friends Finnegan and Philpot. Oh, yeah, they're upstairs, in a safe place. Wanna say hello?"

"I don't know those dudes."

"I understand. If they see you with me outside the cage, they might have the impression that you've been spilling your guts. I suppose that could be a problem. Finnegan is crazy. You know that, don't you?"

Top Dog stared at the table, thinking hard. "You got a cig'rette?" he asked.

"Sorry, Eugene, I've been trying to quit. Franklin has some butts, but that can be tricky. He has what we call his cigarette punch. I've seen it. With his right hand he offers someone a cigarette and when you open your mouth to take it, he hits you on the side of the jaw with his left. See, when your jaw is open, it breaks easily. It takes timing and you need to know the exact spot to hit, but Franklin has got it down. He practices."

"Where my lawyer?"

"Eugene, the public defender is rushing to your side, even as we speak. I suppose we might as well take it easy until he gets here."

Dwight Franklin reentered the interrogation room. He appeared to have calmed down. "Say, man," he said to Top Dog, "let's start over and be friends. Investigator Sands thinks you're going to do the right thing, so let's calm down." He reached into the pocket of his leather jacket for a pack of Chesterfields. "Have a smoke."

Top Dog looked pop-eyed. "No thanks!"

Franklin still proffered the pack. "C'mon, man, relax. Light up and be somebody."

"I don't want no cigarette!"

"Take one," Franklin insisted.

Top Dog's eyes began to fill up. "I got nothing to say until I talk to my lawyer."

"Let's face it," Sands said to Franklin, "this guy is too smart to jerk around. I hope Finnegan appreciates how cool you are. And seeing that the money hasn't been accounted for, I hope he's not the kind of guy who assumes the worst of people."

Tom Castleton slipped away by himself and drove to Lansing in the rain to talk to Mike Tomack, the brother of the murdered detective. He worked on the State Pardon Board, appointed by the governor. His job was to recommend candidates for parole and pardons to the state legislators.

The office was decorated in an ultra-macho

mode. A bear's head and a nine-point buck were
mounted on the wall. A reproduction of a Reming-
ton sculpture and a model cannon lay on the big
desk, and big red leather chairs were placed
around the room. Behind Tomack's chair a window gave a view of the state capitol dome.

"I wanted to express my condolences. Ed was a
friend of mine."

"I know."

"How are Cynthia and the kids doing?"

"As well as can be expected. It still doesn't seem
real to me. I can't believe Ed is gone."

That was the nature of sudden death. Even when
death is long anticipated, the actual absence was
always a shock.

"What can I do for you? What brings you to
Lansing?"

"I wanted to talk about Ed. Had you been in
contact with him during the last weeks?"

"No, we'd both been busy. We would have gotten together at Thanksgiving, of course. Now . . ."

"Then he gave you no indication that he was
involved in anything dangerous."

"No. Of course, I've tried to be helpful to the
Homicide detectives. They asked a lot of questions. You'd think Ed was the criminal."

"It's just that no one can connect what happened to Ed to any investigation he was involved
in."

"This has been a hard time, and frankly I'm
tired. You're not participating in the investigation, are you? Officially, I mean."

"No. . . ."

"I mean, Mr. Castleton, you're not a Homicide
detective. I understand you have a desk job at the
precinct." His tone was clear.

"That's right."

"So officially, the case is none of your concern."

"Officially."

"Forgive me, I don't quite understand what you're doing here."

"I'm being a friend of the family."

"Does your commander know you're here?"

"No, I'm off duty."

"I have the sense you have something to prove. Am I right? No doubt you have the best of intentions, but you're intruding on our grief."

"Then I'm sorry. I'm sorry that there seems to have been no positive developments in the investigation into Ed's murder."

"We may never know. That's something we have to deal with, unpleasant as that is to contemplate. But I'm sure that the best qualified people are doing everything they can. Now, if you'll excuse me, I'm not off duty today, and I have an appointment."

Castleton shrugged, rose, and left.

In the hall, he passed Racine Latimer, the state representative for a Detroit district. He was a black man, bald, with a mustache, jug ears, and tired eyes that seemed to pass judgment. Castleton glanced back. Latimer was entering Mike Tomack's office.

Castleton had parked his gray '81 Dodge in a municipal lot across the street from Mike Tomack's building. Once back in his car, it was no longer clear to him why he had come, what he thought he might accomplish other than to be given a humiliating reception. He put the key in the ignition, but his hand fell to his lap. He felt no desire to go anywhere, do anything. Despair came over him, familiar now, and he felt no more alive than a stone falling through space.

He lost track of time, and wasn't sure how long he had been sitting there when he saw Tomack come out of the building, followed by Latimer. The body language was odd. They were not together, exchanged no words of parting, and walked in separate directions. Racine Latimer walked into the parking lot, to a deep purple Pontiac. He opened the passenger door and got in. Someone was already sitting behind the wheel, his image obscured by reflected light. Yet there was something oddly familiar about the dark shape, something in the set of the shoulders. Scarcely a minute passed before Latimer got out of the car and went to a white Cadillac, apparently his own.

Both cars pulled out of the lot. Castleton's instincts were aroused. Without questioning his actions, he followed the Pontiac as it tooled along a commercial strip and pulled into a Denny's restaurant. Castleton drove down the block and parked. He found his dark glasses in the glove compartment and put them on. He had the same queer sensation that had come over him that terrible morning at Handy Andy's when his daughter died, the certainty that something was very wrong.

Old techniques came into play as if of their own volition. When he entered the restaurant he affected a limp. Affliction can provide a kind of invisibility. People generally try not to stare at a cripple. And a waiter gave him prompt service when he sat at the counter.

His subject had taken a booth. Castleton used his peripheral vision, careful not to watch straight on at such close quarters, and then for only a moment. Then he used the mirror behind the counter. The man had a big head and sunken eyes with bags under them. The left eyelid drooped, hooding the eye and creating an asymmetry to the face, as if the two halves didn't properly fit.

He felt, then, he had made the subject.

He'd have to get closer to verify. Castleton finished his coffee and headed for the cashier. As he limped abreast of the booth, he let a quarter fall from his hand to the floor. When the subject's eyes were on the coin, Castleton looked directly at his face.

Carby. Vincent Carby. He had started out burning down businesses for insurance money. Later he became a strong-arm man for Jason Lemons. The last Castleton had known, Carby had been in the Detroit House of Correction, serving a term for second-degree murder. Tomack, Latimer, Carby, Lemons. It added up to something.

He let his gaze linger a fraction of a second too long. When he picked up his quarter, Carby was staring at him suspiciously, trying to remember where he had seen him before. Castleton stared right back. It was the only thing to do when the subject was suspicious.

Castleton sat in his car and waited for Carby to finish his meal. At length the subject came out. He was short and waddled when he walked, but he carried himself with authority. Carby got into his car without looking around, unworried, and headed for the freeway. Castleton followed. The freeway was relatively flat and open. Rear visibility was good, and that was bad, but Carby seemed unaware of his tail.

After a while, Carby turned off the freeway onto an access road. The access road forked. One fork led to side streets, the other back onto the opposite lane of the freeway. Castleton slowed as Carby made his exit, then committed himself, making the exit and turning onto the access road.

Suddenly, Carby accelerated ahead, and turned onto the fork that led back to the freeway. Castleton was caught dead. He couldn't follow Carby onto the freeway without being made. He couldn't follow Carby from a side road. Carby had burned Castleton's tail so adeptly it was almost arrogant.

* * *

Patrol Car 7 stopped along Grand River, in front
of Najib's, a Mom-and-Pop grocery store where
O'Hallerin got the light cigars with the wooden
tips that he liked. Not that Sue Mallory let him
smoke in the cruiser. The store was one of the
places they checked out nearly every tour, and it
had become practically a ritual.

Najib was a tiny, ancient man who wore wire-
rimmed glasses and an apron that must once have
been white. He gave the impression that he never
strayed from behind the cash register. He called
O'Hallerin Hot Shot and treated Sue Mallory with
deference as he sold Deck his cigars and pressed
a yellow rose on Sue. Someone in his extended
family was a florist and his wife always kept a
bouquet on a shelf behind the counter.

As they walked back to the cruiser, O'Hallerin
asked, "Is Najib flirting with you? Is that what's
going on? I get the feeling he thinks that he and
you might have a lot in common."

"Don't blame me for the way your mind works,"
Sue said. "Najib's not a lover, he's a working machine."

"He'll die behind that cash register, that's for
sure," Deck agreed.

They turned off Grand River just before the
bridge over the John C. Lodge. O'Hallerin deliberately drove the wrong way up Brooklyn with the
headlights off. This was a simple ploy used to gain
an element of surprise when scanning the buildings and side streets for miscreants.

O'Hallerin abruptly braked the cruiser. He put
the car in reverse and backed up several yards,
then sat motionless, staring into the darkness.

Sue Mallory looked around. She didn't see anything. "What's the matter?" she whispered.

"Okay, come outta there," O'Hallerin ordered in
a command voice. He unsnapped his gun, resting

one hand on its grip as he got out and stood behind the open car door.

Sue was out of the car on her side now, still wondering what Deck was talking about. He beamed a shaft of light from the cruiser's spotlight into an alley and brought it to rest on a pile of wooden fruit crates. She saw movement as two black figures stepped slowly from behind the crates and stood in the spotlight's glare.

"Hey, fellas, c'mere. Like to talk to you."

They began walking toward them.

"Watch the one on your right," O'Hallerin said.

She could see them both clearly now—two black youths in their late teens. "What did they do?"

"Don't know. They were walking along being real cool back there. Then they saw us coming from behind and ducked into that alley. On the car," he said simply to the man on the left as he walked up.

The man quickly assumed the position—feet wide apart, palms flat on the car.

"You've done this before."

"Shake the other one down," O'Hallerin said as he began running his hands across the first man's shirt and trousers.

"Say what, baby?" He came toward her with both hands in the pockets of a windbreaker jacket.

"I said—"

"He said to get your ass on the car! Now move!"

Sue turned and saw that Deck's revolver was out of its holster, pointed directly at the man. The man's eyes grew wide when he saw the gun.

"And take your hands outta your pockets nice and easy or I'll blow your head off! That's it. Now get on the car like that officer told you."

She started frisking him.

"Well, well. What have we got here?" O'Hallerin said. He reached deep in the first man's groin area and emerged with a small nickel-plated revolver. "How about the other one?" he asked as Sue finished running both hands down a pantleg. He handcuffed the first man and made him get into the back of the cruiser.

Sue stopped. She felt something soft and spongy in the second man's left sock. "There's something there," she said as she stood up. "But it's too soft to be a weapon. I think it's a plastic bag of some sort. Shall we run a records check on him before we let him go?"

Deck looked at her with a puzzled expression on his face. "What the hell do you mean, 'let him go'? Find out what's in that sock."

"We can't do that," she protested.

It was legal to frisk the man's outer clothing for weapons but it was illegal to go beyond that extremely limited search and examine the man's sock without first having actual grounds to make an arrest.

"Here, keep an eye on this one," he said. He walked over to where the second man was still spread-eagled against the patrol car. He reached inside the sock and withdrew a plastic bag filled with small, tightly folded coin envelopes. "Smack," he said as he opened one of them and examined its contents. "Four, five, six decks. You're under arrest, too, friend. Gimme your handcuff, Sue."

The one who had been armed was off and running.

Sliding over to the driver's seat, O'Hallerin plucked the receiver off the radio and called for backup units as he hit the gas.

Screeching up the street, O'Hallerin and Mallory caught up with the youth as he turned west on Spruce. Suddenly, he lost his footing and tumbled to the pavement. At almost the same instant, the speeding patrol car skidded right past him into the intersection and screeched to a halt. O'Hal-

lerin was out of the car in a second, his revolver
drawn.

The youth picked himself up and tried one last
run for it. But O'Hallerin jumped, grabbed his
shoulders, and slammed him roughly into the side
of a building.

"Fuck you, man! I didn't do nothing!"

He stopped struggling and went limp when he
felt O'Hallerin's .38 in his ear.

Just then two more squad cars pulled up and
more officers jumped out to assist.

They transported both men to the precinct and
booked them.

Once they were back inside the patrol car
O'Hallerin looked at Sue and said, "Don't ever
hesitate to draw down on assholes like those two
if they don't move when you tell them to."

Sue said nothing.

"And another thing," he added a block later as
they pulled into a drive-in restaurant for coffee.
"Why'd you let that guy walk up on you with his
hands in his pockets like that? If he'd had a gun
inside that jacket he could have blasted you before you had time to bat an eye."

A waitress brought them their coffee. Sue sipped
hers slowly, not saying anything.

"Something on your mind, Sue?"

"Yes, there is, now that you mention it, Deck."

"Well, go ahead, get it off your chest."

"You know as well as I do that searching that
guy's sock back there was illegal as hell, don't
you?"

"So that's it."

"You're damn right that's it."

Deck shrugged. "So it was illegal. So what?"

"So what? My God, how can you say a thing like
that? We're supposed to be police officers. If we
don't follow the law, how can we expect anyone
else to respect it?"

"That what you think those two back there were doing, respecting the law? If we hadn't busted them, you can be sure they'd have knocked over Najib's or another one of those all-night markets by now with the gun the little guy had in his jeans. Maybe hurt somebody, killed somebody doing it."

"I'm not talking about that. I'm talking about making a patently illegal search, then turning around and using the illegally obtained evidence to justify arresting a man. Now, that's wrong!"

Deck frowned. "Okay. Let's say we did it your way—let the guy with the heroin go because we didn't have legal grounds to search him. What then?" He leaned back against his chair and folded his arms across his chest.

"Then—"

"Then he'd be back on the streets pushing the shit in his sock next morning, wouldn't he? You heard the check that came back on them. They both did time for selling drugs."

"Sure. But that's got nothing to do with it. We're police officers. We can't go around like a couple of vigilantes meting out curbside justice. We—"

"Hey, don't talk to me about justice . . ."

"But a cop can't go around punishing criminals just because the justice system doesn't work as it should, Deck!"

"The system doesn't care about us. You're a cop, you're nothing. The D.A.'s office, the judges and jurors—they don't give a damn if you and I get our heads blown off out here. What they do care about is protecting the rights of punks like the two we arrested tonight. Well, I say fuck their rights! And fuck the courts, too, if they're too damn stupid to know the difference between right and wrong anymore! What about our rights, dammit! Don't cops have rights, too!"

* * *

After two days Finnegan and Philpot walked.

They went directly to the pad Philpot shared with Zahara. Zahara was cooking a pack of heroin, brand-named CBS when they arrived. JoJo, her sometime supplier, was there also. "Hi, baby," Zahara said.

"Shit, look at you."

"Baby, I missed you. I needed something for the pain," Zahara said, and passed out.

"What you doing here?" Philpot asked JoJo.

"Keeping Zahara company until you got back, that's all," JoJo said.

"You give her too much."

"She's just coasting, man, no harm done."

"Get your white ass outta here," Philpot said. "Next time I see you hanging out with my woman in my place, I'll kill you."

"Hey, I was just trying to help somebody." JoJo was scared of Philpot, but what made him cringe was the way Finnegan just smirked at him. He got out quick.

Finnegan looked at Zahara for a minute and then went into the back room without saying a word.

About an hour later, Zahara was slumped over the table in her little kitchen alcove. She heard someone coming into the room. Then she saw Finnegan with a thin-bladed knife in his hand. Zahara wondered if this were really happening or if it were a bad reaction. She fell back on her bed, trying to clear her mind.

"Where the money, bitch."

"What money? What money you talking about? Where's my man?"

"I told him to find a car. You and me got important business. I know Top Dog was here. Now where's the money?"

Zahara tried to jump out the basement window

but he pulled her back in. She screamed and Finnegan struck the base of her neck with the inside of his forearm. He smiled as he felt the vibration in her body. It was a blow intended to stun and cause pain without doing heavy-duty damage. Finnegan hadn't decided whether or not he was going to kill Zahara, and he didn't want to mess up her money-making face.

He threw Zahara to the floor and pulled off her pants. "You move, you die." He heated the knife over the gas stove flame and held the blade close to her eyes. Every so often he would ask her where the money was and deliver more diffused blows.

He inserted the tip of the blade in her anus. "How do you like this?" he asked. She screamed.

"Why you doing this to me? Please, please don't kill me. I'm just trying to get over like you are." Tears streamed copiously down her cheeks.

"I am a professional, dirty motherfucker and you are guilty until proven innocent. You took the money for dope."

"JoJo turn me on, that's all. I never seen any money. Top Dog didn't have no money I ever saw when he come in. Maybe the cops took it off him. Maybe he stashed it someplace else."

Finnegan paused, then withdrew the blade. He looked thoughtful.

"Okay, I believe you. Don't tell Reggie about our little talk."

"I won't say nothing," Zahara promised. "Can I get up now?"

"One more thing," Finnegan said.

He made her perform fellatio on him. Then he let her up.

There had been six attacks. Four times the women managed to get away. Twice they were raped and murdered. The Sex Crimes Unit had turned the squad room into a war room. There was a large map on the wall with color-coded pushpins for the locations of the attacks. There were charts and graphs and computer printouts describing typical offenders and typical victims, days and hours of the incidents, locations, moon phases, weather, even barometric pressures.

"The fact remains," Claire Hopson observed, "that we're looking for a man who has left no clues."

"Not entirely true," Lieutenant Wartiainen said. "We have some input from the Serology/Trace Evidence Unit. The technicians found some hairs that were not the victim's. Semen and blood specimens taken from the body of Miss Mills indicates that a single assailant was responsible. The crime lab has developed a biological profile of the rapist. Now, this profile fits only two percent of the population. A positive match would be strong evidence."

"Terrific," Vern Szabo said. "Now all we need is a suspect."

Lieutenant Wartiainen didn't react to the jibe. "We also have input from the FBI. The crime lab sent pictures of the murder scene to the psychological profiling team at the FBI Academy. The profiling program combines police work with psychology. Using what they know about repeat offenders, they employ known patterns to analyze new crimes."

"Are we talking shrinks, Lieutenant?" Claire Hopson asked.

"We're talking computers. The computer has given us a description of the attacker. Here's the profile it printed out:
Race: White.
Sex: Male.
Age: Late 20s.

Personality: Quiet, loner, manipulative, calcu-
lating, bright, middle class.

Relationship to victims: Knew first victim.

Residence: Lives nearby.

Dress: Dark clothes.

Job: Semiskilled night work.

Transportation: Car with a shortwave radio.

Pets: Large dog.

"No address?" Szabo muttered to Claire Hopson. "What about the tattoo on his dong, does it
read "Mother" or "Death Before Dishonor"?

"How often are these profiles on target, Lieutenant?" Claire Hopson asked.

"About fifteen percent of the time. So it might
be at least helpful."

The team was filing out of the squad room when
Claire stopped short under the big map.

"Look up there, Vern. What do you see?"

"A lot of pins."

"Look," she said, jabbing at lines of pins that
sliced the precinct east-west on Vernor and then
cut north. "Most of the attacks are along this line.
Here, here, and here."

"Yeah. So."

"Lieutenant? Miss Mills' car was stolen three
days before her death."

"That's right."

"None of her boyfriends—or her girlfriend—
gave her a ride home that night."

"Unless someone was lying a little bit," Wartiainen conceded.

"And none of the cab companies have produced
a driver who had Miss Mills as a fare."

"Right."

"So, she took the bus. This line," Claire said,
pointing to the map, "corresponds roughly to a
bus line, doesn't it?"

Wartiainen looked at the map for a long time.

"What do you think, Lieutenant?"

"Investigator Hopson, I think it's time to mount a decoy operation."

Sinker Barnes could not believe that the fear he had felt throughout the Civic Club incident had gone unnoticed. By the time the collars were made, he was finding it hard to breathe, as if steel bands were tightening around his chest. When Finnegan and Philpot were released he suffered a paranoid flash that the Big Guy was out to get him. It was like a nightmare in which the ghouls were laid low, but after a brief respite it began all over again. Sinker Barnes was living in a world in which, from time to time, it was necessary to get stoned.

When he came off his shift at midnight he cruised Erskine instead of driving straight home. At the corner of John R., without leaving his car, he made a quick purchase of a small zip-lock bag's worth of marijuana from a black youth.

Barnes pulled away from the corner but had to stop at the light. He felt guilty and introspective. Maybe he wanted to get busted. Then he wouldn't have to worry about Finnegan and Philpot, about his inevitable disgrace. While he was thinking these thoughts, the hooker in a fur-lined Pakistani jacket stepped off the curb, opened the passenger door, and climbed in.

"Want a date?"

"No! Will you get out of the car, please? Jesus." She started crying.

Behind him horns blared and the light had changed. Sinker stepped on the pedal and wondered what the hell was going on.

"Your name's Tish," Sinker said quietly.

The blond woman looked surprised. "How'd you know?"

"We talked once. I was driving a taxi."

The girl began to blow her nose. Out of the corner of his eye Sinker saw her lean forward to see his face.

She sighed heavily. "Sorry about that. I remember, now. How you doing tonight?"

"Less than great myself."

"Are you lonely? You want a date?"

Damn it, he was lonely. "Maybe," Sinker said, surprising himself.

"I have to make some money tonight or I'll be sick. We can help each other. You look like you could use a date." She found a filter cigarette in her pocketbook.

The dashboard lighter popped and he reached for it. She held his hand lightly as she drew on the cigarette.

He parked the car on Cass and the girl led him a short distance to a building. The ground floor windows were sealed with cinder blocks.

"You wait here a minute," she said, and continued to walk down the street until she was nearly out of sight. Left on the steps, Sinker was as filled with resentment as a jilted teenager. Had the girl become paranoid and abandoned him? He thought of going back to his car.

The Pakistani jacket came into view. She walked past him, looking over her shoulder before unlocking the door. They stood in a hallway with dirty yellow walls, facing green elevator doors. Mirrors were fixed to the narrow walls on either side. Considering his multiple reflection, he had a powerful feeling of unreality.

Ignoring the elevator, the girl began to climb the steep stairs. Sinker caught up to her at the top, where she paused mysteriously. Her nostrils flared, but not from effort. She seemed to be listening for something.

They climbed another flight, where she actually raised a hand and quietly hissed at him, her eyes scouting the long, narrow corridor ahead. The pas-

sageway was absolutely still. If a man jumped
from some recess, Sinker knew he would shoot
him.

They seemed to pass countless doors before the
girl put her key to one, and they entered a single
high-ceilinged room in which a bare lightbulb was
suspended, lighting more dead-yellow walls. A pile
of gray sheets lay on the bed. The only other piece
of furniture was a low stuffed chair in the far corner. The girl shrugged out of her jacket and hung
it on a nail. Underneath she wore a sheer black
turtleneck. She opened a door onto a closet just
large enough to house a small sink.

"What are you waiting for?"

"What?" he asked. His voice sounded strangely
thick.

"Take off your clothes," she ordered, turning a
faucet. "Then get in here."

He undressed to the sound of running water.
Removing first his denim jacket, he slipped his
leathered Walther off his belt and placed it underneath his jacket.

"Come over here," she said. Sinker obeyed and
stood next to her. She was lathering a bar of green
soap.

"Don't you know what I'm doing?"

"What?"

She took his limp prick in her hands and began
to soap it. "You know what I'm doing." She
smiled. She was hoping to avoid intercourse. But
Sinker felt numb, and his body was only dimly
conscious of pleasure.

The girl sighed, sat on the edge of the bed, and
wiggled out of her slacks. She lay down, resting
her head on an uncovered pillow.

"Let's see the money, now."

The floor was cold under his feet as he walked
over to the chair and took the bills from his bill-
fold without letting her see his badge and ID. She

put the money under the pillow and spread her legs. She still wore a thin pullover and a bra underneath.

"Aren't you going to take that off?" he asked.

"You don't get tit. Come on in."

"Wait, let's talk."

"Okay."

"Where are you from, Tish?"

She sighed. "Muskeegon, before I came here."

"Why'd you come to Detroit?"

"To die, I guess. This city eats people."

"So get out."

"I'm trapped." She said it simply and without hope.

Sinker knew the sensation. He felt so bad that he turned to sex in desperation, hoping to achieve a few minutes of mindlessness. The motions soon began to produce real feeling in him, and Tish's body seemed marvelous, warm, and full. He insistently kneaded one breast.

"Oh, what the heck," Tish murmured, and she willingly bared her breasts for him. His hips began a pounding motion and he shuddered and groaned.

He lay still and watched her as Tish took a cloth and began to wipe off slowly, staring into space.

"You ever think, we're free, we're not dead? I mean, what if you and I just decided to get in my car and drive to the Upper Peninsula? Someplace green, with clean air and little towns. I could get a job, we'd never go back to the city. No one would ever know what we might have been before. We could invent ourselves, know what I mean?"

Tish looked at him like she was taking him seriously, but at length she said, "No." She seemed upset and angry.

After a long silence, he rose reluctantly and began to dress. He lifted the jacket off the chair, revealing the pistol. He let it lay while he put his arms through the jacket. Tish's eyes widened when she saw the gun.

He looked at the girl and smiled. "Not to worry. I'm a police officer."

"Now I've seen everything."

"Could I see you again sometime?"

"Sure, but don't talk a lot of shit like that, getting me going."

Sinker didn't know what to say anymore.

"Goodnight, Tish."

"Goodnight, foxy cop."

From his cell on the eighth floor of the Wayne County Jail, Top Dog asked for an interview with his lawyer and Nick Sands.

Sands and Franklin arrived to find Top Dog already huddled with the Public Defender, Jack McRitchie. Tall, with a trim beard and mustache, McRitchie was handsome but pale from spending too many hours inside. His business suits were always a little disheveled, the knot of his tie always loose. He walked in a slight crouch, his shoulders leading his body. Sands and Franklin had to like him, he was so open, friendly, and rumpled.

McRitchie was a good lawyer with a reputation for aggressive and emotional advocacy. He was verbal and could think on his feet. He excelled in the theatrical atmosphere of the courtroom and considered himself the last line of defense of the Constitution of the United States. Sands and Franklin considered themselves the last line of defense between perpetrators and victims. Seeing how McRitchie's clients were invariably guilty, they wished he weren't so damn good.

"We have your client dead to rights on the Civic Club robbery, however he may plea," Sands said. "We saw him driving the getaway car."

"Sure, but my client is willing to cooperate with your ongoing investigations."

"He'll have to put his heart and soul into it." Sands turned to Top Dog. "Are you ready to identify your accomplices?"

Top Dog looked to McRitchie, who said, "He is."

"Eugene, were you part of the Chez Lila robbery?" Sands asked quietly.

Top Dog stared at the cops, his face impassive.

"Eugene, the more you tell us, the better it's gonna look for you. There are judges who will look at this as a public service, and I'm sure the D.A. can be convinced to recommend that you be shown full consideration for your cooperation. Am I right, counselor?"

"I've discussed it with the prosecutor's office," McRitchie said. "Full cooperation means my client can plea-bargain the felony assault charges away in exchange for a rollover on the robbery second charge. With the possibility of bail."

"Imagine that. Top Dog, you were born lucky. Now, did you take part in the restaurant robbery?"

"Maybe." Again Top Dog looked to McRitchie. "Yes."

"Don't you feel a whole lot better now?" Franklin asked.

Top Dog didn't look entirely convinced of it.

"Okay, let's get a typewriter in here," Sands said. "Eugene, you're going to give us a statement telling us how Finnegan and Philpot did the robberies at the restaurant and the social club, and maybe some other things."

They guided Top Dog through an affidavit. He signed and they witnessed.

The warrants came down for Finnegan and Philpot in the morning. 14th Precinct detectives went to the Hotel Atlanta and to Zahara's subterranean apartment and found not a feather. An A.P.B. was issued. The results were zero. Finnegan and Philpot had gone to ground.

The fact that Finnegan and Philpot were on the loose put the 14th Precinct detectives in a bad mood. Off-duty men came in without being asked. Case loads got juggled and court dates were rescheduled. Detectives shook up all their finks. The Patrol Section clamped down on all the minor operations, making life in the street grim until the criminal community pushed the quarry out into the middle of the street. A certain amount of low-level crime in the precinct, such as prostitution and illegal gambling, was tolerated. Normally the detectives didn't shut it down, because most of their tips and information came from these people.

In that regard, Sands and Franklin decided to drop in on Skeets. They drove to a hovel situated right below the giant red Stroh's sign over Exit 11 on the Fisher Freeway. Skeets was home, but he wasn't alone. Sands and Franklin were shocked to see Raccaniello browbeating him, pressing him to the wall with his short stick. Nothing more than a key ring with a six-inch, grooved stick. It didn't look like much but it produced plenty of pain when pressed against bone.

It was a rule in the detective brotherhood that a man's snitch was his private property, and he had to be asked if another detective wanted to relay a few questions.

"What do you think you're doing? Get away from our snitch," Nick Sands yelled angrily.

Raccaniello chewed gum with unimpeded high energy. "Hey, I'm trying to do my job here. I'd like to know why you've been coddling this piece of shit."

The detective's trade consists as much in forming friendships with criminals as in pursuing them. Raccaniello was an exception to the rule. Skeets was family, and Franklin was also enraged. He put his face up to Raccaniello's and shouted, "You're not a detective! You don't even do your own legwork! You're just another fucking thief!"

"All right, all right, the scumbag's all yours. You boys have fun now." Raccaniello walked to his car with deliberate slowness. Sands and Franklin watched him pull away.

"The fucking nerve," Sands said.

"You okay?" Franklin asked Skeets.

"Yeah, yeah. But keep that fucking creep away from me! How can you stand working with people like that?"

"It won't happen again," Sands assured Skeets. "Gotta ask you, you know either of these men?" He showed Skeets a copy of Finnegan's mug shot.

"Nope."

Next he showed the mug shot of Philpot.

"Hey, that's Reggie."

"Seen him around lately?" Franklin asked.

"No. We used to hang out together, but we don't have the same outlook on life. He a new jack."

"I'm hip," Franklin said. "Where did he used to hang out, then?"

"Hm. Lemme think. Used to be a candy store on Seward. Had a pay phone there, it was like his message service."

"Thanks, babe," Franklin said, pressing a five spot on him.

"Let's ride!" Sands said cheerfully.

When they found the place, it turned out be one of the Chaldean establishments. Though to most people Chaldeans were barely remembered people from the Bible, they existed in greater numbers in Detroit than anywhere outside the Middle East. Clannish and shrewd at business, they had little stores throughout the city.

The clientele, however, was black and young. The kids sensed who they were as soon as they walked in. Sands focused on the dominant personality, a young man who carried his suspicious wealth in the form of gold chains around his neck.

"Hey, bro. Where's Reggie Philpot?"

He looked at Franklin and slowly let his smile grow. "I haven't seen Reggie for quite a while. I heard he's been living in California, studying to be a acupuncturist."

His friends laughed.

"You want to go for a ride with us?" Franklin said. "I think maybe we can clear up a few things a little easier if you go with us down to the station house." He turned to his friends. "I'm gonna ask each of you the same question." But the kids were no more helpful. They could not remember when Philpot was last around.

The pay phone on the wall rang. One of the kids jumped to answer it.

"Leave it, I'll pick it up," Franklin said.

"Hello . . ."

"Um . . . is Jimmie there?"

"Sorry, he's not. Who's calling, please?"

"It's just a friend of his . . ."

"Reggie, baby—is that you?"

"Yeah. Who's this?"

"It's Investigator Franklin, Reggie. I want you to come down here so I can talk to you."

"How come you want to talk to me?"

"We're looking for a guy. We thought maybe you could help us out."

Silence.

"Come here now, Reggie. It'll be better for you."

Franklin could hear Philpot thinking hard. "Okay," he finally said. "I'll be over in ten minutes."

Sands and Franklin waited. A pall had settled over the store. The phone rang.

"Dwight's Place," Franklin said heartily.

Silence on the other end.

"Hey, Reggie, it's Investigator Franklin again. How come you didn't show?"

"I'm just tied up and I can't."

"Why don't you come over and talk with me? Then we can let your friends go home."

"I'll be there in half an hour. It's not that I got something to hide, you know."

"Okay! Ciao, baby."

The detectives didn't expect Philpot to show, and indeed he stood them up. At least they knew he was still in Detroit, within their grasp.

While Sands and Franklin were cooling their heels at the candy store, Barnes and Raccaniello were entering the Sugar Shack, a topless bar on Woodward which Zahara Lane had been known to frequent. Raccaniello, heedless of regulations, ordered a bourbon and branch. They stood for several minutes watching a girl with striking red hair and small breasts as she undulated atop a platform. She stared vacantly around the room, dancing zombielike amid the smoke and laughter.

"Broads like that are trouble," Raccaniello said. "Half of 'em are hookers and the other half fuck scumbags."

Sinker thought about Tish, remembering his fantasy. "Some people say ex-hookers make the best wives."

"Never get married, Barnes. All a broad wants is to get her fucking mitts in your loot. Take it from me, there's nothing in the world that'll get a cop in trouble faster than a broad. I got to fooling around with a topless dancer a few years back. A twenty-five-year-old. I shoulda had my head examined. Guys are idiots when it comes to broads, you know. I went with her pretty regular. Even had a key to her apartment. Anyway, one night I come to her place unexpected, and there she is sitting in the middle of the floor—with a spike in her arm, shooting up!"

"What did you do?"

"I dropped the key on the floor and walked out. I never went back."

Sinker was taken aback by the sadness in Raccaniello's voice. Jesus, he had been in love with the girl. Raccaniello in love. It was a new concept, and it made him grin.

"What the fuck are you looking at?" Raccaniello asked.

They hit the street. Raccaniello seemed to regret having told his anecdote, and they rode in silence until the radio crackled a ten twenty-two, reporting a robbery that had gone down at a funeral home on Martin Luther King, Jr. They were close enough to respond. Raccaniello punched the accelerator. Sinker's stomach drew up as he changed in three seconds from a state of relative relaxation to a state of total intensity. As they drove, the dispatcher put out a description of both the car, a blue or gray four-door Ford, and the suspect, a heavy black male in sweats and a hooded sweatshirt.

On busy Grand River, Raccaniello flashed down a blue Buick driven by a black male, a small man who looked to be about forty. It seemed to Barnes that his car and physical description weren't even close to the suspect's, but that didn't matter to Raccaniello. Barnes was coming up along the passenger side when Raccaniello went crazy. He hauled the suspect right out the window, slammed him against the side of the car and started calling him a no-good nigger. The man just stood there with his hands up. The short stick appeared in Raccaniello's hand, and the man cried out as Raccaniello poked the hollow of his left shoulder. He spun him around and used the stick on his kidneys, leaving him draped over the hood. He stuck his stick at the touch pressure point under his left earlobe, and the man screamed in agony. "Get off the hood, scumbag!" He slid his stick under the man's neck, drawing him up in a bar arm hold, a hold prohibited by department regulations because it too often crushed the suspect's Adam's apple or larynx.

Sinker recovered from his shock and went running over to Raccaniello. The man had fallen to the pavement and Raccaniello was handcuffing him, still cussing him out, asking him where the gun and money were.

That was when one of the patrol units came on the air and said they had both the suspect and money in custody. Raccaniello turned his attention to Sinker. "Okay, I made a mistake. It happens. But I still got to make the collar and charge him with resisting, to protect myself in case he decides to file a brutality complaint. Are you with me, Sinker?"

"This stinks."

"Hey, we're brother officers. I'm not gonna tell you any fairy tales. I could lose my shield over this."

Sinker looked away from Raccaniello's pleading eyes.

"You don't give up another cop," Raccaniello said.

"I know."

They put the man in the cage and headed for the station house.

"Jesus," Sergeant Kalina said when he saw the still-moaning figure that they half dragged up to the booking area. He shook his head. "Fellas, I've got news for you. This one's going to have to go over to Detroit Receiving before we can take him.

I'll bet he'll take a half-dozen stitches on his jaw alone." He studied the limp form and looked at Barnes. "What happened?" he asked. "He resist?"

Raccaniello and Sinker stared at each other for several seconds before Sinker finally said, "That's right, he resisted."

Chapter Eight

"ACCORDING TO SERGEANT Raccaniello's report," Commander Rivers said, "the prisoner began complaining that the handcuffs were too tight on the way to the station house?"

"Yes, that's right," Sinker said.

He frowned slightly, pulling at his ear like Bogart. "You didn't have the cuffs double-locked?" he asked.

A tiny metal pin on the side of every handcuff makes any adjustment of the mechanism impossible once it has been pushed in by a key. It was a standard departmental procedure to double-lock the handcuffs of every prisoner, in order to prevent allegations of police brutality by a person who might tighten his own cuffs to the point where they cut off circulation or injured his wrists.

"No, I thought we had, but I guess we must have forgotten to in all the rush," Sinker said. "We had a rough time getting him handcuffed in the first place."

"Now, you stopped the car and one of you went back to loosen the guy's cuffs—" Rivers said as he studied the report. "Which one of you was that?" he asked abruptly.

"Raccaniello. Sergeant Raccaniello."

Cal Rivers had been reviewing Raccaniello's file. There was the past trouble with Internal Affairs for his shootings. Since he had been dumped in the 14th Precinct, there had been lesser matters. Once he had talked back to Inspector Campbell. Twice he was caught in a country bar while on duty. Seven other times he was cited for such infractions as slovenly appearance, insulting a superior officer, and failure to follow proper arrest procedure. Specific citations referred to "unnecessary force" and insulting a citizen.

"Uh-huh. As soon as Sergeant Raccaniello unlocked one of the cuffs to loosen it, the suspect jumped him and a fight started. That right?"

"Yes."

"Now, what did you do then, Investigator? What happened? Just tell me in your own words."

"Well . . . I jumped out and tried to give Raccaniello—Sergeant Raccaniello—a hand. You know, get the prisoner back under control." Sinker was conscious of an increasing tightness in his stomach as he went on. "We really had our hands full. I mean what with him struggling."

I'm lying to Cal Rivers, Sinker thought. Lying to protect another policeman who had committed what amounted to a felony assault.

"Did you personally hit the prisoner, Barnes?"

"No, sir. It all happened so fast. Sergeant Raccaniello did all the . . . restraining, I guess."

"You guess?" Rivers leaned forward in his chair and looked at Sinker. He struggled to meet his gaze.

"Did either one of you use a weapon of any kind on him—a slapjack or a stick?"

"No."

Rivers took a paper out of the folder and handed it to Sinker. "This is the medical evaluation they made on the guy after you took him over to Detroit Receiving," he said. "I'd like you to take a look at it."

Sinker took the report and scanned it. "Fractured ribs . . . concussion . . . multiple bruises and abrasions on face and about head . . . lacerations . . ."

"It takes a hell of a lot of resistance to justify using that kind of force," Rivers said, his brown eyes drilling into him.

"I—"

Rivers got up and walked across the room, poured himself a cup of coffee. "I've seen this guy's rap sheet," he said. "He has a list of priors as long as your arm. Everything from wife beating to grand theft auto. Hell, he probably deserved everything Raccaniello gave him."

"I didn't say Raccaniello gave him anything, Commander."

"Oh, knock it off, Barnes," he said. "Why don't you cut the crap? Now I want to know what happened out there last night! What did that guy do or say that got Raccaniello hot enough to beat hell out of him?"

Sinker sat there without saying anything.

"Was it you, then?" Rivers said. "Are you going to try and tell me that it was you that made the guy look like somebody worked him over with a steam shovel? Please, tell me what the guy did, for your own sake. There's a chance—a damn good chance—that this one will go to the chief's disciplinary board for review. From there it could very easily wind up in court. You could be called upon to testify under oath about what happened out there." He looked at Sinker for a long moment.

Sinker looked at Rivers, conscious that he wanted to tell him what had really happened.

"Sir, do you have any more questions?"

"No," he sighed. "Barnes, there are four kinds of cops. There are bandits who are brilliant in the street but terrible in the station; stand-up cops who play by the rules as much as they can; management types who live by the book and think police work is paperwork and judicious ass-kissing. And punk cops. I wonder which you are. You can go."

Sinker stepped out of Cal Rivers's office feeling two feet tall. His attitude toward Rivers was one of total, unqualified respect, and yet the cop's code had required that he lie through his teeth to his commander. He felt even more a coward than the night he first encountered Finnegan and Philpot.

He wished he were dead.

Nick Sands was on the phone in the squad room, talking to Inspector Claude Shaver of the 5th Precinct IOS squad. Shaver was one of the best, a cop's cop like Commander Rivers, and Sands had seen to it that Skeets's tip about the Clarke burglary had been passed on to him. This was a follow-up call, to ascertain that Inspector Shaver owed him one. Sands like to keep score.

"Dwayne Fernald? We took an interest, sure, but we haven't been able to find him. We talked to his wife, and I can see why Dwayne might have cut out. This is the sort of woman who inspires a need for a sudden vacation."

"That's too bad."

"Why are you so disappointed? Is there something you didn't tell me?"

"We got word on the street that Dwayne was bragging about his parole. Like someone bought it for him. My curiosity was piqued. I'd like to ask him about it."

"I looked at Fernald's sheet. He was out on the

street in record time. I sometimes wonder why we bother chasing the bad guys."

"Right," Sands agreed, "we should get rid of the police department and the judges, and just pay the animals off directly! It'd be a lot cheaper and we could vacation with Dwayne in Florida or wherever."

"Well, it's been grand chatting with you, Sands. We get a lead on Dwayne, you wanna know?"

"I'd appreciate it, Inspector."

Dwight Franklin was sitting on Sands's desk. "Our tip was for naught," he said.

"Shit, and we paid for it out of pocket. I'm gonna have to get a hack license just to maintain Skeets's habit."

"Nick, Dwight." They turned to see Castleton.

"Lieutenant."

"I overheard part of that. Lieutenants have a right to snoop. You know something about sticky paroles, Nick?"

"I don't know anything, except that something stinks."

"You remember Vincent Carby?"

Castleton had always had that way of asking unexpected questions. "Sure, Dwight and I busted him for extortion a few years back."

"I saw him sitting in a car with a State Representative in the parking lot of the Parole Board the other day. I didn't see them French-kissing, but they were talking about something."

"Where was this?"

"Lansing."

"Lansing?"

"I was on private business." Castleton wasn't ready to bring Mike Tomack into the picture. He could have had any number of perfectly valid reasons for meeting with Racine Latimer. "Carby was exhibiting all the characteristics of a bag man, and that includes shaking me off his tail like an expert."

"Hmm," Franklin said.

"And hmm again," Sands said.

"What can we lowly, overworked precinct grunts do about it?" Franklin mused.

"Let's take it to the commander," Nick Sands said.

"Not much to take," Castleton said. "Let's see where we stand when Dwayne pops up."

JoJo was frantic. His woman, a hooker named Tish, hadn't come home the day before. He had been on the streets all night trying to find her. He worried that she had taken a hot shot somewhere, and he was at the point of going to the morgue at Brush and Monroe to look for her. He had found missing friends there on past occasions.

When the phone rang he leaped for it.

"Hello, honey."

"Tish! What the—"

"I was afraid I wouldn't be able to get hold of you. I'm at the Greyhound, and I'll be going in fifteen minutes."

"Going where? What is this? I want you home *now*. I need you here, baby."

"It's too bad the bus is crossing at night," she said. "I like to see the farms."

"Where are you going?"

"Maybe I'll write you. I was going to leave you a letter but it had too many lies in it. If you don't hear from me, remember I know that you love me beautifully and everlastingly and I'll always know how good you are."

Tension pretzeled JoJo's stance. He crossed one leg against the other and leaned his forehead against the folding door. "Then why are you leaving me? I need you here."

"Baby, I'm doing what I have to do. I'm going

in the only direction I can go, and I could only make it harder on you, so try not to be sad for too long."

"You're not telling me anything! Are you going with some guy?"

"If I could be anybody's old lady, I'd be yours. But I'm nothing, JoJo, and sometimes I feel myself going fast. Everything is so hollow inside. I've got to change."

JoJo no longer knew what to say.

"JoJo, your love for me is like a vast, undiscovered country. I wish I could go there. Try not to be too sad." Her voice was cut off by an annihilating dial tone.

It took JoJo ten minutes to drive to East Congress and double park in front of the station. He found Tish sitting in one of those plastic chairs with a little TV. He sat next to her and grasped her arm tightly.

"Stupid idiot!"

"Don't call me that."

"What kind of a person are you?"

"I'm not a person at all."

"Yah!" JoJo snorted. "What are you then?"

"I'm a junkie."

JoJo put his arm around her shoulder and she didn't resist.

"I love you, JoJo." Tish let her head hang down, her blond hair obscuring her face. "I think a lot about when I was a kid," she said, "but that kid's not there just because I can think of her, is she?" She looked up at JoJo's face as if she were looking at the night sky.

"People just are what they are," JoJo said, but Tish was not comforted.

"I'm done for either way." She closed her eyes.

"Come on, baby," JoJo said. "Let's go home and boot up."

* * *

Sue Mallory walked into the squad room wearing a full-length raccoon coat, high heels, and a diffident smile. Given the opportunity to work as a decoy, she had volunteered without hesitation. Claire Hopson introduced her to District Attorney Bodner and Lieutenant Wartiainen.

Sue felt good being with Claire. She trusted her instinctively, and they had the bond of women who had broken and entered into a man's world.

"Are they taking me on because I'm tough, or just because I'm the shortest female officer in the precinct?"

"I recommended you to Lieutenant Wartiainen, Sue. I'm sure you can handle it. You weren't selected just for your height and light frame. In fact, your normal walk won't do at all. On decoy you need to be vague, relaxed, unalert. Try to give the impression that you don't know which way is up. Send out helpless vibes."

Sue laughed. "I will."

That night they initiated the routine. Every member of the detail, including Sue, was assigned a two-way radio. Sue would ride the bus while a special van followed a block behind. When she got off, she would walk six or eight blocks while detectives followed her progress with binoculars.

It was a tricky business, the first runs full of frustration and incipient boredom.

Three times Sue rode the bus, got off at an arranged point, and walked a predetermined route before the team picked her up. All without incident. The high heels were killing her feet as she neared the end of the third route.

Before returning to the station house to log in their report for the night, they decided to do one more route, one which required Sue to get off the bus at Vernor and Scotten, walk the fringe of Clark Park, and proceed as far as Holy Redeemer High School. There were dogwalkers in the park.

High school students spilled out of the gymnasium after a basketball game in a surging mass, moving toward the pizza parlors and video arcades near Scotten.

By the time she cleared the park, Sue's heels were chafed and a distinct limp became part of her decoy repertoire.

Some distance ahead, a car that had passed flashed its brake lights and pulled over to the side of the road. The lights went out. She strained her eyes and thought she saw a man getting out of the car, but her view was obscured by a tree. She was tired and her attention had slipped for a moment.

Then she saw another form emerging in the darkness. It was a long moment before it was apparent that the person was walking away from her, and that it was a woman.

Sue quickened her pace, the damn heels sounding on the sidewalk. Painfully, she gained.

Ahead of the woman, the dark form of a man stepped out from behind a tree. Sue gulped involuntarily. She didn't know her heart could jackhammer the way it was at that moment.

Before the man could move the woman turned and ran back to her, asking "May I walk with you?"

The suspect sped away.

Only then did Sue remember to use her radio. Claire Hopson and Vern Szabo ran to them, and the van followed up behind, disgorging Lieutenant Wartiainen and Investigator Tibbets.

"What happened?" Wartiainen asked.

"Our decoy fucked it up, that's what happened," Tibbets said.

Chapter Nine

KALINA TRANSFERRED A call from the 5th Precinct to Nick Sands. It was Inspector Shaver. "You still interested in Dwayne Fernald? Got time for a scenic drive? Better take down these directions."

Sands signaled to Dwight Franklin. "Let's take a run by and see what they've got," he said. They put on their black leather jackets. The elevator, as usual, was out of order and they hustled down the narrow staircase, encountering Roger Campbell on his way up.

"Where you going?" he demanded.

"Gotta see a sick friend, Inspector," Franklin explained.

"Taking care of your own business on department time, huh? You're both in violation of department rules and regulations. Getting back at the system, is that it, is that what makes it all right?"

"We deliver when there's a job to be done, and

you know it," Nick Sands said. "Of course, Franklin's kidding. We just had a call from Philpot's cousin, might be a lead."

They shouldered past Campbell and got out through the lobby without further challenges.

After two days of autumn drizzle and showers, Detroit was gray and unlovely. The sky cleared as Sands and Franklin drove across town, the low light assuming a clarity that pared things down and made one think thoughts appropriate to the season. Like how things die, for instance.

Shaver's directions led them to one of the numerous private piers along Lake St. Claire. A number of other police units were parked in front of it as they pulled up, their radios blaring. There were two wagons from the Harbormaster Section as well.

The Harbormaster Section was responsible for the patrol of Belle Isle Park and the twenty-eight statute miles of waterways within the city limits of Detroit. The section was responsible for the recovery of drowning victims, and the investigation of boating accidents and water-related fatalities.

They worked their way through the crowd of people on the pier, mostly kids on bicycles, staring, and saw officers floating on a ten-foot flatbottom pram, close in to shore. Beyond, the heads of two scuba divers from the Underwater Recovery Team periodically rose and sank like seals as they searched the murky bottom for evidence. Far beyond, a vast oval of bright light fell upon the water.

Sands and Franklin found Lieutenant Samuels, the officer in charge.

"Homicide?"

"Fourteenth Precinct."

Samuels's face closed up. "Slumming in reverse?"

"We got an interest."

"Okay. Kid in a canoe thought it was a turtle. Until he poked at it with his paddle. Guy's rear end was up in the air."

The pram had brought the body close in to the pier, and the detectives stepped down for a look.

Aquatic plants had held the body under until bacteria germinated in the intestines, producing methane gas and bloating the body until the belly exploded. The skin was green. The stench was nauseating. Crabs had plucked at the body. Fish had nibbled ragged holes. As the Harbormaster people had dragged it, spongy hunks of flesh had sloughed off and floated back down in the water.

The eyes were sunken and shriveled like a mummified corpse. Most of the hair had fallen away, but the bloated face was not yet beyond recognition. The corpse's mouth was open in a look of surprise.

"Dwayne Fernald!" Franklin exclaimed with feigned anguish.

"You know him?"

"Did I know him? He was a good burglar. And you guys let him get killed! What the hell kind of a police force we got in this city when a decent thief like Dwayne Fernald here can't even walk the streets without getting knocked off, huh?"

Tom Castleton got a nice smile from the female guard in the lobby of the *Free Press* building on West Lafayette. He took the elevator to Ralph Thomas's floor and walked down paneled corridors until he found the partitioned cubicle where Thomas worked.

It was a crowded space, with stacks of paper and folders and books piled high on the desk, the floor, the chairs, and, most precariously, on the narrow windowsill. The window gave a view of the opposition, the *News* building.

Thomas was sitting behind a tall, antique L.C. Smith Super-Speed, pecking at the manual keys. No word processor. The reporter looked up, evincing no surprise. "Take a seat, officer." He didn't have to be told that Castleton was a cop.

"My name is Tom Castleton. I used to work with Ed Tomack, years ago."

"Yeah? Is this official police business?"

"No, I'm here on my own."

"Sounds like trouble. You got a problem?"

"The press conference. You were obnoxious."

Thomas smiled and leaned back in his chair. "I'm very hurt. The complaints department is downstairs."

"I'm not here to fuck you over, Thomas."

"Many have tried. That's when I know I've been doing my job."

"I want to talk to you like a human being," Castleton said, "if you think you can manage it for five minutes."

Thomas looked at him with a new regard. "I remember who you are now," Thomas said. "You used to be a good cop, considering."

"Meaning?"

"We all know the Fourteenth has a reputation as a dumping ground for misfits. Don't get me wrong, I like misfits. And Rivers is for real. So, if you didn't come to lean on me, what is it?"

"A deal. An exchange, if you will."

"You show me yours and I'll show you mine."

"I want you to plant a story."

During the discussion that ensued, Thomas sent out for beer—Tab for Castleton—and sandwiches.

Thomas told him that any such article would have to be approved by his city editor and managing editor. He took the plan to them while Castleton waited in his office. "It's fine with me," the editor said. "But every word has to be true."

Castleton shook Thomas's hand as he left. "Thanks. You be straight with me and I'll be straight with you."

William West hadn't worked for three years—not since a relative had pawned his radio and reacted to his protests by bashing him in the face with a brick and cracking his skull. Seizures started soon after that, and he could no longer function in his job jockeying cars at the Ford plant's parking lot.

After his wife left him, he didn't bother obtaining his medical entitlements, replacing his stolen Social Security checks, or seeking legal advice when his landlord evicted him. He became a habitué of Riverside Park.

That night he was arrested by Officers Popovich and Witoski while walking along the N&W railroad tracks cradling a tape deck he had lifted from a Pontiac TransAm.

While at the station house booking desk, West said that in exchange for his freedom, he would offer information about the killing of the detective in the park.

Kalina called upstairs to the squad room, where Inspector Campbell listened to West. On Devil's Night, West said, he had been walking toward the river and had seen a bright blaze glowing ahead of him. There was nothing surprising in that on Devil's Night. What did surprise him was to see a short, fairly smartly dressed white man carrying a briefcase hurrying towards him. As he passed under one of the pinkish streetlights, he called out, "Looks like someone's having a bonfire up there." Thing was, the man's white shirt was covered with blood.

West had continued walking until he saw the

burning car. He stood at the far fringe of the swiftly gathering crowd and watched, volunteering nothing. He wasn't surprised that the cops were looking for black boys when a white man done it, but it was no concern of his. Not until he was picked up with the tape deck.

Campbell notified Lieutenant Jackson, who sent Investigator Johnson to the station house with a police artist. Lieutenant Castleton took them up to the interrogation room, where Johnson guided the interview, getting a feel for West and his mental range. The artist brought a library of pictures of people with different-shaped faces and hairstyles. West looked through the photos until he found one similar to the suspect. With this as a foundation, the artist did his drawing full face, asking questions all the while.

"What was the shape of the man's head? Round? Square? How about the forehead? The eyes? Nose? Large ears? Long or short hair? Is the nose anything like the one I've drawn? Is this close? Are the eyes this far apart? Have I made him old enough?"

When the artist was done, West said, "That's it."

"When you take the drawing back to headquarters," Castleton said, "compare it to mug shots of one Vincent Carby and I think you'll agree that we have a make."

She was being followed.

The task force had focused on the narrow northern border of Clark Park. As Sue got off the bus there, she saw no cars behind the bus and no cars parked down the block. And yet, seconds after Sue began her route, she felt a presence behind her. For a fraction of a second, her peripheral vision caught a man closing in at an angle.

However much she might need reassurance she

couldn't glance around to check her backups. The
street was empty. She listened to the clack of her
own heels on the pavement, thinking the pross and
matron details were not so bad after all. She fin-
gered her .38, holstered in her waistband.

Maybe he wasn't the Beast. Maybe he was an
honors student at Holy Redeemer out for a medi-
tative walk, pondering the merits of entering a
seminary. Maybe he was only a mugger. Even if it
was him, he might not choose her.

As Sue approached the corner of West Vernor
and Clark, she felt like someone walking the last
mile. He was still there, and closer now, she could
hear his steps. She felt his eyes on her. The odds
went down. The cat and mouse game was under-
way.

She took stock. If she kept walking down West
Vernor past apartment buildings under good
streetlights, she'd be prolonging the agony. But if
she turned left onto Clark, he'd go for her. Under
her breath Sue said, "Let's do it!"

Clark Street edged the park. Street lamps made
small pools of light, but with no illumination from
apartment windows, the sidewalk was shadowed
by shrubbery and trees. The back of Sue's neck,
her whole spine, was stiff and prickly, but she
made sure her eyes stayed straight ahead. One
look backward could be enough to tip him off, or
make him nervous. What worried her was that she
couldn't hear anything anymore. Not him. Not her
backups.

Claire Hopson followed the man following Sue,
on the same side of Clark Street. She'd gone half
the length of the park when she realized the man
was no longer in view. She broke the rhythm of
her walk, a fractional hesitation, but in the second's silence she heard a sound, a cough or
sneeze. It drew her eye to a doorway across the

street. Vern Szabo was backed up there in semi-darkness. She breathed again. At least she wasn't alone.

She went on for a bit. Without any sound he was suddenly before her, one arm around her neck imprisoning her head, the other hand pressing something sharp against her cheek. She could also feel the material of the nylon stocking he had pulled over his head.

"If you make a sound, I'll stick you." The breathy voice was at once calm and full of rage, hot against her face. "I'm going to have you. It's going to happen, now."

"No. You can't. I've got my period."

"Women. You're all so messy. I hate you."

He pulled her off the sidewalk, into the deeper shadows. As he maneuvered, she managed to get her hand into her waistband, onto her revolver.

Squirming, Claire tried to make a half-turn. "Don't! Don't look at me," he said. And then he struck her cheekbone with something hard, probably the handle of his knife. Claire felt her knees buckle.

Then a loud guffaw broke the street quiet. There were shuffling steps, the sound of a garbage can being kicked over, its cover spiraling out over the curb. The knife at her head wavered. Instantly she pulled free, ducking and twisting away as he grabbed for her. Somewhere a second garbage can went over. The rapist stared for a brief moment, then turned and ran.

"Stop! Police!" Claire yelled after him.

For the first time in her years on the force Hopson fired at a live target. She crouched in the combat stance, holding her revolver centered with both hands, both eyes open. One. Two. Three. Yellow sparks flew from the muzzle. She was shooting to kill.

The man kept going. Then Vern Szabo, panting

from the exertion of his sprint, was holding her. She was aware of Sue Mallory having doubled back, of Wartiainen and Tibbets thrashing about in the shrubbery.

"What happened? What went wrong?" Claire asked. "Let's get after him!"

"Take it easy," Vern said. "You're hurt. He got cute. He went into the park and trailed you from in there. If I rushed him, there was every chance he'd slash you to death before he ran. But if he heard something nonthreatening in the distance, there was a better chance he'd just run. So I knocked garbage cans around. He got confused. He ran."

Sinker Barnes ordered another shot and a beer from the bartender with the conked hair.

When the legal bars closed, Sinker wasn't ready to stop drinking. But how he had come to the Sportsman's Palace was unclear.

The place was larger than he remembered. He faced a dark room in which round white tables were set, each surrounded by low plush chairs, all a velvety red. The jukebox panel cast a purple glow.

He drank the whiskey and beer, knowing that would put him across the line. He lit a cigarette and swung around on his stool, put his elbows up on the bar, and looked across the room to a table at which two women sat alone. He sauntered over to them, his eyes fixed.

"Hello, ladies," he said. The better looking of the two women looked away from him, smiling coyly, as if pleased but pretending to be embarrassed.

Something sharp slammed into his leg below the knee, and the women smirked. One of them had kicked him under the table. Sinker smiled idiotically and turned away. Boisterous laughter sounded at his back, and as he neared the bar he heard the woman say something.

He didn't look around to observe the reaction to the woman's remarks, but the bartender's expression was so comically incredulous that Sinker threw his head back and laughed. He regained his seat and when he looked over to the women's table a lean man in a suede maxi-coat was bending over the women in conference, looking his way.

"Hit me again," he told the bartender, who looked gray with worry.

"I'm goin' to have to refuse you service. You be leaving now," he said, looking at some stony-faced strangers who were standing behind Sinker. "There ain't goin' to be no trouble here," he said authoritatively.

Probably meaning not here, just outside in the alley. Wasn't that what he was looking for, now that he was too drunk to be afraid?

A black hand fell on his shoulder. Sinker tensed and turned slowly.

It was Franklin. And Sands.

"Hey, guys, didn't expect to see you here."

"Nobody expected to see you here, Sinker," Franklin said. "C'mon, buddy, let's get some air."

Sinker grinned. "I like it here. I like the ambiance."

He felt himself being lifted bodily off his stool, flanked by Sands and Franklin. His feet barely felt the stairs. And then he was sitting in the front seat of a car, wedged like a child between Sands and Franklin, watching the dark streets glide by.

"What were you guys doing there?" Sinker asked.

"The bartender knows me. Knows me and owes me," Franklin said. "He gave me a call."

Somewhere during the course of the ride Sinker had started trembling and crying.

"A crying cop, Jesus!" Franklin sighed.

"I think I know what's eating you," Sands said. "Sure, Raccaniello's a beastly cop, but he's still a cop. We have to protect our own kind. So you're getting it at both ends."

"I didn't tell Commander Rivers a damn thing. When I got called in, I lied just like Raccaniello—lied to protect the bastard! Maybe I just didn't have the guts to stand up and do what was right. I know I didn't. In fact, I don't have any guts at all. Working out of the Greyhound that night? I froze. I chickened. And it hasn't stopped. I'm scared all the time."

There. He had said it. Now they knew the truth about him.

"Listen, Sinker," Franklin said. "Four cops have been killed in the line of duty this year. Every one of those cops had one basic thing in common. They all worried about being able to go home at the end of their shift. Don't ever be ashamed of being scared when you get out there. In fact, make it a point to stay scared. You show me a street cop today who says he isn't scared every time he hits the street and I'll show you a liar or a fool—either way, he's a dumb bastard that I don't want to have to work with."

"You really mean that?"

"We're in this together, Sinker," Sands said. "There's no way any of us would have lasted without our teammates. And you're on our team. Am I getting through to you? Our sense of solidarity is our insurance for going on living."

Sinker was too grateful to speak, and too drunk to stay awake. He passed out with his head on Franklin's shoulder.

* * *

They were in Elroy's secret pad, Finnegan and Philpot worrying about the heat, but most of all about their shattered finances. Only Top Dog knew where the loot from Chez Lila was, and he was in jail. Zahara was sick, starting withdrawal. They watched her as she paced nervously and rapped, talking to JoJo on the phone.

"What say, JoJo? All I'm asking for is a couple spoons' worth on credit. Shit."

"It ain't that your credit ain't good. Someone just ripped me off for ten packs. JoJo just don't have," he said.

"The lying bastard!" Zahara yelled as she slammed down the phone. Her need to get down was obvious. "I spent hundreds of dollars with JoJo and when I asks for a little credit he says no! That's the last time he says no! Somebody ought to slit his throat!"

Finnegan mused, "Yeah, we could get up some dope and some money from JoJo while we at it."

There was a pause. "Hey, I was just frontin'," Zahara said.

Finnegan ignored her, concentrating. He said, "The only problem is getting in there. He got a steel door. JoJo isn't going to let us inside there. We'll have to try to get Zahara inside first."

Zahara felt uneasy with the way they were getting into it. But first and foremost, she wanted to geez up. JoJo would probably be able to talk his way out of it.

"Awright," Zahara said. "If you give me some green to wave, I can try it, but you know that if JoJo don't let me in, I'm not going to push the issue, I'm just gonna leave."

"Don't you worry your frizzy head about that," Finnegan said, "because he's gonna let you in." He gave her a lady's gun, a five-shot .22 Ruger. "Now, when you get in, you wait for us to knock on the door. When you hear us knock you take the pistol

out of your purse and cover whoever's at the
door."

"How we gonna know who's in there? JoJo got
a support group. And besides, they know me."

"Girl, it don't matter if they know you, they
won't be alive anyhow."

Sniffling, Zahara went into the little room she
shared with Philpot, of whom the room smelled.
She changed into an up-and-out bra and a clinging
dress, the better to allure JoJo. On Finnegan's or-
ders she also got some scissors and a towel and
some pantyhose that she stuck in her pockets.
Philpot had got a gun and a hammer and put them
in his belt. It didn't seem real.

Tish was snoring brokenly, still wearing last
night's makeup. She had given herself rosy
cheeks, and the area between eyebrows and eyelashes was smeared bluish-black. She muttered
in her sleep.

"What's that?" JoJo asked.

"The tablecloth is glittering."

JoJo felt a certain inadequacy. "Well, that's all
right, isn't it?"

"Yeah," she murmured. "It's pretty, ain't it?"

They drove to a block of single-family houses on
Seward, most of them abandoned, some occupied
by squatters, others by dealers and thieves like
JoJo. Zahara stepped up to the porch and knocked
on the steel door. It opened a crack. JoJo sounded
cranky and suspicious.

"Hi, baby. I got something. I want to feel good
tonight. I don't care if it's wrong."

"You alone?"

"What you think?"

JoJo unbolted the door and let her in.

Skeets was sitting with his back to the wall,

coasting. He was smiling with closed eyes, legs stretched out and crossed in front of him, humming with the music and saying nothing. His eyes, occasionally open, were streaked with red. He was on a heroin high, drowsy and happy. JoJo was on a coke high, pacing, swaggering, and talking sharp and quick. He had a table with a glass top. The sight of it made Zahara slaver.

"Hi, Skeets, how're you?"

"Hi, Zahara. I'm in the Twilight Zone." He giggled.

The walls were covered with posters advertising concerts and dances at the Fox and the Greystone Ballroom. A Castro convertible, a cigarette-scarred coffee table, and a sink full of blue plastic dishes completed the ensemble. The one small window was covered by a plastic sheet of "stained glass" that projected primary colors into the room when the light was right. Tacked to the door was a photograph of Tish, naked from the waist up, holding both hands behind her head and smiling confidently. The ceiling was painted dark blue with clusters of fluorescent stars.

Zahara sat down at the table and said, "Do me a favor, JoJo. Let me get a half spoon of mixed jive until later?"

"No, I can't do that, babe." JoJo frowned. "You're asking me to front you. I thought we were going to do business."

"Oh, awright ..." Zahara fumbled with her purse. "Lessee. I got my lipstick, my mascara, my pantyhose—"

A knock sounded at the door. About time.

"—my eyebrow pluckers, and Lordy, I got the difference," Zahara said, her hand coming out with the Ruger. She remembered to cock the single-action revolver before waving it at JoJo's nose.

"Open the door, chump!"

She followed him to the door, keeping the gun pressed against JoJo's head. When he drew the bar back Finnegan and Philpot rushed in with their guns drawn.

"Don't nobody move!" Finnegan yelled.

"That's right—don't nobody move!" Philpot echoed.

But there was no one else in the room but Skeets.

"Anybody else in the house?" Finnegan asked.

"Just my old lady," JoJo said. "She's in bed asleep. Take what you need, but leave her be. No need to get heavy, man."

"Go get her," Finnegan told Zahara.

"What for?" She looked at Philpot.

"Get the bitch," Philpot said.

Zahara found Tish in the back room, asleep all right. A pasty-faced white chick, she looked like jailbait. At the instant of awakening she knew she was in grave danger, and she did not cry out.

She murmured, "Let me slide. Let me out the back."

"I got no feeling for you, bitch," Zahara said. "Move it."

Finnegan had set two chairs down in the center of the room. He and Philpot tied JoJo and Tish up with telephone wire and gagged Tish with the pantyhose Zahara had brought.

JoJo looked at everyone. He had a funny smile on his face when he asked, "Say, you're not gonna take me out, are you?"

An uncomfortable silence ensued.

"No, we're not," Philpot said. "We're just gonna make it look good, you know, so you don't get on the bad side of Lemons."

"Leave me a do."

"All right."

Then Finnegan broke JoJo's head open with the claw end of Philpot's hammer.

He stepped over to the girl. She had squeezed her eyes shut when a piece of JoJo's brain spattered onto her cheek. But now she looked. Finnegan said, "Bitch, don't scream or make no noise," and as Philpot stared goggle-eyed, he drew a blade across her throat.

Philpot had no idea there was so much blood in a person, or that it could jet out so far, splattering explosively against the wall.

Tish was still moaning when Zahara went into the kitchen because she couldn't stand the horror and the pain and the agony that Tish was going through. She waited in the kitchen. Some cute pictures of Michael Jackson were pasted to the refrigerator.

Philpot came in and asked, "Do you think they're dead?"

"If they aren't after all that, they will be by the time anybody gets to them."

"Come on back and feel her pulse."

"No way, José."

"Come on back," Philpot insisted.

Finnegan had quickly found JoJo's stash and a quantity of cash as well.

They brought the works into the kitchen, away from the mess, and cooked up. Finnegan did himself first. He sighed and settled back, cocking his bared arm and making his massive muscles bunch up.

"Hey, what about Skeets?" Philpot asked.

Skeets hadn't moved.

"Off him, too," Finnegan said. "I don't want no shit behind this."

"Shit," Philpot complained. "Skeets and me go back."

Finnegan walked over, a cut in his strut, and looked at Skeets with merry eyes. The injection had changed his mood to one of benevolence.

"I'm sorry, man," Finnegan said, "but we only got enough for ourselves." He threw his head back and laughed.

Chapter Ten

TOM CASTLETON CAME off his shift, and instead of heading to his motel, he drove unhurriedly to Highland Park. On the John Lodge he stayed behind a truck upon the grimy back panel of which a message was scrawled.

Don't Like My Driving
Call #1-800-Eat Shit

He got off the expressway and stopped at a McDonald's for coffee, where he lingered until it was dark. To kill time he reread the day's edition of the *Free Press*, which included an article by Ralph Thomas that had the appearance of a sensational news leak.

Thomas reported that two state officials had become the prime suspects in the investigation of the Devil's Night murder of detective Ed Tomack, whose burned body had been discovered in Riverside Park. Law enforcement officials had

not confirmed that suspects had been developed
in the Tomack case, and the identities of the men
had not been disclosed. But they were the key
figures in the case, and it was proceeding "piece
by piece."

Too vague to be libelous, and innocent of actual
misstatement, the short article had maximum
negative implications for certain parties. When it
was dark enough, Castleton got back in his car
and took Hamilton Street over the Davidson into
Highland Park.

Mike Tomack lived near Ives Field, in a one-
story brick house with an attached garage that
was identical to its neighbors. It wasn't the home
of a fat cat. But neither had Hoffa's been. And Castleton remembered mention of a summer house in
Pentwater.

He parked his car six identical houses down the
block and waited, hoping a Neighborhood Watch
participant wouldn't blow it for him by summon-
ing a patrol car to check him out.

Mike Tomack came out of the house with a border collie on a leash. Castleton slid down on his
seat as Tomack walked down the block toward
Ives Field. Tomack looked up and down the street,
and into every car on his side of the street. At the
corner, instead of heading for the park, Tomack
crossed the street and came back down the block,
again looking into every car. Castleton had to
draw himself into a fetal position on the floor,
hard against the passenger side.

When he dared to unfold himself, Tomack was
unleashing his dog and reentering his house.
Twenty minutes later he was backing a Chevy station wagon out of the carport.

Castleton gave him a good lead. Tomack was an
amateur, but a suspicious one, and the easiest type
of surveillance to detect is when you are being
followed by a single surveillant. Staying close

enough to keep in sight, yet far enough away to avoid detection, was rarely easy to accomplish. Carby had been a case in point.

But the easiest time to tail someone was at night. Though an oncoming car was just another pair of headlights, taillights were almost all different. Castleton hung back three hundred yards on the Davidson and stayed in the right lane as they approached the Chrysler office complex. Tomack slowed suddenly. Castleton sailed past. He wanted to pull over and wait, but he was unwilling to make his own taillights flare when he hit the brakes. Committed to the Chrysler cloverleaf, he turned off and watched in his mirror to catch which way Tomack went. The man was going downtown. Castleton doubled back and caught up with Tomack in Hamtramck. On Russell, Tomack ran a red light, perhaps watching to see if Castleton followed suit. But Tomack was probably a man who ran red lights. Castleton hung back. There was no doubt in his mind now where Tomack was going.

He drove past slowly as Tomack stopped for clearance with a parking attendant, then entered the underground garage of the high-rise in which Jason Lemons lived.

The purpose of the news leak was to send Tomack back to Lemons for a consultation. It had worked.

"Damn you, Mike," Castleton said.

It was a curiosity of the southwestern portion of the 14th Precinct that when prehistoric seas had receded they had left a great salt reserve beneath the ground, which had been mined since the turn of the century. Most of the road salt used in the Midwest came from the mines in the precinct.

The house in which Carby lived overlooked an open mine as well as the railroad tracks that sur-

rounded and ran through it. When the Homicide
detectives Lieutenant Jackson and Investigator
Johnson went there to execute their warrant,
Sands and Franklin were detailed as local
backup.

Carby was outside the house throwing a suitcase into the back seat of his Pontiac when the
unmarked cars converged. He ran back into the
house.

Lieutenant Jackson pounded on the door. Splin-
ters flew as Carby shot through it three times. It
was an act of sheer panic. Jackson had a hole
through his trenchcoat but none through himself.

Sands and Franklin were ready to fire and rush
the door, but Lieutenant Jackson said, "Cool it.
We're going to do this so nobody gets hurt."

They radioed the patrol section to seal off the
street and draw a tight cordon around the house
while they awaited the rest of Jackson's squad—
six men with shotguns and another six men from
Tactical Services with tear-gas guns and gas
masks.

When the men were in position, Lieutenant
Jackson edged to one side of the door. Before hitting the apartment, he wanted to maximize Carby's sense of instant hopelessness. He thumped
five times on the door.

"This is Lieutenant Jackson," he said into a
bullhorn. "We are here to arrest you pursuant to
a warrant. Don't put yourself in further danger.
Open the door at once."

Sixty seconds passed before Carby finally spoke.
"You're going to kill me, whatever I do!"

"We don't want to hurt you, buddy. Surrender
and you won't be harmed!"

"Fuck you!" And then Carby cried, exactly as in
the movies, "If you want me, come and get me!"

"All right!" Jackson bellowed. "Blue shotgun
squad . . . take your rooftop stations . . . Red squad

. . . cover the windows . . . Tear gas unit, break out your cannisters, face masks in place . . . are you ready?"

It was over. The door was opened timidly. Carby was pasty-white, and he had peed his pants.

"Lawyer," he croaked. The detectives raced to see who could be first with the handcuffs.

The Athens Bar on Monroe Street in the heart of Greektown wasn't famous for its Greek food. Close to police headquarters on Beaubien, it was a cop hangout. When Ralph Thomas shouldered his way through the lunchtime crowd, the men outnumbered the women ten to one. He found District Attorney Caroline Bodner sitting with Lieutenant Wartiainen, both of them eating grilled hamburgers.

Thomas took a half-minute to look at Bodner. The woman had class with a capital *K*. She was wearing some sort of navy-blue suit, dressed the way all the women who did men's work dressed, but the cut and weight of it were remarkable—as was the body inside it. With the blue suit she wore a light turquoise-colored silk shirt and, surprisingly, a heavy necklace of turquoise and silver and matching earrings straight from a Navaho reservation. Even Thomas could appreciate what they did to her light blue eyes.

"Any statements concerning the progress of your special task force, Ms. Bodner?" Thomas asked.

"What task force?"

"You know, the one that's been rousting known sex criminals, sending decoys along dark streets, that sort of thing."

"No comment," Caroline Bodner said. "Especially if you're going to write an article that will alarm the population. Kindly butt out."

"I can't do that. Newspapermen are paid to be

nosy. My editors have been grousing about the Julie Mills case. I've got to find out whether the police are trying. If they're not, I'm gonna nail them."

He wasn't surprised when he ran into a wall with Caroline Bodner. She had always been arrogant toward reporters.

"I don't want you nosing around," she said. "I don't want your criticism and I don't want your help. The rapist will read your stories and change his M.O., or start raping in another precinct, and the detectives will have to start from scratch."

Thomas said, "Well, maybe that's good. He's been doing the same things for two months and you haven't caught him, so maybe if we force him to change he'll make a mistake."

"That's just what we don't want. And any information on the case is private until I say otherwise."

"My obligation is to provide the public with the information it needs to protect itself," Thomas insisted. "Give me something."

Caroline Bodner proffered a small bowl. "Here, have an olive."

"Babe, I tole you I can't drink frozen orange juice," Top Dog said. "It's slimy."

"You're a fine one to talk," Melissa said. "*You* slimy."

Melissa was pretty, with high cheekbones that she said came from her Cherokee great-grandmother. She was super-square. Her father was a Baptist minister. She could be a fire-breather, but today the love light was in her eyes. Top Dog hadn't been home in a long time. She knew he had other women out there, but when Top Dog got his, they were going to be married. After all, she was mother to his little girl.

"You know I like my orange juice squeezed and strained," Top Dog said.

"Well, you know where the store at, chump."

"Babe, I can't be on the street just right now. I got problems."

Melissa sighed. "*You* got problems. Awright. You mind the baby, and don't be smoking no dope while I'm gone."

Top Dog didn't do the hard stuff, but Melissa gave him hell whenever he smoked. She thought it was degrading. When she came back, first thing she'd sniff the air. The woman had a nose like a dog.

When Melissa left, Top Dog turned on the ghetto blaster and started to play with his year-old daughter, Debbie, kneeling on the rug and feeding her small pieces of pancake one by one. The radio was playing old Motown stuff like "Stop in the Name of Love." Top Dog danced across the room with mincing steps, holding little Debbie in one arm as he snapped his fingers to each step.

"Yo, Top Dog!"

He started and turned. Finnegan and Philpot were standing inside the door. They could walk in because Top Dog had kicked the door in the other night when Melissa had lost her keys; he hadn't had time to get the lock fixed.

"Hey, buddy." He set Debbie down on the sofa, wishing he had a weapon of some kind, wishing he'd been content with B and E's.

"Didn't Zahara tell you where we at?" Finnegan asked. "Shit, figured you'd want to thank us for putting up the bail."

"Yeah, but I wanted to lay cool for awhile, you know."

"You been avoiding us," Finnegan said. "What's the matter, don't you love me anymore?"

"C'mon, what you saying?"

"You acting strange. You trembling," Finnegan

observed. "Be cool, man. Relax. I ain't making no play." He sat down next to Debbie. "Cute kid. Say, you got anything that will clean paint off my shoe?"

"There's some gasoline been used to clean paintbrushes in the bathroom."

Finnegan went in and returned from the bathroom with a bottle. He grabbed the baby.

"This gasoline, right?" Finnegan asked.

Top Dog said, "Yeah, hey, what's goin' on?"

"I hear you been talking."

"Hey, I didn't tell the cops shit! What the fuck you saying."

"Don't be getting valiant, dude. You guilty, and nobody crosses me."

Finnegan poured the gasoline over the baby's head. Debbie started to cry and rubbed her eyes. Top Dog instinctively rushed forward, but Finnegan pulled out his .45 and a rope.

"Tie him up," he told Philpot. Philpot didn't move.

Top Dog lunged and grabbed Debbie from Finnegan and threw her in the corner. He turned a table over between Finnegan and his daughter and they started fighting, Finnegan hitting him about the head with his heavy gun. Blood streamed into Top Dog's eyes and he made a half turn as Philpot tried to work his way behind him. Finnegan lit a match. Top Dog tried to hit him with a chair, but he managed to throw the match on the little girl.

She burst into flames. Top Dog grabbed his screaming baby and ran to the bathroom, where he tried to put out the fire with cold water from the bathtub water tap.

Top Dog moaned, too transfixed by the shock of grief to turn and defend himself. For the first and last time in his life, Top Dog was moved by love for a creature greater than his love for himself.

* * *

After the wagon took Top Dog's body to the morgue, after the departure of Van Loon and the crime lab technicians, after Debbie and her hysterical mother were transported to Detroit Receiving, the detectives themselves got a little hysterical.

Dwight Franklin was mad. "Why wasn't Top Dog under surveillance? What'd you think was going to happen when he got bailed out? Zahara Lane, shit. Finnegan put up the money just so he could get at him."

"Goddammit," Investigator Johnson said, "there was a screwup at Prisoner Detention. We weren't notified."

"The baby's not going to live, man," Franklin said.

"I know that, asshole!"

Franklin and the Homicide detective had always enjoyed a congenial relationship. In two seconds they were going to come to blows.

"Cool it, Franklin," Inspector Campbell said. "I don't want to hear another word from you. Go hold your partner's hand."

Sands had gotten a good look at the baby. The Ivy League Gunman was leaning against the hood of their unmarked car, experiencing dry heaves.

Aware of Franklin's concern, he drew himself up. "I guess there's no question who's behind this."

"Guess not."

"You know I don't scare much, Dwight, but Finnegan spooks me. I swear he does. If this man isn't pure evil, there is no evil."

Nick Sands went to a party with Marlene Moro. She had asked him to go—it was a birthday party for her boss, Felix Laurent, so it was practically a command performance for her. Nick was al-

ready sorry that he had agreed to go. He was totally uncommunicative.

"Are you in one of your moods?" Marlene asked
in the car.

"Certainly not," Nick said and put on the falsest
grin she had ever seen. Marlene was wearing a
new black-and-white polka-dotted silk dress and
high-heeled red sandals, and she had been rather
looking forward to the event. She knew that Felix
had hired Gorgeous Foods, the hot new caterer, to
do the party.

She sighed. "Good. I'm so glad."

In this mood, they arrived at the party. The
room was decorated in black and white and crys-
tal, with bouquets of bright pink and royal blue
balloons tied to the wrought-iron chairs. The cir-
culating waiters immediately supplied them both
with tall glasses of Mumm's Cordon Vert cham-
pagne. Nick drained his, grinned, and took another.

Marlene sipped hers like a lady. "Look," she
said, "there's what's his name—the painter."

Nick saw a skinny white guy with wide-set black
eyes, a fishing cap, and blue jeans. "How the hell
did he get in with that getup?" he asked, honestly
curious.

"He's an artist," Marlene explained.

Nick himself was pretty uncomfortable in a
rented tux. "Black tie is so much more meaning-
ful," Felix had said, and had spelled it out on the
invitations: Black Tie. Nick felt as if he'd been
taken and muttered something about sending Felix the bill from Mr. Tux.

Marlene knew almost everyone there and
worked the crowd. Nick tagged along, sipping his
drink and scoffing down the hors d'oeuvres, which
were passed out on mirrored trays.

He didn't want to be identified as a cop at the
party. The minute that happened he was no longer

Nick, he was Nick the Cop. People wouldn't give him the option of being who he was. The hell of it was he had gotten to the point where nobody could understand him but another cop.

Presumably, these were his people, and he was of their class. But he had a cop's resentment. To the affluent, cops were servants, like caterers and doormen.

Nonetheless, those few who knew Marlene well also knew what her boyfriend's occupation was. When he drifted away from Marlene's side for a minute, he found himself talking to a young blond girl in blue velvet, the very personification of a bimbo worth a couple of million bucks.

"Are you carrying a gun?" she asked him, without further ado.

"Yes."

"May I see it?"

"No."

"I bet you're like a samurai. If you draw the weapon you have to use it, that it? I imagine you must love that extension of personal power your gun gives you."

"That's right," Sands replied. "I have the power of life and death. In ten seconds I can kill someone or let him live, and I don't have a jury or a judge or anybody there to say yes or no. You give me this awesome responsibility. You cry police brutality without knowing what is happening. You talk about crime in the streets, but you tolerate courts giving criminals a slap on the wrist. You don't know what a cop is for or what he should do."

Nick escaped from blue velvet and found himself in a similar chat with a redhead in pink. He followed her up to the wrought-iron balcony that hedged in Felix's sleeping area and she told him her name was Ginger. It seemed plausible.

Together they overlooked the mingling party

crowd. "Which one is the cop?" the girl asked. "The one whose sister was murdered?"

He said that he was the one whose sister was murdered and turned away. He proceeded to the bar.

Dinner was delicious—filets mignon with Bearnaise sauce and some potato thins that were as good as McDonald's. Nick just kept his hand on Marlene's knee and drained his glass of wine.

"It's an Australian pinot noir," Marlene informed him.

"Delicious. What's for dessert?"

"Birthday cake, I suppose."

It turned out to be a frozen hazelnut praline concoction with meringue on top, crossed with chocolate in the shape of a spider's web. No candles.

When they left, Nick managed to thank his host for a fabulous time.

"Honey, I'm glad we got out of there," he told Marlene in the car.

"Are you drunk?" she asked.

"Ten thirty . . . armed robbery with injuries just occurred at Twelve fourteen Grand River."

"Ten four," Sue Mallory said into the car radio. "Proceeding to location." She turned to O'Hallerin. "Isn't that Najib's?"

Several minutes later they jolted to a stop in front of the store, jumping out, pushing their way past the people gathered at the door. As soon as they entered, they saw Najib. He was lying on his back behind the cash register. The white apron was bright with an enormous blossom of arterial blood. His wire-rimmed glasses hung by a single loop across his face. An ambulance attendant was kneeling beside him checking for vital signs. His wife recognized them and rushed forward.

"He gave him the money! He gave him the money! Why did they have to shoot?"

O'Hallerin said something to Sue, who didn't hear him. She stared at the body, still dazed by the unreality of what she saw.

"Come on! There's nothing you can do. We got two witnesses—give me a hand."

They began talking to a fifteen-year-old boy and a woman who had been in the store when it was robbed, trying to get enough information on the suspect to put out a description. Other units were already crisscrossing the streets around Grand River.

The men from Homicide and the Armed Robbery Unit arrived and went about the tedious business of asking more questions while technicians processed the scene.

"Why would anybody kill that old man?" Sue Mallory asked after they left the grocery and drove off.

"We're dealing with new jacks, a whole generation without conscience, without values," O'Hallerin said. "So they have no concern about people's lives. Life is very cheap to them. You've got to be able to hold people responsible for their actions, and we're not able to do that anymore."

Chief Davies stood at the podium, smiling confidently before the gathered print and television newspersons. He was happy to announce that an arrest had been made in the Ed Tomack case and that the department was looking forward to a speedy resolution of the matter. However, he was obliged to refuse any questions concerning the ongoing investigation. He thanked the press and turned to make his exit.

"Why is the department covering up the rape/murder of Julie Mills and other related attacks?"

Davies froze. He recognized the voice. Mentally

he grasped Thomas by the throat and slowly squeezed, until his larynx was crushed. He turned and smiled broadly.

"Ralph, there is no coverup. What I want to do is assure the public that we're working like crazy on the case. We will provide information on what the public should be doing, and police officers are making an all-out effort to catch this fiend, even donating their off-duty time and their personal cars." To show that his department was working hard to protect the city's females, Chief Davies threw out some figures: "We have expended over eighty-six hundred man-hours on this effort. This represents the work of twenty-two persons giving part- or full time to the investigation. No further questions, please. Thank you." Without further ado, Chief Davies left the podium.

Claire Hopson had nine stitches on her cheek, and the stitches were protected by a length of curved plastic held down with tape. Once the stitches were out, she supposed she would be going to work behind a thick layer of makeup. Claire knew it was irrational, but she felt humiliated by what had happened to her. She was experiencing delayed stress syndrome.

Once a year Philip Linton's division gave a big formal bash which was taken very seriously. Claire had invested a sizable chunk of her take-home pay in a new formal, and she was looking forward to the party. But that was before the incident in Clark Park. She called to cancel.

"You can't do this to me!" Philip protested. "You never hinted there could be a problem. We've planned it for so long . . ."

"Yeah, and I've got the gown to prove it. I feel at least twice as bad as you do. But I had a duty call," she lied. Claire couldn't bring herself to speak of the shape she was in.

"Can't you call in sick, get out of it?"

"Sorry, that's just how it is." She hung up abruptly.

Claire went to bed quite early, but before she fell asleep she felt a man's hands gripping her breasts, his arm lifting her from the grass, his fingers sliding down her throat. She saw his lips under the nylon stocking, and his bulging, angry eyes. She fell asleep after an hour or two and dreamed about rape. At first her dream was a reconstruction of the event, as though her mind were trying to come to grips with what had happened. Then she repeatedly repulsed the rapist. She blew his head off with a pistol. She pounded him with hammers. She severed his penis and dropped it into the Detroit River off the Ambassador Bridge and yelled, "Go get it!" Then she flung him over the rail.

Her son Timmy came into the bedroom and found her sobbing. He was her only salvation. He was sweet and innocent. She grabbed Timmy and held him tight. Nothing else could allay her fear.

There was a loud rap on the front door. "Don't answer!" she whispered. She grabbed her revolver, peeked outside, and saw no one.

"Who is it?" she called through the door.

A muffled voice came back.

"If you don't show yourself," she yelled, "I'm gonna start shooting!"

A man's face appeared at the window. He was holding a badge. She took a good look. It was Vern Szabo. Still trembling, she let him in. He led her to the sofa and took the gun from her hand.

"I swear to God, Claire," Vern Szabo said, "we're gonna catch this creepo. And when we do we're gonna put him away till his thing shrivels up and falls off."

"Fuckin' A," Claire said. Vern laughed. It was his phrase. His eye fell on the *Free Press* and his mood soured immediately on seeing the headline again—RAPE/MURDER INQUIRY PUSHED.

The members of the task force had been outraged. Their quarry wasn't stupid, and anyone could tell from the wording that a massive manwatch was under way. Otherwise why so many man-hours?

He might be warned off, unless he only reads *USA Today*.

"Why'd the Chief do it?" Claire lamented.

"Because Thomas put a lot of heat on him," Vern Szabo said. "And the chief's a fucking politician."

They were crowded into Cal Rivers's office—Jackson and Bodner, Campbell and Johnson—to review the taped confession of a hopeless and demoralized Vincent Carby.

The statement was made without benefit of his attorney, who was looking for his client at 1300 Beaubien while Carby was in fact still being detained at the 14th Precinct.

His story was that Mike Tomack had introduced Racine Latimer to Jason Lemons, who had let Latimer know he would pay well for early release of convicts he felt would be useful to his organization. Carby was the bagman for the operation. The trouble started when Mike Tomack's brother got suspicious and started nosing around. He leaned on Dwayne Fernald, one of the cons who had gotten an early parole under the scheme. Fernald and Ed Tomack met at various locations in the city, usually at Riverside Park, where Fernald reluctantly apprised him of current events. When he, Carby, got suspicious in turn and followed Fernald to one of the meetings, he informed Jason Lemons that Tomack's brother was on to them. But he wasn't doing official business. It seemed that Ed Tomack was hoping he wouldn't have to bust his own brother.

Jason Lemons made two quick decisions. First, he put a paper out on Fernald, and second, he offered Ed Tomack sixty thousand dollars to forget what he had learned. Carby set up the meeting in the park and brought the money in a briefcase. He left his car beyond the railroad tracks that bordered the park and walked to the meeting place. He sat with Tomack in his car and explained the situation.

"I told Tomack, 'You just can't hurt people. You have to use common sense, reasoning.' I told him, 'We're men, we're friends, we should try to help each other.' I told him, 'Jason Lemons will never embarrass you. When you know him better, you'll see he's a nice fellow. He don't want to hurt you. If you should ever have a problem, he can be helpful to you.' He laughed at me. I could tell he'd been drinking. Tomack was bent out of shape. He said he was going to shove the money up my ass and set fire to it, then he was going to send me back to Lemons in parcel post packages. He pulled his gun. I tried to grab it so the cylinder wouldn't turn. We struggled and the gun went off. The bullet hit him in the face. Funny, when we were wrestling, it was like his heart wasn't in it."

"That's it," Rivers said. "He knows he's not safe from Lemons now, not even in prison. When he siphoned gas and set the car on fire, it was an act of sheer panic."

"Do you think he'll give the same statement in court?" Caroline Bodner asked.

"He wants a deal."

"Twenty-five years to life. Nothing less."

Downstairs, a man identifying himself as Carby's attorney was confronting Sergeant Sudol and demanding to see his client immediately. The attorney was a short, white-haired man in a three-piece suit, with designer eyeglasses and an expensive haircut. He had parked his white DeLorean a block away. They brought him upstairs and allowed him to interview his client privately in an interrogation room.

Sudol had also given a visitor's pass to Ralph Thomas, who was greeting Lieutenant Castleton when Inspector Campbell caught sight of him.

"What's that scumbag doing here?" he asked loudly.

"I authorized his presence," Castleton said. It was their deal. In return for planting the article in the *Free Press*, Castleton had promised to keep Thomas abreast of developments in the Tomack case.

"Hi, Roger," Thomas said. "Having a nice day?"

Campbell ignored the reporter and closed on Castleton, all but stepping on his toes. "I don't know what you think you're doing, Castleton, but I know I don't like it!"

"Get out of my face, Inspector," Castleton said evenly.

Campbell flushed. "What do you think you are, Castleton, a cop? Everybody knows you're a case. Any other precinct would have pressured you into early retirement. But here, I know what you're doing: hanging in for the pension, right?"

Before Castleton could answer, Caroline Bodner interrupted impatiently. She had been pacing holes in the linoleum waiting for Carby's attorney to finish and psyching herself up for his inevitable accusations concerning statements made under duress.

"I haven't got all night. What are they doing in there?"

"I thought Carby was back in the cage. I saw his mouthpiece heading downstairs a moment ago."

They looked at each other.

"Mother of God," Campbell said.

He rushed to the interrogation room and threw open the door.

Vincent Carby was sitting upright in his chair, staring at them. The silenced bullet had made a small entrance hole in his forehead, but the wall behind him indicated that the exit wound was quite another story.

Chapter Eleven

IT MUST HAVE been in the stars, a negative planetary influence that affected everyone. The precinct detectives were mad at the downtown detectives for failing to keep tabs on Top Dog and for blowing a chance to nail Finnegan and Philpot before they committed further atrocities.

Chief Davies was mad and held Commander Rivers responsible for letting a killer get at Carby right in the station house. The D.A.'s task force was made at Chief Davies and Ralph Thomas for publicizing their activities. Inspector Campbell was mad at Lieutenant Castleton for being chummy with Ralph Thomas. Cal Rivers was mad at the Homicide Section for snubbing his detectives and allowing them no major role in the search for Carby's killer. And Barnes and Raccaniello were mad at Inspector Campbell for making them deliver pizzas.

A series of pizza deliverymen were getting held up as they made deliveries. They would go back to their car and there would be two guys waiting to take them off. Sometimes they took the pizzas as well.

After the eighteenth time, Inspector Campbell contacted all the pizza places in the precinct and told them if they got a suspicious call to inform the IOS squad. Precinct detectives could become their deliverymen and try to catch them. Thinking it likely that the perps would be leery of a Chrysler as a cop car, a battered Buick Skylark with a hatchback, delivered from the city pound, was kept ready in the lot behind the station house.

That night the manager of Rocco's Pizza called the precinct with a delivery that was a block away from where their driver had been robbed before. He was sure he recognized the voice of the caller. Barnes and Raccaniello got in the Skylark, went to Rocco's, and then to the address on Pingree. Barnes had taken off his tie and put on an apron. He had his Walther underneath the apron. Raccaniello was hiding in the back with his arsenal.

Some distance behind, Popovich and Witosky followed in a patrol car. It was a dark street. There were streetlights on the block but none were functioning. Driving down the street Sinker said, "There's two guys standing over there. Looks like they could be waiting for me."

"I hope they like anchovies," Raccaniello said. "Keep on going."

Sinker pulled to the curb and glanced back once. "I don't know where the guys went to." He got out of the car and lifted the pizza out of the back. When he went up to the house, an elderly black lady said with considerable irritation, "Mister, we didn't order no pizza. This is the second time this has happened in a week."

Bingo.

Sinker went back to the car. Just before the opened the hatch, he saw two dark forms reflected in the glass. They were walking out of the darkness, separating to flank him.

"Get ready," Sinker said. "Here they come."

He put the pizza back inside and closed the hatchback. He backed up against the car. They were there, closing in fast. A guy in a pink shirt with a machete in his hand. He seemed underdressed for the cold. The other guy wore a Max Julian and had a gun in his hand.

"We want the money, turkey," he said.

"Give it up, sucker," the other said. He raised his machete.

"Okay, okay, take it light," Sinker said. He didn't take time to identify himself as a police officer. He pulled his Walther out from under his apron and fired. The guy with the machete folded up and went down. The other one took off without using his weapon, running like a deer down Pingree.

Raccaniello jumped out of the car and took a snap shot at the running guy. The guy kept running and he took off after him.

Sinker was staring at the man in the pink shirt. He had been hit square in the middle of the chest and appeared to be quite dead. Sinker had never shot a man before. He couldn't quite believe that he just had. He had shown restrain in firing once. Others would have emptied their clip. In the following weeks he would suffer irrational guilt, nightmares, insomnia, and gastrointestinal problems, but he didn't know that yet. He just felt nervous.

The backup came roaring down the street with red-and-blue lights and siren, and mounted the curb to cut the perp off. The officers jumped out of the cruiser. Popovich saw someone running. He cranked off a shot and the guy dodged then fell, as if he had deliberately leaped forward. He crashed in a heap on the sidewalk, his head lying in the gutter.

Raccaniello and Barnes came running up. The kid looked too small to be the perp. In fact he looked to be about ten years old. Popovich was visibly shaken. "I figured he was the bad guy," he said.

People were spilling out of houses up and down the block.

Sinker ran to the cruiser and reported a major injury accident, calling for an ambulance. By the time he had completed the call, a large crowd of people had gathered in the street around the boy. He had to push his way through the throng.

"That's my brother!" a child's voice shouted from the crowd. Sinker caught a boy of about seven by both arms as he rushed forward. "Let go! He's my brother!" the boy sobbed.

Every police car in the area showed. They couldn't find the second perp.

After they finished helping the attendants put the boy on a stretcher and place him in the ambulance, Sinker noticed the hand he had held behind the boy's head. It was wet and sticky with blood.

"Well, there's one it looks like we won't have to worry about," Raccaniello said.

The look on the little kid's face told that he had heard Raccaniello's remark. Sinker left the crying boy with a woman in the crowd and walked back to his partner.

"Do me a favor, Raccaniello."

"Anything for you."

"Shut up."

The two men glared at each other for a moment.

"What's the matter?" Raccaniello taunted. "Afraid of the natives?"

"You fucking creep!" Sinker cried. "One more

crack and you'd better be prepared to back it up
or eat it."

Raccaniello noted that Sinker had stuck his
automatic in his belt and that his hand had
remained in the general area of his buckle.
He looked ready to draw. His eyes told Raccaniello that this was not a moment to make a mistake. Barnes had his limit and they had reached
it.

Raccaniello backed off and walked away.

The theory was that the Beast had a thing about
Clark Park. One among several, it involved the IOS
squad.

"He may not change his M.O., but we better
change ours," Lieutenant Wartiainen had said.

"Listen," Vern Szabo suggested, "why doesn't
Sue be a dog walker? You could bring Sturdley
with you when we stake out."

"Sturdley?" Sue asked.

"He's my Lab. We call him Sturdley because we
had trouble house-training him. Name's a cross
between—"

"I get it," Sue Mallory said. "You mean I'm going to be counting on Sturdley for protection?"

"C'mon, Sue," Vern had said with a cheery slap
on the back. "I've been trying to lose him for
years."

Now they were crowded into the van. Sue was
wearing a jacket, sweater, and skirt. Her legs were
in knee socks, her feet in good solid shoes for a
change. Sturdley couldn't wait to get out. Parking
the van, they made a last check of radios and
guns—her .38 was in her shoulder bag. Then the
only thing left was to do it.

Sue and Sturdley got out. She checked her
leash, fiddled with his collar, and gave him a pat.
"Come on, doggie. Let's go get us a homicidal
rapist."

They began their stroll. The team let Sue get a bit forward and then headed unobtrusively for their positions. Vern and Claire Hopson followed a path that led through bushy trees. It offered some concealment. The others took the right flank, staying on the far side of the childrens' playground. They would have to fix themselves farther from her than they liked, but the park was too open and there was no good cover any closer.

Once everyone was deployed, the crew tested their radios. The plan called for everyone in the team to be in constant communication. The only thing wrong with the plan was that Sue's radio was malfunctioning, and there was no way for her to know that the check was in progress and had failed.

"We ought to abort right now," Claire Hopson said into her radio.

"No, no," Lieutenant Wartiainen said. "Let's hang in there."

Unaware of all that was happening, Sue strolled on behind Sturdley, her lips dry, eyes and ears doing double duty.

Sturdley led her down the path toward the playground. Here the path curved, then offered her a left or a right around a set of swings.

A high whistle—an alert—floated on the air, barely heard over the muffled roar of the Fisher Freeway. One of the team had seen something. Sue decided on the turn to the left. She was able to pivot casually for a look behind and to her left. There was something. A shadow. A sound. A shifting.

Now it was real, and she suddenly realized how far away the crew was and how scared she was.

Another faint movement in the shadows wiped out all doubt. Breath deeply, she reminded herself. She thought she could actually hear the beating of her own heart.

She dropped the leash and Sturdley rushed ahead, soon stopping to lift his leg. As Vern had promised, Sturdley was utterly useless as a watchdog, entirely concerned with his own affairs. He wasn't the type to challenge strangers or scare away prospective rapists. Sue walked more slowly. Ahead, a tree trunk changed shape as the man behind it moved out, coming toward her.

There was a knife in his hand and a nylon stocking pulled over his head. She began to back off. But at once he was on her, the knife at her throat, the other hand twisting up her blouse so that she was immobilized.

He yanked her down the path. In all her judo and karate experience, Sue had never been exposed to such strength. She brought her heel down on his instep, and his grasp momentarily weakened. She swung from side to side, hands to her face, her elbows tucked in, and jabbed at him. When he brought his hands up she punched him just above the belt. He seemed stunned for a moment, but he closed in with his knife. Sue rolled in the direction of his lunge and crouched. As he recovered, Sue went into a rage and forgot her training. She clawed at his eyes with both hands, rending the nylon stocking.

Shots rang out, shattering the night. Sue jerked away, twisted, plunged off the path, and was free.

One more shot and the rapist was running away. Vern broke out first from the bushes, followed by Claire.

"I'm going after him!" he shouted.

She could hear Wartiainen and Tibbets pounding up the path. "My God," Claire exclaimed, "that was close. Did he hurt you?"

"No, I'm fine," Sue said. She could feel her legs shaking.

The team gave chase but couldn't close the distance. The creep had burst out of the park at the exact spot where he'd left his car. The team saw him leave, noted the color and make and the first three numbers on his plates.

The backup units tore down Clark to give chase.

Back at the van, Wartiainen radioed base for a vehicle trace. He described the car by its make, model, color, and the license numbers.

"What about you, Sue?" Claire asked. "You okay?"

Sue sat up straighter. "Sure. I got a piece of him," she said. Sue opened her clenched hand to reveal a shred of nylon and a tuft of auburn hair. "I wish we'd collared him."

"Not to worry. He won't make it."

But he did. The backups radioed that they had lost him on the Fisher. They thought they had him when a civilian had cut in front of them and the pursuing cars had piled up on one another.

Downtown was back already with the car trace they wanted—name and address.

"Right in our precinct," Claire said.

"Hell, let's go get the fucker," Vern said.

Lieutenant held up a hand, palm out. "Patience." He called in to the D.A. and gave his report.

"Do we go?" Claire asked.

"We do not. D.A. wants the hair. We're not going to let him go anywhere, and she wants an analysis of the polypeptides in the hairs."

Vern cried, "For Chrissake—"

"Ours is not to reason why," Wartiainen said.

Inspector Campbell just couldn't accept the black leather jackets that Sands and Franklin wore in lieu of sportsjackets. And both detectives had come into the squad room without ties.

"You call that office attire? Regulations don't exist for you, right? You both look like hoods."

"I'm sorry, sir," Franklin said. "I'll try to improve."

"Don't say try, say will."

"Yessir."

Franklin left the squad room and walked down to the lobby. There was a pay phone next to Sergeant Sudol's desk. He dropped in his quarter and called the station.

"Fourteenth Precinct. Sudol."

"Inspector Campbell, please," Franklin said.

Sudol knew who it was, but he transferred the call upstairs, "Inspector, phone call for you."

"This is Inspector Campbell."

Franklin dropped an octave and spoke in a husky voice. "Fuck you, you fat-assed prick!"

Franklin hung up, walked out of the pay phone, and went back up to the squad room. He looked Campbell in the eye, his face innocent and free of tension, as he returned to his desk.

"What's with the Inspector?" he asked Sands. "He look all red in the face."

The light blue telephone on his own desk rang. Franklin picked it up.

"Dwight?"

"Skeets, baby! What's up?"

"Finnegan is going to buy an Uzi from a dude named Maben at a place called the Sugar Shack."

Sands took note of Franklin's suddenly intent expression. He sat on the edge of his desk, expectant.

"Pretty public place to do business," Franklin said.

"Maben's afraid of Finnegan. Thinks he'll be safe there."

"Sensible dude. When's it going down?"

"In about twenty minutes."

"For Chrissake! You don't give us much lead time."

"Sorry about that. The fuck you want? I just found out."

"Okay. Thanks, Skeets."

"Do one thing for me."

"What?"

"Cap the motherfucker."

"The game ain't promised to nobody, Skeets."

Franklin put down the phone. "Battle stations!" he cried.

Sands opened his desk drawer and began filling his pockets with spare 9 mm clips.

The detective burst into Commander Rivers's office, where he was listening to Campbell's complaints about the attitude of certain investigators, and shared the information they had just received.

Campbell found their excitement less than infectious. "Could be bullshit," he said.

"This is for real, Commander," Sands insisted.

"Okay , I'll notify Thirteen Hundred Beaubien," Campbell said.

"Fuck them," Franklin said. "Finnegan is ours."

"Make the call." Rivers said calmly. "But first order all available personnel out there."

The Sugar Shack was on a disreputable stretch of Woodward, an area of cheap hotels, shabby apartments, and boarded-up buildings. Some of its large old homes had been converted into halfway houses for the mentally ill. Neighbors frequently complained about hearing weird screams at night. Pedestrians ambled on the sidewalks with the slow walk of people who have no particular destination. Most of the cars parked on the street seemed abandoned, although every now and then someone drove one away. In the liquor

stores counters were completely screened by
transparent bulletproof plastic. Money and bottles were exchanged through a rotating panel.
Despite the cold, a noisy group of craps shooters
had gathered in a lighted parking lot, their ani-
mated voices carrying far on the underpopulated
street. In the far distance the Ren Cen towers
rose surrealistically, as if the Land of Oz lay beyond.

A vertical red neon sign spelled Sugar Shack
over the door, its lurid glow giving unnatural color
to the pavement and Maben's white DeLorean, a
real eye-catcher, parked in front. Sands and
Franklin were parked across the street and two
patrol cars waited a block away on John R. Sands
had mug shots of Maben in his lap. They were to
intercept him before he got inside.

The Sugar Shack had a back door that opened
onto a vacant lot where a house had once stood.
Only a low concrete wall remained. Barnes and
Raccaniello were hiding behind the wall with Inspector Campbell. Campbell started when he
heard someone crossing the broken ground behind them. It was Castleton.

Campbell hissed. "You're not supposed to be
here."

"But I am here," Castleton said evenly.

"Is your gun loaded tonight?"

Castleton didn't answer.

Some children who had been crossing the lot
must have heard Campbell. They came walking
right up. "Hey, are you police officers?" An older
teenager asked, "Hey, you guys want some
broads?" He laughed and walked on. Another
young man approached Raccaniello, who was
kneeling with his gun in hand.

"Hey, someone just broke into my house."

"Can't you see we're busy?"

"You guys don't do shit! You are never fucking there when anyone needs you."

"Your trouble is going to get a whole lot worse if you don't beat it," Raccaniello said.

The youth believed him and walked away without another word.

A Buick Skylark came down the street and parked near the Sugar Shack. A man and a woman, casually dressed in sportsclothes, got out and walked to the entrance, the man courteously holding the door. They were Szabo and Claire Hopson, with whom Finnegan was not acquainted.

The place was half full. Zahara Lane, wearing a G-string and a red wig, was shuffling on the platform, languidly turning from side to side, vaguely in time to music from the jukebox. Finnegan and Philpot were sitting at a table with their backs to the wall. Finnegan watched for the entrance of Maben. Philpot watched Zahara. Finnegan noticed the man who had just come in, and especially the woman who accompanied him. She didn't look half bad.

Finnegan looked as icy as he felt, but he knew the Uzi would improve his mood. It was getting so that even a few days without action depressed him. He had to know by constantly reinforced experience that he was capable of affecting the world, most importantly other people. When no one was available for him to victimize, he felt dead, fell into inertia and even critical depression. His only life, his only identity, came from moving other people around. Without that he was nothing.

Maben was at the bar when they came in, a skinny dude with long white hair and a narrow face, a leather bag at his feet. Finnegan had to wait for him to give the high sign and then follow him into the bathroom to make the transaction.

Finnegan was convinced that Maben enjoyed making him wait.

The white couple that looked like Shirley MacLaine and Walter Matthau paid for their drinks and left. Must have decided it wasn't their kind of place. And then, at last, Maben slid off his stool, picked up his bag, and headed for the men's room.

Outside, Vern Szabo spoke to Sands and Franklin. "Use the walkie-talkie. Maben got there ahead of us."

"That's bad," Sands said.

In the men's room Finnegan took off his knit sweater.

"Hot in here, bro." He flashed his cash and listened politely as Maben took out the Uzi, inserted a clip, showed him the safety, the folding butt, and the sights.

"Let me demonstrate how quickly you can break it down," Maben said.

"Don't get into that," Finnegan said. "Lemme get the feel of it."

"You'll love it." Maben handed over the weapon. He smiled to see Finnegan grin appreciatively as he hefted the Uzi.

"This is how you cock it?"

"Yeah. Careful, it's loaded now."

"I be careful," Finnegan assured him.

Finnegan came out of the men's room, casually holding the Uzi at his side. Suddenly he went into a combat crouch. Maben heard someone yell, "Police! Drop that weapon!"

Philpot stood, his arm coming up with a nickel-plated gun. Maben slipped out of the men's room and edged toward Philpot. The hit man drew his High Standard from the clip-on holster on his belt.

Philpot's eyes widened. "Who the fuck are you?" he asked.

Maben shot him.

The bullet struck Philpot square in the chest. He fired off a wild shot of his own, but Maben's bullet had cut his aorta. Philpot sat down heavily on his chair. His chest filled with blood. He grinned stupidly, then fell straight back.

The detectives behind the Sugar Shack leaped over the wall to rush the back door, but people were coming out and getting in the way. Campbell waved his hands and shouted, "Get the fuck out of here!" They looked at him, stupefied, and scattered in every direction.

Finnegan was coming out the back door.

Raccaniello yelled. "Freeze, motherfucker!"

Finnegan had the gun cradled. He was strutting. He brought the Uzi up. The detectives ducked, heard the pop-pop-pop and bullets ricocheting off the wall.

Sinker stood up to return fire. A bullet nicked his shoulder, spun him around and knocked him down. Raccaniello fired over the wall without aiming, then crawled over to Barnes.

"You okay?"

"Yes!"

"You may think you got something to prove, kid," Raccaniello said, "but I'm more than satisfied."

Meanwhile, Maben was coming out the front door behind the general rush, having paused to kill Philpot. He saw the detectives rush him from across the street and started shooting, forcing them to retreat behind their car. He opened the gull-wing door of his DeLorean, hastily firing in the direction of the cops to force their heads down. The DeLorean pulled away, leaving behind several yards of rubber, the gull-wing door flapping until he pulled it down at the end of the block.

Finnegan, still firing the Uzi, began to edge back

to the rear entrance. Campbell tried for an end run, firing harassment rounds as he sprinted for the corner of the Sugar Shack. Tom Castleton followed, and saw Finnegan turn. The Uzi muzzle flashed as the new jack swept the weapon from right to left. Castleton lunged forward desperately and pushed at the small of Campbell's back, knocking him flat.

In a split second the 9 mm bullet hit, fragmented, and caused major damage to his chest, stomach, liver, and the small and large intestines. The immense force of the slug carried Castleton into the air and threw him to the ground.

Instead of retreating backward, Finnegan suddenly pivoted and ran.

Barnes and Raccaniello stood up and emptied their weapons rapid-fire. Their bullets followed Finnegan, powdering the brick wall. Then the bullets caught up. One slug hit him in the upper chest, the other entered at his right elbow and traveled up his arm to his heart.

He stopped, and with apparent calmness, started to load a fresh clip into the Uzi. Finnegan did not know he was dead. Slowly, he dropped the clip, then the Uzi. He fell, finally lifeless.

Castleton struggled to his feet and covered the hole in his chest. He fell back as the intense pain in the middle of his chest started spreading down to his hip and burned to the core of his body. Campbell caught him on the right side and Barnes rushed over and grabbed his left shoulder. Together they trudged to the front of the Sugar Shack. Castleton's face was twisted in a grimace. He continued clutching his chest, trying to staunch the flow of blood that was seeping out from between his fingers, staining his white shirt with a blossom of bright red blood.

The ambulance that had been called to stand by still had not arrived. Campbell gestured toward the nearest of the patrol cars that had rolled up and said, "Let's go."

Sinker got into the back seat first to help Castleton in. Campbell jumped into the driver's seat and took off.

Campbell was murmuring words of encouragement. "Come on, hang in there. Don't go to sleep."

"I don't think I'm gonna make it."

"Tom, don't let me down. Stay with it—don't let me down."

"Don't think so," Castleton whispered. "At least Mary will get a good pension after I'm gone . . ."

Maben made it to the Edsel Ford. Sands and Franklin started gaining speed in the pursuit. Approaching at seventy-five miles per hour, they heard gunfire from two patrol cars ahead of them. Traffic slowed. Maben was weaving between the first and third lanes, intentionally ramming several cars to temporarily block the road. The collisions added up, no less than seventeen of them in four and a half miles. The patrol car ahead of them got blocked in a slow lane. The other patrol car attempted to get on Maben's side. It immediately was rammed, and the driver forced to slam on brakes and head to the side. Sands and Franklin found themselves the lead car. They followed directly behind the DeLorean, gaining.

Maben slowed to thirty, like he was coming to a stop. He got off the gas and cranked the wheel to the left a half turn. At the same time he hit the emergency brake hard. When his car was at ninety degrees he released the emergency brake, punched the gas pedal, and straightened out. He had made a 180-degree turn; without stopping, Maben regained speed quickly and headed against traffic.

Sands performed the same maneuver. All four hubcaps flew off the Chrysler. The car puked transmission oil but kept going.

Franklin yelled, "Watch out for this one! He hit another!"

"Why don't you shoot out the tires?" Sands suggested.

"Why don't you get closer to the sucker?"

Maben rammed a new Chevy Cavalier and demolished it.

The perp was going to kill someone, if he had not already, but there was no way to terminate pursuit. After seeing the Cavalier demolished Sands decided to shoot.

"I've been thinking about that," Franklin said.

"He's going to kill someone."

"Or already has."

They thought of sideswiping him but weren't sure they had the angle or power to knock him off the freeway. Franklin leaned out of the passenger window with his S&W .45 held in both hands. Maben drew back. Sands saw Maben lean forward and shift his hands as if he were to going to sideswipe them.

Franklin fired three rounds at the left rear tire. One .45 penetrated the tire, but it merely began to deflate slowly. Sands cut the wheel and hit the guy's rear-wheel section. He hit the brakes and countersteered to break contact. The DeLorean went sliding sideways down the highway until its tires regained traction. When that happened, the car continued in the direction it was pointing, crossing in front of the Chrysler and going off the road. The DeLorean spun to a smoking stop, and Maben climbed out.

Franklin dove from the car. Sands bailed out the driver's side.

Maben fired three shots. Sands fired eight. Franklin fired three.

Maben was blown back to a sitting position, his back resting against the median divider.

Franklin pulled the High Standard out of Maben's hand.

"Who are you?" Sands shouted. "What's your name?"

Maben looked at them for a long moment. "Santa Claus," he said. He bled from the mouth and died.

Chapter Twelve

INSPECTOR CAMPBELL FLEW the patrol car to Detroit Receiving in an amazing five minutes. While dodging cars, Campbell managed to contact the hospital to alert them to the fact that a wounded police officer would be on their doorstep momentarily. A doctor coordinated a team of four other doctors, as well as nurses and technicians who were ready to receive Castleton at the emergency room entrance. They took him out of the arms of Campbell and Barnes and had him on a gurney in a matter of seconds. Immediately they put tubes in him to replace the blood he had lost.

"You better do everything you can to save this guy," Campbell said.

The doctor was black and beautiful and one of the most experienced emergency room doctors in the world. She quietly replied, "We'd put the same effort in, even if he were Jason Lemons."

Castleton's vision was blurred, and all he could

see were the bright patches of light overhead as he was wheeled around. He could barely respond to the doctor's questions. Still, in the emergency room Castleton asked Campbell to make sure that Mary was given the two manila envelopes that were in his desk back at the precinct. They contained pictures of him holding Kate and a letter he had been writing intermittently for two years.

The pain was becoming unbearable. He whispered a short prayer. Then he heard the familiar voice of Reverend Leo Harris. Harris had caught the emergency transmissions on his scanner and rushed to the hospital.

"Tom, do you want a priest?"

"Do you think I'd make a priest come out on a night like this?"

"Very funny, Tom."

"Okay, yeah, but don't you go."

"I'm staying right here, babe."

Castleton was convinced he was going to die. He had always thought he would die on the job.

More lights flickered overhead as he was taken down a hall. He glimpsed a corner decorated with round, silvery balloons. He thought, "So this is death." He was transferred from the gurney to the table. He was in the operating room. Two nurses in green stared impersonally at him, leaning against the wall with their hands behind their backs.

Then he heard a new voice which reassured him, "You're going to make it."

The anesthesiologist went to work. Castleton's vision swiftly doubled and he fell into blackness.

When he came to, he thought that he had actually died and come back to life. He became aware that he was in the recovery room. He was in a great deal of pain, and he couldn't make any part of his body move. Yes, he could, the fingers of his left hand. He felt it necessary to signal that he was alive. He raised his left hand a few inches and wiggled his fingers. It seemed a silly gesture.

Someone grasped the hand gently and held it. He couldn't move his head to see who it was, but he knew the hand that held his.

"Mary," he said.

Caroline Bodner wasn't about to go to bat with no more ammunition than Carby's taped confession.

There was no case against Mike Tomack. There was no case against Racine Latimer. There was no case against Jason Lemons.

However, she felt it was her responsibility to disclose to the public the identities of persons under investigation, even though she knew she lacked sufficient evidence to indict them. Bodner wrote a press release that, in effect, identified the suspects. Mike Tomack and Racine Latimer's names appeared in the next day's *Free Press*, under Ralph Thomas's byline.

Within days, both men resigned "for personal reasons."

District Attorney Bodner was not remorseful over the fact that she had destroyed the reputations and careers of men against whom she did not have an indictable case.

"Justice comes to those who deserve it," she said. "I don't know that these men were unjustly treated. I think they should have been indicted. We were unable to do that. But a person who is corrupt should not hold public office."

Claire Hopson, Vern Szabo, and Sue Mallory had desperately wanted to be in on the big moment, but they lacked an invitation.

Satisfied that she had sufficient evidentiary angles, Caroline Bodner had given the go-ahead. The Sex Crimes Unit got their warrant to arrest one James Jay Madison. He worked as a groundskeeper at Tiger Stadium and lived with his mother in a house on Regular Street.

When he came to trial, his attorney would successfully establish that Madison had suffered a psychotic depression since the age of seventeen, when he had cracked up the family car on the Jeffries, killing his two younger sisters. He felt so guilty for killing his sisters that he developed a hatred of all women.

One by one they parked their cars on Regular Street and got out to watch. They were sad and they were angry. It had been a point of honor with all of them that they deserved to be present to put the gotchas on the scumbag.

He came out of his house surrounded by Lieutenant Wartiainen and two other detectives. The Beast was startlingly handsome, with an actor's profile. He wore a dazed smile. They saw him duck his head and get into an unmarked car for the ride downtown. The party was over.

For a long moment, no one knew what to say.

"Ah, fuck it," Vern Szabo said. "Let's go out for some fucking drinks."

When the Patrol Section was ready to turn out, Commander Rivers asked the IOS squad to follow him downstairs.

He stood before the men and women of his precinct. "I have something to say."

They fell silent.

"You'll be happy to know that Lieutenant Castleton is expected to recover fully from his wounds, though he won't be returning to active duty for some time. Chief Davies tells me that Lieutenant Castleton will be awarded the Detroit Police Department Distinguished Medal of Valor."

There were cheers and scattered applause.

"Medals are baubles," Commander Rivers said

sternly. "The job, hard as it is, is its own reward, and you all share in that. Policemen will get shot, and policemen will get killed, but it's still the greatest job in the world. We exist for the purpose of guarding the life, rights, and property of the people of this great city, the city that put the world on wheels.

"The job demands wisdom, patience, humor, integrity, and courage. It asks you to subdue a good measure of your own identity in order to protect those who need protection—to help the helpless, care for the lost, and assure those who are in fear.

"On the other hand, it offers enormous rewards. You will find strength and reassurance in our participation in a larger life. There can be no doubt about the significance of that life, and when the knowledge of that settles in your minds and hearts then there can be no doubt about your own significance."

Cal Rivers paused. He seemed somewhat taken aback by his own eloquence. He turned to Lieutenant Starks. "Turn them out."

"All right, people," Lieutenant Starks said. "Nail 'em and jail 'em."

Deck O'Hallerin and Sue Mallory were driving down Second when they heard the emergency tone followed by their car number.

"Oh, hell, here goes," O'Hallerin said.

Sue picked up the mike.

"We have an unknown injury at the Jeffries Project," the dispatcher said. "Ambulance en route." Sue ten foured.

"Okay, you tell me, which one is it? The buildings all look alike to me," O'Hallerin said over the siren's wail as they pulled into the project.

Intact street signs were rare in the neighborhood, and Sue recognized the turn by the Chaldean market on the corner.

The ambulance had just turned onto the street behind them. As they entered the apartment building, they saw a girl who looked to be about fifteen lying on her back in the hallway. Her face was contorted in pain and she clutched the worn fabric of her dress over her swollen abdomen. A middle-aged black woman knelt beside her.

"Oh, Mama! Mama, it hurts!"

"What happened?" Sue asked as an an ambulance attendant began taking the girl's blood pressure.

"She fell down the stairs," the middle-aged woman sobbed. "Oh, baby, I tole you to stay off them stairs. They give way right under you."

"You're her mother?" Sue asked.

The woman nodded, continuing to cry.

Sue crouched in the urine-spattered hallway and looked at the girl. She knew without asking that the girl had no husband and had probably never seen a doctor in her life.

God, babies having babies. What would become of them? What was the answer to the poverty, the waste, the cycle of hopelessness?

Suddenly the situation became intensified.

"Sue," O'Hallerin said, "the paramedics got a heart attack over on Seward and they say that the shocks in that meat wagon out there are too rough for her. We gotta take her in the cruiser."

Sue could tell from the girl's cries that the pains of hard labor were coming closer together. O'Hallerin slid one hand under her back and another under her legs.

"Oh, please! Don't lift me, please!" she cried out. She clutched his uniform shirt tightly in one fist.

"Easy, now, honey, you're going to be just fine," he said gently as he motioned for Sue to get the door. A strange tenderness came into his voice as

he walked toward the car, still reassuring the
girl. He eased her onto the back seat and got in
after her, handing Sue the keys.

"Head for Detroit Receiving," he said.

They pulled away with the siren and the bar
light flashing red and blue.

A sharp cry of pain came from the back seat.
Sue pushed the patrol car faster, fishtailing as she
took a corner.

"Listen, you got nothing to worry about. There
ain't nothing to it," O'Hallerin said. "Just take it
easy. You're gonna be okay."

As Sue listened to Deck calm the girl, she mar-
veled. She thought she had the measure of O'Hallerin, but this was a man she hadn't known. She
wasn't calm. She felt ready to jump out of her
skin.

"Just relax. Take short breaths," O'Hallerin
said.

Only a few more blocks. Sue could already see
the lights at the hospital's emergency entrance
ramp.

"It hurts so bad!" A scream of pain. "Am I dying?"

"No, honey, what you're doing isn't dying."

Up ahead a car started into the intersection.
"Don't do it, asshole!" Sue yelled as she worked
the siren control.

The woman arched and thrashed, grunted and
yelped. She let out a piercing scream and Sue bit
her lip so hard she drew blood. As she glanced
back, the crown of the baby's head appeared.

She braked at the entrance ramp moments later
and turned into the hospital. As she cut off the
siren, she heard a squall coming from the back
seat.

"Deck . . . she didn't—" She turned and looked
through the cage. The baby had slid out.

"The hell she didn't." He laughed.

O'Hallerin lay the child on the mother's breast and cleaned the mucus from his nose and mouth. The baby wasn't black, not yet, but a sort of lavender-and-cream. O'Hallerin counted fingers and toes. "All there!" he said with satisfaction.

Sue sat there watching the tiny figure on the back seat. She started laughing also and felt tears spill from her eyes.

After the medics had wheeled mother and child away, Deck and Sue took a moment's rest in a hospital lounge furnished with beverage machines and orange molded-plastic chairs.

A woman doctor came into the lounge looking for them.

"You did this all by yourself?" she asked.

"Well, yeah," O'Hallerin said. "My wife is pregnant and we've been going to this home birth class."

"You did an excellent job," she said.

After a while they left the emergency room and walked toward the patrol car.

It was getting close to dawn and the eastern horizon was a deep blue. The lights of the city appeared in subtle tones of blue, pink, and yellow. They could see the white and red of the broadcast tower of the Fisher Building, and the tubes of the Ren Cen reflecting the first rays of dawn. Sue wondered how many had died in the night, how many lives had been snuffed out in violence that had no meaning other than its own rage. And how many others had been born.

It was a tough town.

God, she loved it.